This Is Yesterday

ROSE RUANE

corsair

CORSAIR

First published in the UK in 2019 by Corsair
This paperback edition published in 2021

1 3 5 7 9 10 8 6 4 2

Copyright © 2019 by Rose Ruane

The moral right of the author has been asserted.

A CIP catalogue record for this book
is available from the British Library.

ISBN: 978-1-4721-5400-2

Printed and bound in Great Britain by
Clays Ltd, Elcograf S.p.A.

Papers used by Corsair are from well-managed forests
and other responsible sources.

Corsair
An imprint of
Little, Brown Book Group
Carmelite House
50 Victoria Embankment
London EC4Y 0DZ

An Hachette UK Company
www.hachette.co.uk

www.littlebrown.co.uk

For everyone who was ever made to
feel as if their difference was a bad thing.

Chapter 1

The phone ringing in the dead of night can only mean sex or something terrible. Or maybe both. Even in the deep sludge of sleep her body registers shock. Cold sweat and a kick in the chest.

It's Bella. Her sister. Not being awkward. Not stacking the odds against her with a complicated preamble.

Immediately she knows there will be fluorescent light and waiting, the crunchy flex of an empty plastic cup in her hand, inadequate words to fend off silence. Dad's had an accident, a bad one.

The clipped, urgent call ends. She ransacks her brain for names. People who might be sober enough to drive, kind enough to stumble into their clothes, solid enough to take charge and deliver her into this moment, to her family. This is how it begins.

She chooses Joseph. Joseph who she used to sleep with. Who she almost loved. Until she realised: on the ground, looking up, indebtedness is almost indiscernible from love. Joseph got tired of waiting for her anyway. He married someone prettier than her. Prettier, and a much better person.

Recently she has acclimatised to dread, the hovering

anticipation of crisis. Over the last two years Dad has become slower, vaguer, his conversations disjointed. Creeping suspicion grew insistent and troubling. Then last Christmas, he mistook her six-year-old twin nieces for her and her sister, and on Boxing Day asked where his mother was.

After that they could not fudge and demur. Worst suspicions confirmed. Dad's dissolution had a name. A prognosis. They gathered round the luminous blue scan as a consultant pointed out dirty thumbprints on the creamy cauliflower of their father's brain.

They have flailed through months, watching him become an uncanny remainder. Often so much himself, frequently fading and slipping. A recognisable version of Dad; warped by the funhouse mirror of dementia.

Shock hasn't torn away the muzzy thickness of things she consumed to help her sleep. Yawning in the grip of wine and codeine, she longs for something bright and jaggy to resuscitate her. Instead she cleans her teeth and smokes and cleans her teeth again. And smokes.

In the car, Joseph proves he was the right person to call. He dispenses coffee from a flask of it his wife made and doesn't make her talk. As the orange lights of the motorway bubble across the windscreen, he describes colleagues at the school he teaches in. Tells stories about his pupils and squeezes her hand at junctions.

Outside the hospital Joseph looks at her as if he wishes she was his problem. She realises it was unfair to ask this of him. When he says goodbye, call him if she needs anything, she knows she won't. At least not until next time panic bypasses decency. Or maybe next time she will call Alex or Per or Simon instead.

The hospital doors hush and suck behind her; her sister is

2

pacing the corridor. Bella is first to arrive. Their brother Greg has further to come.

Normally he would be the one to make and receive these calls. He lives closer to Dad, coordinates his care and sees him every few days. But this week Greg has been taking a much needed break, a holiday. Arranged a while ago. He said it was someone else's turn for once. She felt rebuked. Conversations with him always leave her feeling that way.

Regardless, she wishes he was there to fill the space between her and her sister.

Greg will ask searching questions – only about Dad, only of the medical staff. Compassionate and practical, he would show them the right way to behave. But, for now, there is only her and Bella – what has happened tonight that she doesn't understand and the events that caused their rift twenty-five years ago that she still can't fully comprehend.

Twenty-five years. In all that time, the sisters have never been alone together. There have been family get-togethers. Christmases, birthdays and weddings: impersonal gifts, a rote performance of brittle pleasantries accomplished with the earnest hesitance of a school orchestra trying to stay in tune. Meticulously, they avoid all reminiscence.

But now Dad has become disoriented, they have all begun to hold their breath. Dislodged, he slips between time streams. Interleaves past and present, interpolates his child-hood with theirs. Another waiting has taken hold, another anticipation: the inevitable moment his disease will blunder into the minefield they have skirted so long, detonating buried ordnance.

Cemented to the spot, she watches Bella, whose clothes whisper obscene wealth discerningly spent, tasteful individuality.

3

Her own hint at nothing but haste. She has used the grease in her hair as a styling product. Yesterday's smudged eyeliner underscores the fatigued look which has lodged round her eyes over the last few years. A grey dereliction which no longer improves with good sleep hygiene and proper hydration, making it easy not to bother with either. Her fake leopard fur coat, limping into yet another winter, is doggy with damp and smoke. Licking her finger, she rubs a red wine spot on her jeans. As she scrubs and tuts, her sister turns around. She feels caught. Tricked.

'Bella,' she says and holds her arms out. They feel like they belong to someone older and heavier. Her sister makes a sour mouth round the name she gave her, 'Peach', but she gives her a look from before; sad and tired and full of love. Something from 1994.

Suddenly the fact that Dad is hurt is very real. Suddenly they are crying. Suddenly they are holding one another. This is how it begins.

'What happened? How is he?' Peach coughs muffled questions into the bowl of Bella's collarbone. Her own breath comes back to her: coffee, cigarettes, toothpaste.

'Bad. He's in surgery. A car. He got hit by a car.' Bella's voice vibrates her thin body; it travels down Peach's arms.

'How? What happened?'

'Don't know. Apparently, the driver said Dad stepped right out in front of him without looking. But the weird thing is: he was back home.'

Peach knows Bella means home where they grew up. Home as in the past. Home as in when they were young.

Bella lets Peach go. Methodically scoops tears from the corners of her eyes with polished fingernails.

Peach lets her own tears cool and evaporate on her cheeks.

4

'What was he doing there?' Peach asks.

Bella brushes nothings off her clothes. 'I don't bloody know.'

'I was just asking. Where's Douglas?'

Douglas – Bella's husband. Utterly pleasant, breathtakingly thick, impeccably mannered and impossible for Peach to relate to. His simpleton handsomeness makes him look like an advert for whatever he is wearing or doing. Something weird and plastic in his manner, like an android running an algorithm, doing its best to produce an impression of a real human man thinking real human thoughts.

Eight years ago, Bella met Douglas at a Future Leaders in Internet Business seminar. The kind of networking event where, Peach imagined, everyone quoted Sun Tzu and bragged about imaginary companies which would bankrupt them in very real ways. Peach took Douglas to be an amusing plaything; a rich, fleshy Ken doll. But within six months Bella had married him, and a year later she was pregnant. Part sperm donor, part hedge fund, Douglas trots after Bella like a child wanting to please. He is completely beneath her, and this, Peach assumes, is what makes him her sister's ideal husband.

'Douglas? Where do you think? With our daughters obviously. Remember them? Octavia and Anais? It was their birthday last month, *thanks so much for the presents*.'

'I was busy at work, I—'

'You can't just *forget* children, well, apparently *you* can, seven by the way, they're seven now. Anyway, you can't just *leave* children. They're not cats.'

'Actually, Richey went missing a couple of months ago, I don't know how he got out. I put up posters, but I never heard . . . no one ever—'

'Just like his namesake, asking for trouble really, calling

him that. Anyway, it wasn't really fair to keep a pet in a place as poky as yours, no wonder he ran away.'

Peach misses the little black cat, tripping her with figure eights round her legs, chirping for biscuits, the soft heft of him on the bed at night. Doesn't know how he got out. Probably her own fault. Probably pissed.

'I miss—'

'God, how can you think about a cat at time like this, Peach? Dad's in surgery. He could lose his leg.'

'What?'

'His ankle is broken. Shattered actually, in several places too, bone tore right through his flesh. Doesn't bear thinking about.'

'But what—'

'*Doesn't bear thinking about.*'

Peach takes out her phone to check her messages. She takes out her phone to avoid talking to her sister, looking at her even. The battery is dead. The screen is black. It offers Peach nothing but a shadowy reflection of her face.

Then their brother Greg arrives. He smells like mud and grass. He asks questions calmly, listens to the answers attentively. He was camping with his partner Marcus, who has stayed behind. Tonight, alone, Greg has run down the side of a mountain with only the ghostly beam of his head-torch to guide him, yet he is equal to this. Adequate and practical.

Peach looks at her siblings. They have each brought their lives here, carried in their clothes. Bella's artful and composed. Greg's waterproofs implying wholesome activities. Peach's ripped jeans with a bloodier, more extensive spattering of red wine than she noticed before. Attired like her adolescent self, she has arrived with pockets full of the past, spilling mess and offence into the sterile supportiveness of the hospital.

'What was he doing? Why was he even there?' Greg asks as if there will be a benign, sensible explanation for their father being in a place they all diligently avoid.

There is silence as the three of them begin to understand that there will be no more benign, sensible explanations for anything Dad does. Only the clumsily malign chaos of his condition, spiralling further out of hand. Other hospitals, more worry, care homes. A funeral.

'Do you think he got confused? Do you think he thought he was going . . . home?' Greg asks.

He looks at Peach. Bella looks at Peach.

Greg looks at the ground. Bella carries on looking at Peach, and Peach could swear she smirks at her as she puts her arms around their brother and says, 'Oh, Greg, sweetheart, I don't know. Maybe, probably, I mean he's never really had a proper home since . . . '

Bella lets the ellipsis turn eggy.

Anger and fear nudge up against the slurry of Rioja and codeine and Peach can't help herself. 'Nice. *Nice*, Bella, thanks. Now is definitely an appropriate time to—'

'Don't,' says Greg. '*Do not.*' Her brother squeezes his hands together.

You always did that when you were upset, Peach thinks. Ever since you were little, you comforted yourself that way. She watches Greg pulse his flesh and imagines doctors performing chest compressions. Her eyes fill with tears again and she sobs noisily.

'Stop making it all about you,' Bella spits.

'I'm not! I'm upset! Your attitude isn't helping.'

'My attitude? I didn't say anything, Peach, I can't be held responsible for the way your guilty conscience interprets things.'

'Stop it. Just stop it. Both of you.' Greg, hands squeezing his own hands.

All the time while Joseph was driving her here Peach was thinking it is time to be better, this situation *must* make us *be better*, Bella and me. There is a long sad journey ahead of us, we must put the past aside, stop accounting for every bitter penny of fault and this is how it begins – it has to be.

But instead this is Peach behaving as she promised herself she wouldn't.

This is her sister with poison in her eyes.

This is her brother with disappointment and bemusement in his.

This is an unseemly scrabble for the moral high ground: even now, even here, with Dad cut open on a table behind one of these doors.

This is Peach and Bella carving up who is the worst here, passing fault back and forth between them like a hand grenade with the pin pulled.

This is everything being wrong and nothing being safe.

This is Peach assaulted by things she's tried so hard not to think about, so she can carry on trying not to be the person who did them.

This is everything she's tried to forget hulking into view like a destroyer heaving into port. This is the summer of 1994 rushing into the present: the terrible things which happened then pushing her out to the edge of the terrible thing which is happening now.

This is a door opening.

This is a doctor in blue scrubs walking towards them with her hands outstretched and her lips already parted for the words she is going to say.

And *this* is how it begins.

Chapter 2

As the doctor approaches, Peach feels the corridor rush away, the familiar focus-pull under her sternum. She scrambles to remain in her body, in the moment, to listen, to speak.

Greg holds his own hands, left wrapped in right. Bella has carefully taken herself into her arms. Peach wishes that they were the sort of siblings who instinctively reach for one another.

But they are not.

So she permits the untethering. She merges with the tide as it comes in white and absolute; like a seizure, like a blinding. Familiar now; frightening the first time it happened on the last day of school.

School corridors wrap themselves round hospital ones. Vines pulling the present down into the past, like the floors of a dying building collapsing into one another. And suddenly she is there on the last day of school which was nothing it was supposed to be.

The weather was wrong. No sun, no rain: just thick heat trapped under grey cloud.

Peach perched on the edge of a desk in the art room, inhaling damp scents of clay and egg tempera, balled up into herself like a crumpled tissue, holding a Polaroid camera. Pointing and shooting with a mixture of desperation and disinterest.

It was Mr Wilcox the art teacher's idea for her to take Polaroids of them all. It was his camera.

Peach was used to her own: the methodical balance of focus and exposure her mother had taught her a year before.

Mum had showed Peach how to adjust the aperture, a cautious twist at a time.

'The camera is greedy for light,' she'd explained, 'it'll starve the image of detail if you don't control its appetite. Always remember you're in control of it, it's not in control of you.'

Peach carried her camera all the time. Took rolls of film to Snappy Snaps once a fortnight unless she could wangle an hour in the school darkroom to be bathed alone in red light and chemical haze, at once magical and scientific. Coaxing images out of the fluid. Sometimes delighted, sometimes disappointed. Always fascinated.

At home, she'd covered a whole wall of her bedroom in photos. Still lives, landscapes, family and friends. She could track the improvements in her skill, in her eye. See where she started to take charge of the images she created.

The Polaroid was impulsive and haphazard. It offered no control; snatching up images, spitting them out.

All around Peach, classmates signed one another's shirts. Hugging and crying, promising to be friends *forever*, even though most of them had never been friends at all. The prevailing hysteria was seductive and intoxicating. For reasons she didn't understand Peach felt immune: flat and separate, with the camera on a plastic strap round her neck.

At first, the others had jostled to pose for Peach, clustering round, eager to see. They giggled excitedly as they watched themselves emerge from blackness. But the pictures had nothing to tell them about who they were.

Bleached and featureless, instant and ancient. The Polaroids turned their urgent aliveness into fuzzy, ageless spectres. The white border barely contained them. A pale arc of shoulder where a face should be, a mouth reduced to a magenta smear. They grew incurious and wandered away.

It was the first time Peach felt the slipperiness: something firm inside her becoming crumbly and soluble. Disgraced by the pile of disappointing pictures, she traced compass-carved graffiti with her fingernail. U.K. SUBS and RICK HEARTS CHERYL IDSTL. Old marks, insisting strangers had once been here, been young, made it seem like nothing happening now really mattered.

Mr Wilcox held court to a group of girls, regaling them with wild tales of art school in the sixties. Mr Wilcox reminded Peach of her father. Both art teachers. Both garrulous. Both embarrassing.

She began to visualise the family ritual that marked the last day of school and the start of summer. Dad would stop at the Panda House and bring home more Chinese takeaway than her family could possibly eat.

It was different since Bella had gone away to university. She returned for holidays exuding flamboyant disdain, looking subtly different each time. Less like the sister Peach had always known, more like someone from a band or a film. Bella's clothes grew ever more gothic and bohemian – the outfits of someone unafraid to tell the world what to think of them. Bella wore swirly velvet dresses and crochet cardigans that Peach tried on in shops and was never bold enough to buy. Sometimes, in a fit of bravery, she'd spend her pocket money on dangly silver earrings that reminded her of something her sister would wear. But by the time she'd worked up the nerve to wear them, Bella's style would have moved on. Feeling silly and immature, Peach would bury them in a drawer with other trinkets and lipsticks she'd bought to try looking like someone she always concluded she was incapable of being.

Greg had grown into a monosyllabic lump of not quite man or boy, lowing constantly about hunger as he passed through the house, dumping one set of sports kit, picking up another, shedding mud and grass, leaving a miasma that was fifty per cent barnyard, fifty per cent Lynx and a hundred per cent disgusting.

Still, it pleased Peach to picture her sister setting the table while her brother peered out the window. She could almost smell umami steam; see her father at the head of the table, her mother smiling as she doled out plates.

Suddenly she desperately wanted to be at home.

Mr Wilcox was still wind-bagging about doing his best paintings on acid and looking smug about being the kind of teacher who'd tell students that.

Since there was nothing else to do, Peach lifted the camera and trained it on Karen Casey – an unpopular girl, with a reputation for being a bit of a bike. There were rumours that on a geography field trip she had let several boys do what-ever they wanted to her, including Mr Hannon, the head of department; a teacher renowned for drinking in the Cross Keys at lunchtime and stinking.

Karen's hand was up at her face. Pudgy fingers: dimples for knuckles like a baby. Tearfully, loudly, she exclaimed to no one in particular, 'I just can't believe it's the end of school forever.'

And although Karen was usually socially isolated, she

disappeared into a scrum of comfort. The poignant occasion had infected even the terrifying, alpha girls with sentimentality.

Peach felt her own indifference to the end of school *forever*. She *did* have a place at university but hadn't yet anticipated the experience with either excitement or trepidation. Her mind hadn't wandered in that direction. Recognising it made her wonder if something was wrong with her. She lifted the camera, aimed it at the knot of girls cooing over sobbing Karen.

Peach remembered changing next to her in PE: Karen manhandling her breasts into mumsy cups as big as cereal bowls while Peach concealed the disappointment of her flat chest in a tiny bra. The pneumatic plumpness of Karen's body radiated heat. A sad private smell underlay a cheap floral one: bad teeth, old shoes. It had summoned a vivid picture of Karen, knickers round her ankles letting Mr Hannon hump her in a youth hostel cupboard.

Peach had felt assailed by the image.

Disgusted by her recoil, knowing it illuminated nothing about Karen, she brought her finger down on the red button and let the camera swipe the image out of the air. It wheezed out another Polaroid. She chucked it onto the desk, didn't bother watching it develop.

School was already healing up around her absence like water closing over the momentary hole a dropped rock had made in it.

Once, in the early years, she had almost been popular. Shamefully laughing with her mouth and apologising with her eyes as girls she'd been calling friends threw a bespectacled classmate's underwear into the shower and stuck chewing gum in the hood of her anorak.

The guilty scrabble to maintain their acceptance had ended after a thirteenth-birthday party, where Peach misjudged the magical permission a game of dare provided. And, although the scandal which secured her exile had been more the fault of a boy called Barry Jones and his intrusive fingers, she'd been judged a slut and was briefly bullied herself.

There had been horror and humiliation: a used tampon thrown into the bathroom stall she was peeing in, *her* underwear in the showers, catcalls and whispers. But there had also been relief. Freedom from complicity in things she had wished she wasn't taking part in all the time she was. Liberation from spinelessness and self-reproach.

After that she had slouched into easy companionship with a group of nice girls and, more recently, decent boys. Pleasant. Unremarkable. Almost interchangeable. Neither cool kids, mature and tough; nor outcasts harassed for things they couldn't help – glinting orthodontics, trips to bible camp.

Her group had been fortunate in their blandness. Kids in class whose names were hard to remember. Smart enough not to be troublemakers. Not academic enough to have their schoolbags hurled up trees for being swots.

They were all released from it now: the boys who'd had pubes since the start of secondary, who bought single cigarettes from the ice cream van at lunchtime. The girls with primary school shoes and love bites on their necks despite no boy ever having touched them – the result of zealous violin practice. The boys whose acne looked like a biblical punishment. The ones who went to computer club and played chess at break. The girls whose whispered secrets echoed through the toilets on breath scented with Silk Cut and Juicy Fruit. All of them were emancipated from those versions of themselves.

14

The thought was so sudden, Peach's unimportance so claustrophobically substantial, that she felt insubstantial herself.

She reached for the photograph she had just discarded on the desk: the girls in it appeared as a pink mass, human blancmange. Why had she trusted Mr Wilcox's stupid Polaroid? Why hadn't she brought her own camera? She felt like she was boiling alive inside her skin.

Overcome by an urgent need to feel cold and clean, Peach grabbed her bag and stumbled from the classroom.

She bowled out into the playground gulping at the soupy air. Humid black sky hovered above the buildings. Her clothes stuck to her body. Pink rivulets of melted ice lolly groped the asphalt like dirty fingers.

Peach told herself she was just popping home to get her camera. Even though she knew there wasn't enough time to go and come back.

Hesitating, she imagined the relief of letting herself in before the rest of her family: the low, reliable pulse of the dormant house, the faintest toast smell suggesting hours ago when the house pounded with breakfast and Radio Four.

Peach screwed her eyes shut and opened them again. Loud light; the school buildings squatted in front of her, familiarity set aslant. She hastened away.

On the walk home, Peach began to think she should have gone back inside, wondered if, in an adult future she couldn't imagine, she would regret having bolted.

Probably not, she thought. She planned to hang out at Pamela's house later. Pamela had *Fire Walk with Me* on video and Colin was going to get lots of cigarettes and cider. He could always get served in Spar because he had looked old enough to be his own dad since he was fourteen. Pamela's mum and dad were already off visiting cathedrals in Northern France or some other boring middle-class parent crap.

Peach felt like she was being watched as she passed through the streets of the sixties estate where identical grey houses crowded together like gossips. Big front windows underscoring their nosey appearance.

Unsettled and dislocated from herself, Peach shivered. She had always felt she was okay. Decent, smart, just fun enough not to be boring. Not especially beautiful, not particularly ugly. Apart, perhaps, from her nose, which she was convinced was too conspicuous. Just like her name.

Her parents had let her four-year-old sister name her: their way of trying to turn Bella's dismay at news of a sibling into delight. Bella, enchanted with the sweet soft baby once she came, chose Peach. She couldn't be persuaded to select something more conventional, wouldn't accept it as a mere nickname.

At any suggestion it might not be the name on the baby's birth certificate, Bella drummed her feet and fists, refused to eat, held her breath until her face turned blue and screamed 'You promised I could choose' until their parents let it stand. Bella's iron will always had ruled the roost. And Peach was stuck with her ridiculous name until she learnt, if not to love it, then to own it through defiance.

She developed a stubborn way of telling people what she was called which implied there was nothing unusual about it. And while popular mean kids persisted in calling her Plum or Pineapple, they found it more rewarding to torment Debbie Brassiere or the boy in Peach's history class whose parents had seen fit to call him Hilary. Eventually Peach stopped envying Lauras and Susans and Katies and got on with being who she was.

Now the slippery feeling made it seem like she could slide under the skin of any of those names and become any of those people.

Peach lived in a knot of cul-de-sacs on the edge of town, where the weave of buildings loosened and fractured into fields. The street was new when they moved there.

Once there had been woods and fields on every side of their estate, wide fields she ran around in with her siblings, but they were narrower now. Old stomping grounds blocked by new fences, pallets of brick and bulldozers. She once heard a man in a hard hat, who she knew was not a nice man because he was smoking and nice people don't smoke, saying to a man with a clipboard, 'They call it greenbelt – I call it missed opportunity.' She hadn't known what that meant but she didn't like the greedy way he'd said it. Then he'd chased her away shouting about private property.

Over time, there had been more and more diggers and scaffolding. More houses. Perfunctory bungalows, grandiose mock-Tudor piles. The handful of cul-de-sacs she lived in no longer felt like an island. The edge-lands of the town were beginning to creep across the pasture into the next village. Which, in turn, was outgrowing the name village and becoming a town.

A town virtually indistinguishable from this one. Just like here: uniform streets made of blonde brick. French doors, car ports, porches and patios. Identical houses which looked like the idea of a nice home in a nice street; built to project the impression of a place where nothing bad could happen. Houses to make people imagine that lives follow the courses set for them like a building society advert.

Close to home, the sky began to suck up inside itself, like the deep breath before a scream.

Thunder bellowed. Peach ran as rain began sluicing down.

Soaked, she tumbled through the front door, kicking her shoes off. The house had a used, live cadence where only the companionable hum of the fridge should be.

Understanding someone else was at home, she called, 'Hello?'

No one answered but she detected movement above.

Carefully, she slid her bag onto the newel post. She stepped onto the threadbare orange stair carpet, stirring the leaves of an enormous cheese plant that grew out of an ugly brown pot on the bottom landing. Over the years it had colonised the blown vinyl wallpaper, supported by an increasingly baroque system of nails and string. Soon it would reach the top of the staircase.

Her brother's door was ajar. She heard rustling and wondered why he too was home early from school. Realising she had the upper hand, she readied herself to give him a scare, suppressing giggles as she peered through the gap in the door.

Her brother was standing with his back to her, but she could see his school trousers were open, his back was hunched, his arm was moving. A fat catalogue propped up on his chest of drawers. Open at the underwear section.

'Shit!' she said without thinking.

Greg jumped, turned around while zipping his flies, cheeks red.

'I was just changing my trousers. I, I spilt something on them.'

'What did you spill on them?'

'Ehm ... Vimto.'

'Really? They look fine.'

Peach hadn't seen Greg look so ashamed since he wet himself with too much pop and excitement at Alton Towers when he was eight.

'Can you get out please?'

Malice tickled under embarrassment. But she saw the outline of her brother's shrinking hard-on through his trousers and felt sick.

'Sure, you get back to *changing your trousers*, it was obviously taking *a lot of effort*.'

'I spilt Vimto on my trousers, so I was changing them and then the zip was stuck, okay? Shut the door.'

'Zip seemed fine to me.'

'*Shut the bloody door, Peach.*'

She began to shut it but couldn't resist throwing it open again at the last moment.

Greg lunged at the door and slammed it, yelling at her to piss off.

And as he did, she noticed the Great Universal catalogue had fallen open to a page of men modelling vests and pants.

She rushed back down the stairs cringing, muttering 'oh god' under her breath. As she went, the cheese plant nodded agreement that today was definitely the worst, weirdest day in the entire history of the world.

She went into the kitchen where the dog lay motionless in his basket. 'Solomon? Solly?' she called. Solomon's nails clattered on the lino as he hauled himself upright.

He was big and brown; rough-coated, with the sage, human expression old dogs often have.

She hunkered down on the floor and put her arms round his neck, still cringing at what she'd seen. Solomon sat down with a punctured wheeze. Nuzzled into his neck, Peach remembered clambering on him, subjecting him to the indignities of ribbons and hats while her mother remonstrated, 'You'll break that dog's temperament.' She never did, though: Solomon was placid from nose to tail.

For a long time, she embraced Solomon in the middle of the kitchen floor. Rain hosed down outside, throwing jittery shadows on the walls; the clock shunted time forward with a soothing tick.

Sick-sad with love for Solomon, Peach was sure he was more her pet than anyone else's. Listening to him breathe, she wondered how days and weeks had heaped up into enough months and years for her brother to be pulling himself off over boring undies in Mum's mail order catalogue, for school to be over forever, and for her to be cradling her beloved dog who had grown old and slow without her noticing until now.

Peach was beset by a rebarbative itch: uninvited wondering, twinned with a confident presentiment that no good could possibly come of it. What else had she been failing to notice?

Chapter 3

Greg is mute, very still in a way that reminds Peach of the poised quiet their mother assumes in crises.

It always appeared to Peach as an automatic nobility of reaction, a native grace far preferable to her and Bella's own prating histrionics. Yet, over time, she began to allow the possibility that it was instinctive animal calm. Playing dead in the jaws of whatever threat had snatched her. Hoping to be released unharmed.

The hospital light is unforgivingly utilitarian. But where Peach first perceived hermetic perfection, she now sees that although the corridor *is* scrubbed and hygienic, there is an ingrained shabbiness. As if sad news and exhaustion have accumulated in the paintwork. Nothing is actually white. The walls are the pale mushroom of moist skin under a plaster.

The past flickers and glows like a magic lantern. Its beam is shame, dirty old light. Hers, remembering Greg and the catalogue. She had never explained that only the confronting bodiliness of the act had repelled her. That his hunger had appeared obscene only because he was her little brother.

Years later, she understood what it must have been for him.

Exploring his own desire, what and who incited it: those male frumps – mild smiles in plain undergarments – it must have seemed to him that *that* was what was abhorrent to her.

Peach opens her mouth to speak, there is too much unsaid here, yet now is not the time. The doctor is talking. She closes her mouth. *The doctor is talking.* She puts the whole shoulder of her being into listening. Or trying to.

Dad is alive. Not in any way which can be depended on. Not alive in any way Peach recognises when the doctor cups her hands round the air to describe a skull, spreads them out to describe a leg, leaving her prone and queasy.

The doctor explains that things which should be kept apart were crumpled together in the crash. Solid things were shattered. In Peach's mind, crockery strikes a concrete floor and flies apart, red wine lunges out of a glass as it tips and spins.

The doctor is charting out possible futures: tougher, more demanding than the tough, demanding one they were already doing a poor job of adjusting to. Inappropriately, Peach is hungry. Why can't she listen to the doctor?

She can't stop thinking of Mum's lasagne: lethally molten and tempting, huge in the middle of the table, impossible they should finish it, but they do. Or roast chicken: fingers moist, mouth shiny from the best part, prime morsels, sensuously gobbled while helping strip the carcass. Or birthday cakes: chocolate hedgehogs spiked with candles and Cadbury's Fingers, dementedly green buttercream and Subbuteo players on a sponge football pitch for Greg, why can't she listen to the doctor? Or buttered toast and tinned tomato soup under a blanket on the couch or the rude suck of the ladle penetrating the Christmas trifle or fizzy Coke and salty crisps in a pub beer garden while Dad swigged a pint or Chinese takeaway, the remnants of a Chinese takeaway, plates smeared in lurid sauce, congealing like blood and paint, falling back into the past like a chunk of cliff face shrugging into the sea.

Peach resurfaced from a fitful nap, her head aching. She looked at herself in the mirror. Even though the last day of school had been mediocre she half expected to look more grown up. Naturally, she was just the same: paper-white skin which embarrassed her by going red in the heat, red in the cold and scarlet when she was embarrassed. Big blue eyes she really liked, big long nose she really didn't. She ruffled her bob, wished it was longer, shorter, red or blonde instead of brown, then gave up. She poked her tongue out at her reflection, stuck up two fingers at it, then tried something she'd never done before.

She lifted her camera from the bedside table, held it at waist height and fired off a couple of frames towards the mirror. And wished she hadn't. It felt like playing with herself. Her brother's arm fast pounding, knees bent, panting. Jesus. She put the camera down and walked away.

Greg and Mum were in the kitchen. Peach helped herself to a Coke from the fridge, enjoying the blast of cold and light. End-of-term treat; Coke in the fridge – the Lewises were not usually a Coke in the fridge family. Normally it was all green vegetables and natural yogurt.

Outside it was still raining. In the garden, plants flailed and dripped. Spoilt sky, bruisy with premature dark, made the kitchen feel cosy. The cracked terracotta tiles and tired yellow units were fruity with light from the lamp in the corner. The tall beige shade with fraying brown trim, the big ceramic base, shaped like a bomb or amphora with pointless handles, glazed in shades of baby poo and compost. It was part ancient Greece, part sixties drug den. Her parents had carried it from student flat to family home. Even though it was ugly it gave a kind light. Trustworthy and familiar.

Solomon was asleep in his basket, forepaws twitching as he chased squirrels through his dreams.

'Hungry?' Mum asked Peach. She smelled of soap and something baked; the slightest hint of outside – earth, leaves.

'Starving.'

'I hope you starve to death,' interjected Greg.

'Get stuffed,' Peach pouted.

'What's the problem here?' asked Mum, threateningly measured. 'Why are you antagonising each other?'

Mum never shouted; extensive, articulate reason was her weapon of choice. She was handsome rather than pretty. Tall and mannish, with a long nose Peach and Bella both resented her for passing on. She was intelligent and quiet; even her clothes and hairstyle were carefully subdued.

Sometimes Peach was sad that there was nothing unpredictable about Mum. Unlike Jade's mother, who sometimes smelled of bad fruit when they got in from school and was talkative and friendly in ways that felt a tiny bit dangerous. Or Colin's who was in an episode of *The Bill* once and had affairs.

'Earlier, Greg—'

'Shut up, Peach.'

'Greg what?'

'*Shut! Up!*' Greg grabbed Peach's shoulder. She yelped.

At that moment, Dad stepped through the door. 'Grub's up! Who's for Chinese?' Unruffled by the war zone he had stumbled into.

'Look who I found, walking up the road with her worldly goods,' he exclaimed, placing bulging bags of takeaway on the worktop. 'Sly old Bella didn't tell us she was coming today.'

Bella entered, already looking sick of them all. 'What are you doing?' She glared. 'Fighting like immature twats? Classy.'

Greg released Peach's shoulder. A second seemed to stretch for long silent minutes. Everyone stood there, waxen and strange. Rain chuckled in the gutters outside.

In the hospital corridor they are the same, placed like chess-pieces waiting for the next move. Why can't she listen to the doctor?

'Bella!' beamed Mum. 'Never mind this daft pair. Why didn't you tell us you were coming home? Dad would have picked you up from the station.'

Bella shrugged and the frozen instant thawed.

'Hey Bella,' Peach said shyly.

'Sis.' Bella smelled of cigarettes and perfume: a distant, adult smell.

Bella's full name was Isabella Lewis. In baby photos she appears plump, golden and contented as a bee. Sitting on a mat in the garden she gives the impression of emitting sun from her skin. At two, on the beach at Camber Sands, she laughs and waves – paper flag in each fist, sand flocking the candies of her toes. She appears so full of goodness she might split with bliss.

The second she'd been allowed to name her sister like a toy, Bella had been convinced having a sibling was a good thing after all. Naming made Peach *her* baby. *My* baby sister. She was almost four when Peach was born. They remained close until hormones and pretensions etiolated Bella into someone prone to weeping, rage and silence.

Bella had always had a spectacular temper. But after her twelfth birthday she evolved a hair-trigger, weapons-grade fury everyone lived in fear of.

Peach had watched Bella screaming at their parents in response to imaginary crimes and decided drama wasn't something she planned to bother with.

Bella had not wizened into absolute unpleasantness. Rather the dark end of her spectrum of light and shade was *so* gloomy that she was difficult; an unsettling presence. Geysers of goodwill sometimes burst from the deep core of her old self. Yet it was impossible to predict how the capricious tectonics of Bella's temperament would structure the surface of her moods.

At the table Dad made everyone join in with the game they'd played since childhood: guessing what was in each foil tray before he opened it, making deliberately preposterous suggestions. 'Egg fried otter brains! Sweet and sour bison! Spare ribs Shoeburyness style!' As every member of the family entered the game that was barely a game, self-consciousness slipped away.

'This is nice,' smiled Mum. 'What a lovely surprise, Bella. I'm glad you didn't wait 'til next week.'

'Well,' Bella sniffed, dangling a prawn cracker between her fingertips, 'wouldn't miss the end-of-term banquet for the world, would I?' The statement was delivered with sarcasm, but Peach saw a gleam of sincerity open and close in her sister's demeanour like a crafty wink.

Peach was grateful to them all for being so exactly themselves; the way they looked in her head when she imagined them. Mum and Bella chatting about books. Mum exuding interest while Bella furrowed her brow, measuring out words in frugal bursts. Dad and Greg clowning for each other, laughing at nothing but noises and gestures. Solomon sniffing round, ostentatiously sitting, hoping to have his good boyness rewarded with scraps.

'I was telling the guys about Colour Wheel today,' said Dad.

The guys meaning his pupils at St Giles Grammar for Boys. Colour Wheel meaning Dad's band; extant for less than a year in the sixties. According to Mum, tongue sherry-loosened one Christmas, they absolutely stank. 'He wore a cape!' she'd giggled. 'A purple satin cape!'

Sad old twat, Peach thought; out of nowhere, she found herself imagining lopping her father's ponytail off with garden shears.

The thought made Peach titter meanly.

'Hey!' said Dad. 'The guys thought it was cool. A few of my third years are into music, so I said at the end of Christmas term I'd bring in my guitar and jam with them.'

A plug of unkind words clotted Peach's palate, imagining the way those boys would laugh at him, impersonating him in the common room. Dad was cheap meat for cruel jokes. His predilection for loud waistcoats and Status Quo jeans. For thumbs up and peace signs, using words like groovy, calling people folks and chaps and guys and dudes. Worst of all – the ponytail. It started further and further back on his head with each passing year. The less hair grew at the front, the longer he let it get.

Peach wanted to protect Dad then. From his pupils. From herself. From what she later understood was the jealousy the self-conscious have for the freedoms of the unself-conscious. Back then she was unable to name it; it was just a horrible cringing feeling she resented her parents for.

'Daaad!' squealed Greg through a half-chewed mouthful. 'You are such an embarrassment.'

Dad laughed and made devil horns with his fingers. 'Rock on, son.'

'Dad's embarrassing, is he?' Peach broke in. 'Not as embarrassing as you, Mr Vimto Trousers.'

'What's this?' Dad leant back in his chair good-naturedly.

'Nothing! Peach is being a bitch.' Greg put his head in his hands.

'Greg is being a *wanker*.' Peach made a supercilious face as Greg's ears seared red between his fingers.

'Wow!' Bella slouched, stared up balefully through her hair. 'I'm *so* glad I came home, the quality of dinner-table conversation is *exceptional*.'

Mum stood up, pushing her plate away. 'Why can't you just be nice to one another?'

'I'm going to my room.' Bella was already halfway out the door. Something had snapped shut in her like a deadbolt.

Dad burped, reached for his newspaper and declared his intention to read it in the living room with his belt undone.

Mum started to clear the table around Greg who still nosed through the containers. The remnants of dinner looked sad as a promise which had turned out to be a lie.

No good can come of thinking about that summer. She is needed in the now, but time is misbehaving. Like a drunk distant relative lurching uninvited into a reunion, threatening to spew vulgar truths. Why can't she listen to the doctor?

Poor Dad, this must be what it is like for him. What it was already like and now sedation and plaster and rehabilitation. Rehabilitation seems such a strange concept – he cannot be restored, not really.

Bella's hand flutters at her mouth like a scared bird trying to find a hiding place.

Words are said which Peach can hardly bear to hear in relation to her father – pressure and critical, intensive, waiting.

Again, she opens her mouth. Then the doctor asks, 'Is Ian

28

here? Your father was asking for Ian when he first came in, before he was sedated.'

Peach and Bella and Greg all look at one another, punch drunk from the blow of a name they haven't heard in more than twenty years. A name which has no right to exist in this hospital. A name which has no business in the present.

'Sorry,' Peach says.

'Oh, right, no, I don't think there's any need . . .' begins Greg. He gestures loosely in the air: something Dad always did when he thought he ought to say something despite being at a loss.

'Well,' interjects Bella, 'I think we all knew that at some point—'

'Sorry,' blurts Peach, 'I'm going to be sick,' and she races down the corridor.

Chapter 4

Eventually Peach finds a bathroom, blue lit to thwart those searching for veins. The eerie gloom like being underwater. She hangs over the toilet, retches spiderwebs of spit but doesn't vomit.

I'd feel so much better if I could throw up, she thinks. Whole system in revolt. Maybe it was hearing Ian's name, maybe adrenaline or Rioja or codeine or the whole queasy admixture. She'd like to feel it could be purged; flushed away – the spoil and poison of that summer, a familiar disease: always inside her, a chronic condition threatening relapse.

Past and present, two currents meet and swirl. She is unsure if it eddies in her or she in it. Regardless, the pull carries her away from the situation at hand. As she rinses her fingers and prepares to return to her siblings, she wonders if the way forward is back. She can think of it only in increments. One recollection at a time.

The holidays began to feel like a vacuum; rootless and stultifying. So much time to fill. An unknown quantity of days boiled by, each so much alike. The threat of boredom hovered like the possibility of rain.

Peach and her friends spent drowsy evenings sprawled on

the flat roof of a concrete bus shelter. It was a new meeting point: right on the very edge of town. As if they were all subtly testing themselves against the idea of leaving. Sometimes it felt like languor: day's last sun on her skin. Very aware of her skin, she'd put her hands on her body just to gather up sensations. Other times it was tedium: wasted time, running like sand. Mum had begun some very monotonous quacking about how instrumental self-discipline would be at university. 'You've always had a tendency to be lazy. I won't be there, you'll have to police yourself.'

It's true, Peach thinks, scrunching up a paper towel; I have always had a tendency to be lazy. So much of her life is spent wondering when she will next be able to do nothing – she is always tired. She gets up and goes to work regardless of how her head aches with sadness and inertia. How heavy and reluctant her body is.

At Capsule gallery in Mayfair, she does everything expected of her by her boss Ben Gardener, no matter how demeaning or unreasonable. She has undertaken the ninety-minute round trip across London twice a day to cook poached salmon for his choosy Maine Coon when he takes a holiday. Flown round the world to art fairs, existed for whole weeks in foreign cities without visiting them. Long days spent in glorified tents; part waitress, part salesperson, part secretary.

The hardest work is tolerating encounters with people she knows. Performing gracious failure when they ask, 'Oh! Are you showing work here?'

Gritting her teeth into a second-prize smile, 'Nope, working for Capsule.'

Or even worse, absorbing the ignominy of seeing those people see Peach and decide to avoid her because they realise it is the case. Then she feels like a disgraced ex-member of a private club, reduced to begging on the steps.

On those numberless summer evenings, the air was albumen. Milky and warm as bath water. Dusk sneaked over the landscape, amber streetlights described the big-smallness of the place where she'd always lived.

With the distant thrum of the main road murmuring elsewhere, like a dreamer speaking from the depths of sleep, Peach browsed the town, laid out like a constellation. Brightest light in the centre. A froth of illumination radiating outwards, marking paths through different housing estates – posh ones, poor ones, places she went all the time, places she would never think to go. The oily, meandering band of the canal. The ruin, floodlit at night, sticking out of the earth like a broken jaw. She can never remember if it used to be an abbey or a fort or a manor: a site of mediocre historical significance, equal in her mind to the leisure centre and paper shop. Simply a place that had always been there. All of it enclosed in a loop of dark, isolated drips of light where there were still farms, where big houses sat apart, glowering behind gates. Peach's mum worked for an artist who lived in one of those.

These are the days she is surprised to remember. Impossible to tell apart, yet, somehow, they contrived to leave an imprint. Even if it is a lasting impression of indifference.

Colin and Jade were always kissing. So audibly moist, Colin's friends would slither off the roof to caper in the long grass, slow-motion karate with exaggerated sound effects.

The girls, mouths stained and sticky from ice pops, would loll on their backs with the tops of their heads touching, turning the thought of university over and over. They tested out references to getting ready, as a way of admitting they

32

would need to. But independence seemed inconceivable as fiction while childish whoops and laughter slashed the spongy dark. Boys testing the powerful newness of their nearly men's bodies in a violent game.

In Peach's memory, their group was outstanding only in how affable they were and how plain. Everything about them all, herself included, was stunningly average.

When occasionally, now, she looks at photographs she took then, she is shocked by the raw, unspeakable power of adolescence. Their absurd failure to understand the loveliness they possessed, like a secret wealth they had no idea how to spend.

It fills her with tenderness: pity and admiration so intense she has to touch them. Compelled, she runs her finger over their cheeks, their hair. Earlobes and bare feet.

They were taken on top of the bus shelter. Long exposures with the aperture wide open. Luminous as moons, they appear haunted and haunting. So vigorously alive that the emulsion cannot pin them down. Even in the posed ones, where they assume the rictus of people being photographed, nature and artifice commingle to produce honest beauty. As if they were captured in a state of partial undress: the fleeting perfection of beings caught between two worlds.

The taproot of their intimacy was quiet. Not silence – they spent a lot of time discussing books and bands and films – but consistent peace. They were unobtrusive to one another. They never arranged to meet up, they simply drifted together like the sandy dust that collected in the kerbsides that summer.

Frequently, Peach found herself wishing she had a best friend. Someone to scheme and conjure with, not to slouch and mooch. A single co-conspirator instead of this group who felt less like friends, more like a habit as the shared context of school receded. Spending time with them, a way of being lonely without being alone.

Each evening repeated itself: the boys' game would turn brutal under darkness. The landscape would distort their voices into animal cries. Colin and Jade would kiss as if it was keeping them alive, kiss like divers sharing oxygen.

Then the last bus out of town would judder round the bend, sweeping them all with an arc of light, making them sit up and blink like rousing sleepers, Peach always the first to say, 'I'm going home.'

Swinging her legs over the edge, letting gravity take her, dropping from sight. The minute she began to fall it was as if she was completely by herself.

She flopped through hot afternoons, devouring a book about suicidal sisters in an imaginary summer years ago, oceans away, until sleep slipped it from her hands. She meandered across fields with Solomon and her camera, grasses rasping against her ankles, sun pinking her shoulders.

She snapped anything that caught her attention. Ducks squabbling over a crust by the canal. Empty swings entertaining themselves in the breeze. Two old women on a bench, creased with chuckles: savouring a rude joke. A child's shoe overturned in the gutter like a crashed car. Taking pictures felt like trying to understand something evasive and enigmatic; always just beyond reach. Something indelibly alive in the moment, desiccated and dead when she collected the photos. Like a butterfly pinned to a card.

Drifting round like tumbleweed, time and again Peach found the edges, the stuffy limitations of the small town. Still she couldn't visualise a life outside it.

*

Maybe she still can't: sometimes she feels like an important part of her snapped off that summer, got stranded. She can believe that her lifeforce was shocked out of her and left behind.

Stagnancy in her stalled life: studio flat, stopgap gallery job she's had for a decade. Addictions she can't deny. Not ruinous enough to deal with (yet). Good sex with bad lovers. The same handful these last few years since no new men are looking at her (she considers herself a feminist and loathes herself for minding). She carries on since loneliness is too hard. Since sometimes the closest thing to love is loyalty. Mutual, reliable forgiveness for predictable misdemeanours.

Advancing down the corridor, her brother and sister are small and clear as if viewed down the wrong end of a telescope. She is ashamed of the little jag of spiteful glee she feels when she observes Greg looking annoyed with Bella.

Bella keeps saying, 'What the fuck?' Repeating it over and over, like she's trying to break the world record for saying it the most. 'Ian! I mean, what the fuck?'

'Dad has dementia, Bella, *dementia*. He can't keep things straight in his head. *And* he's got *severe concussion* now! I mean, if you saw him more often you'd know that he already—'

'Yeah but *Ian*, Greg, it's still weird.'

'It's completely irrelevant.' Greg looks at Peach. His dismissal given as a gift; permission not to consider past wrongdoing. 'There are so many more important things to think about and talk about and sort out because Marcus and I will *not* be doing all this on our own from now on. I can promise you that.'

'Yes, Greg's right, we'll need to—' Peach begins.

'Convenient, Peach. Very convenient for you to just hand-wave Ian away,' Bella snaps.

Greg pinches his nose between thumb and forefinger and sighs. 'Thank god Mum is on her way.'

Peach says, 'Mum?'

Bella says, 'Mum?'

Greg says, 'Yes; *Mum*.'

And Peach thinks what if we all say Mum so many times that it isn't a word any more. What if I call Joseph and ask him to airlift me out of here because I absolutely cannot cope with this.

Bella asks Greg why Mum is coming.

He looks sheepish. 'I asked Mum to come because I've got the car and Marcus can't get a lift with our camping gear until tomorrow and I know I'm going to need some support tonight.'

Outraged crimson splats spring up on Bella's cheeks. She points from herself to Peach, Peach to herself. 'Uh, sorry? What about us, Greg? You've got *us*.'

Greg clears his throat, winkles at suddenly urgent muck beneath his clean, square nails.

And nothing else needs to be said. Since prolonged silence makes a very valid point extremely eloquently.

Chapter 5

In the hospital they have been ushered up to a dingy waiting room. On a spoilt Ikea table, dog-eared magazines splashed with neon disasters. Britain's funniest dog tore my baby's face off! Kinky vicar dad bonked my husband at our wedding!

Restive and forlorn as exhausted children, Bella and Peach fidget and sigh while Greg sits stoically. They wait to see Dad, having been assured it will be soon. They wait for Mum to arrive, having been assured by text that that, too, will be soon.

Peach's head lolled with the motion of the car.

Solomon skidded from side to side in the boot panting, slobbering and releasing ghastly stinks. He was still the least annoying passenger.

Bella struggled with a book. Her elbow jabbed Peach's side.

'I don't know how you can read without feeling sick,' Peach said through dry lips. Bella ignored her.

Greg's big legs swung with the dead weight of sleep.

Bella and Peach jostled in the baking back seat while their father sang along to Roxy Music. Their mother stared out the window. Bella thumped Greg with *Gender Trouble* and hissed, 'Stop taking up so much space.'

Greg woke and punched Bella limply in the ribs. 'You're taking up a lot of space for a waste of space.' He laughed before spreading out and falling asleep again.

Bella shoved Peach. Peach kicked her in the ankle and called her a cow.

Mum threw a glare over her shoulder. 'You're worse now than when you were little.'

'Maybe we actually wanted to go to the seaside when we were little.' Bella shut her book as if she was trying to kill something.

'You're never too old for a family day out,' said Dad. 'We're nearly there.'

They stopped for a red light. Solomon's nails clattered. He wagged his tail. He huffed dejectedly and sat down as the light turned green.

'We could play a game,' said Mum.

'Capital idea,' enthused Dad, drumming on the steering wheel. 'I spy with my little eye something beginning with—'

'"F",' shot Bella, 'something beginning with "F" and ending in "off".'

'Bit hurtful,' said Dad, antagonistically jolly.

'I hate you all.' Bella thudded a fist into her book.

Mum used her palm on her own forehead as a cold compress.

Eventually they tumbled from the car, massaging stiff legs. Solomon shot out the boot. He took off running: smelling things with his whole body. Every limb pursuing a different odour, every part of him emphatically lively. Solomon on the beach was a puppy again. Peach pressed the shutter repeatedly, knowing he was too fast to catch: ten brown frames of blur.

Idling in the grip of pleasant tedium, Peach drew stick men in the sand with a stump of driftwood. Oyster-catchers stalked the shoreline pompously, peeping scolds from red beaks. They scattered before she could take a picture.

Bella lay facing away from the sea; reading to show she wasn't a simpleton like the rest of her family. Peach tucked the image into her camera.

Dad and Greg capered ham-fistedly with a Frisbee at the tide line, splashing in and out of the water. Peach captured a blizzard of frames while their banter escaped, distorted on the wind.

Solomon loped back and forth. He presented Peach with half a decomposing seagull. He offered her a perished tennis ball slick with drool. She ruffled his sticky coat. Threw his gifts into the dunes.

Peach grabbed some shots of Mum as they sat side by side. 'Don't do that, Peach. Put my . . . put the camera down. Have you got much planned? For the next few weeks.'

'Months, Mum.' Stabbing her stick into the sand, Peach looked at her mother haloed by sunlight.

'Months then, have you?'

'Haven't thought really. Relax. Read. Watch films. Take photos.'

Mum picked up the stick and watched sand slide into the hole it left. 'You don't fancy getting a job? Earning some money?' She snapped the stick.

'Maybe. Do I have to?'

Mum poked absently around the fragments of wood with her toe.

'No. You don't *have* to do anything. It was just a thought.'

It was a thought. Not one Peach had had before. With her left foot she banked up sand round her right.

Half of her mother's face had rich light pearling on the edge of it. She batted something invisible away from her cheek. 'There might be some extra stuff to do at Ian's.'

With her right foot Peach banked up sand round her left. 'Like what?'

'Nothing very exciting.'

'Wow, Mum. That sounds great.'

Mum shook her head as Peach stood up and took off against the wind.

Spinning into a backwards run she looked back at her mother and sister. Bella looked hopelessly thin. Mum gazed out to sea. Light collected on her profile highlighting *the nose*. Mum called it a Virginia Woolf nose as if that was a good thing. Peach poked her own version of it with her index finger: massive.

She was glad to lose herself in the simple roughness of a game with Dad and Greg. Solomon frolicked and leapt, trying to snatch the Frisbee out of the air between them. Kelp straggled from his beard like a massive bogey and he looked like his dignity had been offended when they laughed.

For a while Peach busied herself picking up sea glass until her shorts pocket rattled. Miraculous how it entered the sea jagged and lethal and came out soft and opaque. A comforting illustration of how time blunts keen edges.

On rare occasions when she musters the appetite, Peach mudlarks by the Thames. These days, weekends are a test of character. Hours gape like starving mouths.

Once, Peach craved weekends. Now leisure time is a slog: two long days to fill with activities worth recounting. She keeps her idleness secret like a shameful complaint; incontinence or haemorrhoids.

But some Sundays she wakes early and slips into streets empty as a blank page. Church bells peal. Nostalgic timeless summoning that makes her wish she believed. At least enough to go inside and raise her voice: let it mingle in the air with faith and dust motes. To feel part of something bigger than herself. Rather than just waiting for Sunday night to become suffused with Monday morning so at least she'll have a locus for her non-specific dread.

At low tide, she picks up fragments of pottery and glass, gentled by the river's heedless susurration. Arrangements sit in pockets and corners round her flat: the bowl of a clay pipe, the ornately patterned lip of a plate, a jewel-blue bottle stopper. She balances them against old postcards and knitting patterns, found photos bought from car boot sales. Assembling them, uncomplicated pleasure gives way to a sense of being pitiable. As if the act of making confronts her with the stubborn delusion that she might yet become a different person, live another life. Like a barren spinster scuttling from a shop in a fugue, plastic bag in hand, tiny sleep-suit flat and breathless inside.

The journey back was silent and peaceful. The family piled into the car, salt on their skins, full of fish and chips. Solomon exuded the smell of soggy blazers after a rainy break time. The joy of never having to go to school again surged inside Peach. She wondered if maybe she would like to get a job. The words 'I'm going to work' tasted sophisticated as she mouthed them to herself.

The sun melted into clouds tinted plastic pink and lilac.

Slices of light brushed the sleeping faces of her siblings in and out of focus. Bella looked as if she had let go of something or as if something had let go of her as she slept; one hand up behind her head like a care forgotten.

Greg's chin was pale blue with stubble, but his features were still childish. He was much more made of Dad than

Mum. Snub nose Peach could only dream of. Skin which tanned. Eyelashes like a mascara advert. Wasted: all wasted on her brother. Livid pimples on his forehead compensated Peach for advantages he was indifferent to.

He kicked and twitched in his sleep. Even at rest, Greg was on the go – just one of the things that kept him remote from Peach. Her brother was a member of every possible team and club in every sport going. She maintained a suspicion of kids who enjoyed PE – an arena for thickos and bullies to thrive in. She assumed people who enjoyed physical activities did so because their brains were insufficiently stimulating. Even if Greg wasn't bright he was nice, Peach thought. She smiled at his sleeping face.

They stopped at a service station, so Dad could go to the toilet. Peach followed him into the bright building.

A businessman was shoving a sandwich into his mouth and shouting into the payphone, 'Tell your bloody manager I'm not putting up with any more of his crap.'

Two girls in sequins and fun fur were asking a wasted-looking crusty if he knew where the rave was. The girls were probably her age. Her age but nothing like her. They appeared to Peach as peacocks or parrots: colourful, fabulous and on their way somewhere.

All of a sudden, Peach felt sick of everything. So sick of her family, sick of her life, sick of herself: she could walk away and keep walking, walk right out of her life without understanding why. The hazardous feeling of important things dissolving.

She ran back to the car, to the sedative of her family's ordinariness. She loved them intensely in the darkness for helping her climb back into herself and hoped they would never change.

Chapter 6

Bathing suits fluttered on the line in the morning light. Towels flapped back and forth, exposing peeps of Peach's mother weeding her rockery.

Solomon lay down in the sun and rolled onto his back. His liver-spotted belly demanded scratches. He looked like he was grinning. Peach beamed back and called him a lovely puppy.

Earlier, boredom had driven her out for a walk. Solomon had idled in the fields, the tinkle of his collar slower than usual. Thoughts drifted in like ships; small ones and big slid over the horizon as Peach made a detour past the school just to savour the thought of not going back there. Familiar rooms lay dormant behind dark windows. Peach felt giddy and strange at the idea of never moving through them again. Her cutoffs dug and rubbed at the crotch – she wondered if there would be any boys worth kissing at Jade's party later.

Probably not: there never were. Although Nathan Pye would be there, gawping at Peach like a greedy person waiting for cling film to be taken off a buffet. She kept catching him looking at her that way ever since she'd got off with him at a party last summer.

Peach had road tested her sexuality with cautious curiosity bordering on the scientific.

She'd started with Nathan Pye because he had interesting opinions about The Cure. His inept kissing was tolerable to her cider-deadened nerves, until he plunged his hand under her 'Animal Nitrate' t-shirt and started grinding his erection against her thigh.

Long before that, she had begun to feel things, to accept alien possibilities might grow native. Her parents had prepared her. Sort of.

A book appeared in her room. Anodyne cartoons: helpful diagrams explaining she should prepare herself for hair and urges. At first, she'd felt that they were no more relevant to her than the reproduction of the Bayeux Tapestry in her history textbook. No more likely to occur inside her life than an arrow in the eye.

And yet she had begun to explore herself, to understand that in the obscure folds of her body, dormant things had grown restless. The poster on the wall above her bed was of a boy who sang a song she liked. He looked like a man to her.

When she was sure she was alone, she'd crouch on her pillows and rock. Run her tongue over the glossy surface of his grin. Lick his lips which were pink and girlish as hers. His teeth were neat and white as peppermints. She covered them with her mouth, leaving soggy trails she hoped no one would see.

Thrilled and disgusted, she'd wondered if there was something wrong with her. Wondered if she was uniquely dirty. She'd promise herself she would never do it again because it made her feel weird. But then she'd do it again because it made her feel good. Because it was her way of imagining a future of some kind that those hungers would be part of. She

44

was only just starting to become accustomed to them when an incident at a party left her full of self-disgust and reticence. Too afraid to act on her impulses until she shrugged it off and kissed Nathan Pye.

A few months after that, after various unremarkable kisses with boys who liked the right music, she decided she should investigate the darker mysteries of sex, or at least see a real penis up close.

Pamela, Jade and Peach had gone to a party, swigging vodka and orange out of a squash bottle on the way. In the living room of one of the big houses on the new estate, Peach examined the boys like an entomologist studying a beetle colony.

She had taken two or three cautious draws of a joint. Smoke fudged her brain. She noticed a round-faced boy looking over while his friends boasted about feats of daring accomplished on a school trip to Gloucester. A boy with stupid hair and teeth like the keys of a smashed piano brayed, 'Gary and I shoplifted a key ring from the folk museum and Miss Fishlock saw us and started going mental, but I blatantly denied it to her face and she believed me, and she even apologised – it was amazing.'

The round-faced boy gave Peach a look. The Snoopy smile which says, 'sorry my friend is such a dick – please don't assume I am also a dick.'

She invited him upstairs. They found a bedroom, furnished in pink satin, cluttered with a menagerie of china puppies and kittens.

The boy, Dan, was shaking. His words kept tripping him. He started to quote dialogue from *Reservoir Dogs* in an American accent and make finger guns. Peach shut his mouth with a kiss before he got too embarrassing to do anything with. As his hands explored her body, she experienced a rush of unfamiliar intensity.

Fumbled attempts to unhook her bra disrupted her enjoyment. The shock of burrowing fingers chased it off entirely. Dan jabbed in Peach's pants, fiddling where he suspected her clitoris to be. He was nowhere near it, rubbing briskly as if attempting to win a scout badge for lighting a fire without matches.

'Do you like that?'

Peach said yes and unbuttoned his fly with businesslike determination. She was shocked to find something so hard and aggressive in her hand. The only cocks she had seen before had been Greg's when he was younger – rosebud pink, small and plastic as a toy. And on a couple of horrifying occasions, thanks to the useless lock on the bathroom door, her dad's in the shower, waving and jumbling in soap suds, silly as a joke shop novelty.

Dan puffed and shoved and came into her fist in seconds, leaving Peach with a handful of warm slime. She felt disgusted and disgusting. It helped to imagine it was just wallpaper paste and she'd touched it by accident as he muttered she was lovely and that had been amazing.

It felt like a profound mystery of the human condition had been exploded. She resolved not to bother with any other sticky encounters until university, which, at that point, had felt reassuringly far away.

Recently, though, her body acted like a meddler: whispering and goading and shit-stirring. Reminding her that *it* wanted things without wanting any particular person to do them. Constant thirsty-hunger travelled in her blood and stoked her general sense of frustration.

Perhaps it was that very exasperation which made her ask Mum about the job at Ian's.

'I was wondering about what you said.'

'What, what I said?'

'Yesterday. About work. I don't definitely want to. I was thinking about it.'

Mum rattled soil from the roots of a dandelion and threw it into a cracked orange bucket.

'Okay. Well. Like I said, it wouldn't be terribly thrilling but you could make a bit of money.'

'Yeah. But what would I actually be doing?' The sun on Peach's back was heavy as hands.

Mum throttled another weed.

'Ian's got a big retrospective coming up. London. He's making new sculptures, restoring old ones, and a record company have bought the rights to Patty's back catalogue so there's media interest starting up round them both. Some journalist is coming to spend a few days with Ian. He wants archival stuff: photos, letters, stuff like that, so quite a lot of my time will be taken up sorting that out. Ian hasn't exactly been meticulous. You'd take over day-to-day stuff while I deal with that.'

'What *do* you do?' Peach asked. Now she was asking she realised she had never asked, not yesterday, not before.

Ian was an artist. He had been successful: in constant demand, ubiquitous until the eighties when tastes changed but his work didn't. He went out of fashion. Still he seemed to have plenty of money. Still he seemed to need Mum to be his assistant.

His wife Patty had been a folk singer. She recorded two albums that sank without trace apart from a single song. 'The Right Way Home' had briefly been a hit in the seventies. The kind of song that's everywhere for a few weeks then seldom heard again. The kind that only remains important to people who bought it as their first record. Or had their first kiss while it was playing.

Peach once heard it on the radio: she remembered pretty sadness. A melody that swirled and eddied like water. Bells chimed over the chorus, a line she'd liked about dancing with the one who taught you how.

Patty had died in a car accident when Peach was small. She had been gone for longer than she had been around. Peach hadn't really remembered, let alone missed her. When she was that age adults came and went all the time.

Mum snorted. There was a soft ripping as she rooted out something spidery. 'Good question. Lots of things. Well, I'm, well, Ian's assistant. It used to be, when he was more ... when he was busier I dealt with his correspondence and his ... I was more part of him, his ... making the work ... involved in materials, process ... actual sort of daily making things ...'

She hurled the weed into the bucket. 'I've been doing less of that and more of everything else. Housekeeping, paying his bills, gardening, cooking. Domestic stuff. But he's back in the studio again.'

It sounded like a list of pocket-money chores.

'Can I think about it?'

'It's your last summer before you go to university. You can do what you like.'

Peach watched Mum pull out a handful of bindweed with particular vehemence. Her hair was the colour of coins, the dull silver of fish scales. Peach realised she couldn't remember when it had stopped being dark like hers. She reached out and brushed away crumbs of soil that had settled in the parting. Mum startled at her touch.

'I think that rose is on its last legs,' Mum said, 'poor thing.'

*

Mum arrives with her husband, Peter, looking like they never loved anyone but each other. Like they never lived other lives with other spouses, before their narrowboat, watercolours and rescue greyhounds. Happiness they wouldn't have found if Peach hadn't done what she did. Not that Mum and Peter's contentment ameliorates her guilt.

Peach makes towards Mum, who swerves round her to wrap Greg in her arms, and she is only just recovering from the sting when a nurse with a face like a parrot fish comes to take them up to the ward. The nurse's mouth is kissy-pouty round her explanations. Peach wants to see her father. Peach does not want to see her father. Above all, Peach wants a cigarette and *someone*.

Joseph would take this sadness so much into himself that he would leave her with nothing to feel for herself. Per would be deeply Scandinavian in a way that would appeal to Greg. Alex would be drunk or stoned or both. And Simon would be a selfish bastard because that's what Simon is and he's sexy and awful. She'd take any of them back, have any of them here if it meant a hand to hold.

'You can go in. Only two at a time,' says the fish-faced nurse, and no one volunteers for the first attempt at being good enough.

'I need a smoke before I do this.' Peach stares at her shoes because this is profoundly true.

Greg stares at her shoes because he thinks that makes her feeble.

'Me too. Can I cadge one?' says Bella. Peach looks at her sister's shoes. They probably cost more than a month's rent on her minuscule studio flat.

'Cool,' fumes Greg. 'Cool. You two just go for a smoke then. I'll sort this out. It's not like we're a family or anything. It's not like *I* might need support.'

'Well, Mum's here now, *proper support for you*,' Bella hisses through a vicious little moue.

'Oh, give him a break, Bella.' Peach holds her hands up in despair.

Mum mirrors the gesture, palms up as if she's checking for rain, and says, 'Seriously? Seriously you're fighting? At a time like this you're fighting?'

Peter, in his pompous little captain's hat, throws Peach and Bella a look which acknowledges he has no right to rebuke his wife's children, but which does so nonetheless.

'Perhaps it's no bad thing if you pair pop out for a moment.'

This is Mum becoming *Mum*. Instinctively taking charge. Instilling diplomacy they should be capable of without guidance. 'Let's all have a pause and take some deep breaths before we go and see your father.'

Bella and Peach hurry down the corridor. Bella's shoes even *sound* expensive, haughty clicks that imply staff should cringe and tug their forelocks when they hear her coming. The corridor bulges and swims, acid rises at the back of Peach's throat.

'Can you slow down, Bella, I feel a bit dizzy.'

In place of the annoyance she anticipates, Bella slows. 'Sorry, I just – shit. *Shit*, Peach.'

'I know. Shit, Bella, this is so – I'm doing such a – I'm making such a bad job of this, it's like only my body is here or—'

'Right? It felt like I couldn't listen to the doctor, like I'd gone deaf or—'

'Totally! Honestly? It's like I'm hardly here.'

'Of course: we were only just getting used—'

'To the dementia? Not even.'

'Yeah.' Bella reaches out and grabs Peach's wrist.

'No. Exactly: not even. It's like it won't stick, not yet anyway.' Peach makes a little twist, as if she is focusing a camera, so Bella's hand slides into hers. She feels her sister's hand curl up round her own, consolation in her chest as much as her fingers.

'I know!'

'Like if I think of him,' Peach says, 'it's about him doing normal Dad things; noodling his guitar in the corner of his local and calling it a gig, having six pints of something fierce and calling it three—'

'Yes! Even though I know he's not doing that, that he can't. Do that. Any more. It's still how I imagine him.'

'It's so hard, isn't it? Even now I keep feeling as though he's going to walk in at any second.'

'I know! What's that about?'

'So, so tormenting, feeling like he'll just bowl in all tipsy and cheery—'

'Yes!' Bella's index finger draws little circles of comfort on Peach's palm.

'In a garish waistcoat and be like: why the long faces, folks?'

'Hah! Yes!'

'Do one of those massive silent beer burps he does—'

'And launch into a crap joke.'

'Of course, he would, and it's so unhelpful, that thinking, because it's letting me avoid—'

'Oh, me too, it's so messed up.'

'That's families though, isn't it? The older I get the more I realise that all families are messed up in some way or another, right?'

'I suppose.' Bella sounds reticent, and suddenly they are a train running out of track. Peach is not sure which of them lets go first but they are no longer holding hands. 'Ours is.

Seriously messed up.' Bella raises an eyebrow, presses the gigantic diamond in her engagement ring as if it might operate a teleportation device. It glints in the light and Peach realises that a pair of nurses are looking at them, talking about them.

No, not them: Bella. Peach has seen people look at Bella and whisper in the hospital corridor. Peach forgets that Bella is slightly famous, internet famous. Isabella Lewis: the LightPlan Living System guru.

LightPlan consists of costly juice, jogging and mindless platitudes which seem profound as long as they are typeset over photographs of sunsets and mountaintops. It's a multi-level marketing scheme. Her sister is basically as much of a crook as it's possible to be without actually breaking the law.

Peach can see these strangers find her sister magical and inspirational. This makes her feel angry until she remembers LightPlan only works because people are gullible when they feel terrible about themselves. It works because they have no idea what a mess Bella is. They only see happy hashtags and Instagram perfection. Momentarily she hates Bella for it.

Then she realises how crass and irrelevant her resentment is. Their father is clinging to the outer margins of life. How unfair that she should resent Bella any success, any satisfaction after everything Peach inflicted on her. Not just what happened with Ian but also with Dominic. She had conveniently not factored him into all this until now. Since she likes to forget him at every possible opportunity.

Chapter 7

In Peach's dream a doorbell rang over and over, until she woke to find it was a real sound.

Dusk surprised her. She'd dozed the whole afternoon and early evening away. Whoever was at the door was holding down the bell. Peach guessed she was alone, that it was Bella or Greg without keys. Solomon coughed out deep guard dog barks.

'All right!' she bawled. 'I'm coming!'

A few hours earlier, Peach stood in the living room with her family, only half listening to Mum dispensing instructions to live by while she and Dad went camping in Dorset.

Peach's father entered the living room wearing a shirt with a pattern like tropical vomit. He wore a tatty panama hat. A guitar case was slung over his shoulder.

'Will you guys be throwing some wild parties while we're away?'

'Don't encourage them, Kevin,' said Mum.

'Actually, I'm going to be reading for my dissertation.' Bella speared Peach and Greg on the sharp points of a stare. 'These two had better behave.'

'Ha ha! Yeah! "Reading".' Dad made bunny ears with his fingers. 'I used to do some serious "reading" when my parents were on holiday.' He tapped his nose with his index finger.

'No. I *really am* going to be reading.' Bella nearly snapped her neck recoiling.

Dad mimed drawing on an imaginary joint. 'Enjoy!'

'Mother, will you please take your tragic husband away now?'

Mum laughed. 'I think I'd better. But seriously – *please* water the plants, especially that rose. Peach? The rose I pointed out yesterday, the one that doesn't look very well. Peach?'

'Yeah, the rose, will do.'

'Keep the house tidy. Don't alienate the neighbours and don't antagonise one another. Peach? Greg?'

Greg held up three fingers – scout's honour.

'Don't spend all the housekeeping money on cider, the number for the campsite is on the fridge—'

'Come on, Mrs!' Dad tugged Mum's arm. 'They'll be fine.'

Outside, Dad slung his guitar onto the back seat, carefree as a gap-year traveller. He started the car and, reversing out of the drive, rolled down the window. 'See ya later! Party on, dudes!'

Mum shook her head.

'Was Dad quoting *Wayne's World*?' asked Greg.

'He just naturally has a flair for the embarrassing,' Peach cackled.

They stood on the doorstep watching the car disappear.

In that moment Peach felt the three of them to be equal and found herself imagining adult intimacy: Greg with a nice wife, she and Peach with smart, sexy husbands, interesting jobs and a flock of pretty children.

A square white hetero dream she'd not yet interrogated. Having lived surrounded by those exactly like her, she had completely failed to understand the world was equally composed of other kinds of people.

'I meant it about reading for my dissertation. You needn't think you'll be cluttering the place up with your pathetic friends.' Bella disappeared into the house.

'Bitch,' sulked Greg. 'I'm totally having a party.' He loped back inside leaving Peach to stare out into the cul-de-sac, idly petting Solomon, stroking the satiny spot between his eyes.

The familiar landscape was somehow fresh.

Next door, Mr French washed his mid-life crisis sports car. Across the street, through the window, Peach saw Mrs MacArthur pounding away on an exercise bike in front of the television, bottom quivering rudely like pudding, while Mr MacArthur looked past her at the TV. He put down an empty can of lager and smiled at the crack-hiss as he opened a fresh one. Peach had been in their house once; it smelled like boiled resentment: restlessness and soup.

Peach smiled, envisioning nothing but going to familiar places, doing things she had always done with people she had always known.

But now the doorbell was hurrying her down the stairs. The cheese plant shivered.

A shape rippled in streaks behind the frosted glass in the door. And it was neither Greg nor Bella, but a dishevelled young man with long hair. He was attractive in an androgynous way, wearing black jeans specked with many colours of paint.

'Hi. I'm Dominic.'

He proffered his hand. A lacklustre handshake made Peach shudder. 'Hello?'

He behaved like she ought to know who he was. He looked far too old to be one of Greg's friends, but Peach could never tell – some of Greg's friends were hairless pipsqueaks, others were colossal and stubbly as adults.

'I'm Izzy's boyfriend,' he said. He withdrew his hand and hefted a large rucksack from his shoulder onto the step. He looked at Peach as if she was very rude and very stupid.

'Look,' Peach said, folding her arms, 'I have no idea who you are, and I've never heard of Izzy.'

He stared down at his boots which were also spattered with galaxies of paint.

'Isabella. I'm Isabella's boyfriend – Dominic. You must be Peach, right?'

'Bella has got a boyfriend? *You're* Bella's boyfriend?' Peach laughed.

'Yeah.' He jutted his chin sulkily. 'Hasn't she told you about me?'

'Erm ... she doesn't tell me much. She's not even here.' Peach hesitated. 'Do you want to come in and wait for her?'

'Cool, thanks.'

He might be a murderer, thought Peach. Too late if he was: Solomon was already wagging himself banana-shaped in welcome as Dominic stepped inside. He gave Solomon a cursory stroke. One that made it obvious he didn't like dogs but also didn't like seeming a massive bastard in front of their owners.

Peach had never heard Bella called Izzy; such a flighty version of her name. So insubstantial – unimaginable she'd tolerate it let alone choose it. Yet Peach supposed she must have, another name for her other life. She led Dominic to the lounge, which held the heat of the day at its heart like something living.

'Would you like a cup of tea?' Dominic looked like an idea of an artist. An idea of an artist from a good, sad, slow-moving film about love going wrong. 'Or coffee?'

Coffee was cooler, more grown up. He smoked, obviously: fingers ochre-tipped. He probably wanted coffee and cigarettes. Peach had never used Dad's complicated coffee maker. No one was allowed to smoke in the house.

'Well? What do you want?'

'Coffee would be nice, but I could murder a beer.'

Peach was stripped of the ability to deny he was gorgeous. She swaggered to the kitchen, returning with two cold cans of her father's lager.

'Cheers.' Dominic caught the can Peach lobbed in his direction. He smiled lopsidedly using his fringe as a cave to hide in, peeking out.

Peach opened her beer. It spat foam over her clothes. She laughed shrilly and felt redness rush from her chest to her cheeks.

'So . . . ' said Dominic, pulling a pouch of tobacco from his parka, 'you going to uni soon?'

'Yeah.' Peach tugged her cardigan sleeves over her hands, still blushing. 'Glasgow, History of Art.' As she waited for him to ask why there, why that, the fact she didn't know made her seem stupid to herself.

But Dominic didn't ask. He finished rolling his cigarette. Turning it over between his fingers as though preparing a magic trick, he lounged back into the cushions and said, 'Cool, History of Art. Lots to remember. Can't do that stuff – facts and dates and shit. Couldn't, you know? No way. Bor-ing, no offence. I just want to make art, not pontificate about it. Doing painting at Goldsmiths, yeah? Okay to light up?' He waved the cigarette as if doing sign language for someone foreign.

He smiled again, indolent and self-assured. Peach took her scorched face and idiocy to the kitchen for a saucer.

There was a note on the table she hadn't noticed before. Greg's childish scrawl. He was staying overnight at Mitchell's house. Yuck: Mitchell Bennett, Greg's best worst friend. Weaselly, reeking of frustrated pheromones. A spoilt braggart, all spots and surnames. But Greg looked at Mitchell like he was Gazza scoring for England every time he opened his disgusting mouth to say something obnoxious.

Back in the living room, Dominic smoked contentedly. They talked about the Manic Street Preachers; Peach's favourite band – his too. He'd seen them live, of course, a few times. Peach had never been to any gigs, could only imagine sweat and lights and urgent music: the ecstasy of breathing the same air as her idols. It made her feel inadequate. He didn't seem to care.

Cold beer in Peach's stomach warmed her head. It felt heavy with empty pleasure. She rested against the cushions and hoped Bella would take a long time to come home.

Thought performed a jinx: the accusatory crunch of Bella's key in the lock. Feeling caught and dishonourable, Peach jumped to her feet. 'There's someone here to see you . . . *Izzy*.'

Dominic winked at Peach. Peach winked back.

'What the hell?' The door flew open as though wrenched by a force of nature rather than Bella's delicate hands.

'Hey beautiful,' Dominic beamed. He reached for Bella, delighted and greedy.

Bella recoiled. 'I thought I told you to piss off and die.' Her face contorted into a snarl. 'What were you thinking coming here? Oh my god. This just confirms what a complete penis you actually are.'

'Izzy . . .' he remonstrated, trying to put his arms round her. She pushed him. He toppled backwards onto the sofa.

'Get out!' wailed Bella. A prostrate Dominic looked up at Peach, neither of them sure who Bella meant.

'You!' she spat. 'Go to your room.'

Peach went meekly.

Morsels of speech fetched upwards as she threw herself down on the bed. Bella seemed to think Dominic had cheated on her. For the sake of sisterhood, Peach tried to summon hatred for him, but it was hard to have solidarity with Bella's wild unreason when Peach had experienced it so many times, launched by such minor infractions as an unsanctioned 'good morning' or a mistimed offer of toast. She found herself thinking how Dominic's eyes were blue like a swimming pool.

Bella hurtled in. 'Right. I'm going to stay with Katie tonight. That absolute tool can't get a train until morning, so I'm sorry, he'll have to sleep on the sofa. Don't let him in my room, don't let him touch my stuff, don't talk to him and make sure you throw him out the second he wakes up.' She made to leave.

'Are you okay?'

'I will be when he's gone.'

'Do you want a cuddle?'

'Like that's going to make it better.' Bella stamped away, leaving bitterness hanging in the air like a stink.

Next door, drawers scraped and slammed as Bella slung clothes into a bag. Each footfall expressed fury as she thumped down the stairs. The front door banged shut; an exclamation mark of noise.

On the bed, Peach stayed still, listening for movement. She began to wonder if Dominic had been mad enough to go after Bella. He must really love her, she thought. It opened a hollow in her like a sugar craving.

Peach had never coveted romance, presuming it made tears and weakness inevitable. Adult relationships felt separate from teenage melodramas. Girls she knew called having sex being in love – scared they'd be dirty not to. She imagined love might come someday in the form of someone brilliant but as yet faceless. For now, she considered it the preserve of the stupid and unimaginative. Like wearing high heels and liking Take That.

Yet there, in the dark, the thought of Dominic's breath on her neck summoned a private thrill. Maybe it was just sex; a bored curious horniness which felt like deep thirst begging from a serious place. But she imagined holding his hand, watching long films with subtitles without losing interest and impressing him with shrewd opinions about exhibitions, with her photographs.

She rolled off the bed and caught sight of herself in the mirror. She wished she had her Doc Martens on instead of the ugly, comfortable sandals Mum got her last summer.

Her new black button-up dress with the little white flowers, only bought last week, looked dowdy. She wished she'd chosen the long swirly moon-print one she'd tried on in the same shop. She'd felt sexy when she twirled in front of the fitting-room mirror. Looked great, felt great as the fabric swished. And yet, it had seemed too ... something. She wasn't sure what. She couldn't imagine wearing it into her actual life where everybody knew she wasn't the sort of person a dress like that suggested.

On her way downstairs, she tried to make her heart into a fist, tried to put knuckles on her silly soft want.

Dominic was still in the living room, smoking another roll-up, chugging the remains of Peach's beer, his own emptied. Solomon was sitting by the window, policing the comings and goings of the neighbourhood cats.

'Man, this is pretty awkward.' He swilled the dregs.

'Um, yeah.'

Dominic didn't look like he felt at all awkward.

'So, uh, Izzy's pretty angry with me – she thinks I shagged her mate.' He looked at Peach with his palms turned up, like a liar pretending to be honest. 'If you're wondering – I didn't.'

'It's none of my business. It seems like you shouldn't have come.'

He put his head in his hands, cigarette threatening to ignite his hair. I hope he sets himself on fire, thought Peach.

'I didn't do it. You must know what she's like. So angry, so sure she's right all the time. We had a fight and I went out with some mates and ended up talking to her friend, about how upset I was, and I crashed on her couch. Next thing I know Izzy's accusing us of having slept together. And we genuinely, honestly didn't.'

The words floated out on a dejected sigh. The sound of someone realising something very sad is very real. Dominic looked at Peach. So much *at* her, she felt the hook of him asking – please believe me.

Peach wrung her fingers as if counting them.

'We were only arguing because I told her I was worried about her. She works and smokes instead of eating. She's too thin and I was getting paranoid that she's anorexic, so I told her, and she went mental, accused me of trying to control her, like I was being a bastard or something.' Dominic pushed his face into his hands like a child hiding.

Peach thought of all the times her sister had gone ballistic over nothing. Dominic probably received the same punishment every time he was audacious enough to express concern. She offered him another beer.

'Thanks. I really need one.' The cunning of before was no longer evident: in its place just a handsome, heartsick boy.

Smoke drew abstracts in the light. Peach let her sandals fall from her feet as she tucked them up under her body.

'You guys must worry about her surely?'

'Honestly?' Peach took a thoughtful slug of beer. 'I don't think about her very much when she isn't here.'

She knew she sounded callous. 'I think Mum and Dad probably do, though – they know how uptight she is. I mean, how hard she works and stuff.'

Bella ceased to exist for Peach when she left with the leaves in autumn. Her brooding presence and the heat of summer evaporated at the same time. Peach was shocked to realise how little she considered her sister's elsewhere life when she wasn't at home. 'Do you think I'm really horrible because of that?'

'Nah.' Dominic's fingers were stroking papers round a plug of tobacco. 'I've got two little brothers. We get on and everything, but I don't really miss them when I'm away at uni. It's natural: doesn't mean I don't love them.'

Peach searched for a trace of embarrassment in his voice when he spoke of love but was impressed to find none. She'd never met a boy who could talk about feelings. But then she'd never looked for one.

'We were close when we were kids.' Peach touched her lip. She smiled at Dominic across the tip of her finger. 'But she got pretty moody as a teenager and after that we didn't really talk any more. Will you roll me a fag?'

Dominic smirked. 'I'm not sure I should do that – you're Izzy's baby sister, it might make her want to kill me even more.'

'I'm seventeen. I'm going to university in a couple of months.'

'I got up to all sorts when I was seventeen.' Dominic covered Peach with a stare. Crimson rushed from her core.

Solomon sloped out of the room as if he was embarrassed on her behalf. 'I reckon that's old enough.' Dominic put his fingers to work, ferreting in his tobacco pouch. He never once, not for a moment, took his eyes off Peach. She felt like a butterfly in a jar.

Bella and Peach looked sort of alike. Their faces were made from the same ingredients, yet Bella's features existed in a finer geometry, sat in better relation to one another. Peach accepted she was an unspectacular version of her sister. She supposed they had the same marmoreal skin, but Bella's hair was crow-black and glossy where Peach's was brown and prone to greasiness. Peach's hair was short where Bella's was long. Somehow thinking about that made her feel masculine and unpretty when normally she didn't care. Mapping the outline of her mouth with her index finger, Peach tried to resist its instinctive creep towards her nose. She slow blinked as if newly woken.

'Where's your brother, um ...' Dominic searched his memory. 'Greg?'

'Out – staying with his friend.' Truth felt laden and hazardous. Peach's stomach tightened and flipped. Her heart beat wild rhythms of unspeakable situations.

Dominic passed Peach a neat cigarette. Their fingers glanced at the tips, hardly a touch at all.

'Oh,' he said. His lips parted for the tiny word like a kiss. 'Just you and me then.'

'Yup. Just you and me.' Peach recognised this as flirting from trashy films she used to watch before she knew what good films were.

'Unless Izzy changes her mind and comes back after all.' Dominic proffered a light. Peach's reverie turned to paper, blackening and curling in the flame.

'She won't.' Peach exhaled smoke through her nostrils like a spiteful dragon. 'She hates you. When has Bella ever changed her mind?'

She felt like she'd stepped back from a high place after almost indulging an urge to jump. *Just jump.*

'I know. She absolutely hates me, and I haven't even done anything wrong.' Dominic's shoulders heaved. Tears landed on his jeans and made a Rorschach blot. It looked like a skull. It looked like a rose.

Peach was overwhelmed by a desire to lick the tears from his face, to take his sadness into her. Dominic kissed her. And she let him, in the absence of knowing what else to do. He opened her lips with his tongue, filling her with the taste of smoke and salt.

She thought of Bella across town, probably drinking wine and scowling in Katie's bedroom. She thought of Greg and Mitchell hammering buttons in the glare of the computer screen, of Mum and Dad breathing grassy smells as rain drummed on their tent, of the MacArthurs in bed with their backs turned to one another, of Pamela on the bus shelter roof, needled all over with gooseflesh while Colin and Jade stole one another's breath. Of streetlights glowing in the dusk, televisions filling living rooms with the stern tones of men in ties reading the news. Somewhere, a Manics concert; neon animal air, the bassline of 'You Love Us' racing through a thousand strangers, each of them feeling as if the music was their own heartbeat. Above it all, the moon a knowing crescent wink, clouds traversing the sky, scattered stars above the high street with the shops shut, above houses strung out across the fields, the sweep of the top road all the way to Ian's house where soon, maybe, she might go to work. She thought of his dead wife Patty, of blind rocks encased in soft moss, the night bus on an empty road, trees clutching at the sky.

She thought of everyone, everywhere, and didn't know where she fitted in the present which was shaking, flying apart, splintering, so no one and nothing she thought of mattered. Nothing mattered but Dominic's mouth covering hers and how that told her she was *someone, somewhere* and wiped out the world. Everything consisted at that second of Dominic and kissing.

Peach slipped her hand under his clothes, wanting to know everything about the body pressed to her own; charting his back with her palm, measuring his pale arms, tasting his mouth and plotting his flesh in inch-long strokes, drinking up his cigarette smell.

Dominic's hand reached under her dress. A silky electric feeling. His fingers did things she had only managed to do herself before then. He jerked her underwear off and undid his belt.

Back on the precipice she'd been relieved to withdraw from, Peach was aware Dominic was her sister's boyfriend – *ex-boyfriend*. Older, experienced and not hers, yet the liquid sensation carried her. She said nothing as he pushed into her.

Hot bright pain surprised her as he plunged. He took shock for enjoyment. Pushed harder, lunging, gaining momentum.

Peach gritted her teeth. Butted her head into the crook of his shoulder, biting back the desire to push him away, to shout stop.

No, she told herself; I've let him start, I'm losing my virginity: *it is happening now.* I might as well go through with it. She wondered if there was something wrong with her that she should be so practical in the throes of her first fuck. Maybe she had something hard and cold like marble in place of a heart. Then she simply knew this was a stupid idea and was too proud to admit it.

Dominic thrashed and panted. The pain between her legs grew. She clung to his back, inhaling the beer sour taste of her breath as it condensed between their skins. Just when the pain became unbearable, Dominic withdrew, came onto Peach's stomach.

'Jesus. That was good,' he said proudly. He reached down for his tobacco. 'First time?' he grinned, examining his flaccid penis.

'Yeah.' Peach wanted to wash as his come dried scabby on her hip. She pushed her dress down over her legs.

'Nice.' He lit his cigarette and passed it to Peach. She attempted to take it as a chivalrous gesture; hoping any old shit might constitute grace in a dire predicament. It didn't work. She took a long drag and felt like crying.

Dominic relaxed into the sofa with his hands behind his head.

Peach could imagine him in a pub, showing off to friends. Bragging about how he shagged both sisters. She knew she was just the story between smokes. People would buy him pints and call him a legend. His face was mottled and puffy like bruised fruit. Peach couldn't decide who she hated more – Dominic or herself.

Crushing the cigarette into the saucer, she picked up her pants and sandals. 'Um ... I'm going to bed.'

'Cool. Sleep well.' He was rolling another fag.

In the doorway Peach waited for some scrap. An affection-ate word, a nice gesture, an acknowledgement of wrongdoing. He averted his eyes; letting Peach know she was nothing now. A spent match he'd lit himself up with and dropped.

She wanted to slap his face, claw and spit. Melodramatic

thinking didn't alleviate pain. She hefted its immensity up the stairs: so big and real it felt like she was carrying it on her back.

Solomon loped after her. He bowed and stretched, gave her a look like he was smiling in anticipation of a fuss, a game, some ragged nonsense. She couldn't touch him.

Waiting for the shower to warm she scrutinised her reflection in the bathroom mirror. Who are you, Peach Lewis? What the hell have you just done? Steam began to fog her reflection, obscuring her features. She raised her hand to free her image but let it drop to her side. She wouldn't recognise herself anyway.

And she wasn't sure why, because she'd done a terrible thing. But she knew in the mirror she'd look so sexy.

And she wasn't sure why, but she had a feeling in her mouth like a smile round ripe, bitten fruit.

And yes. She remembers now. She felt like that because she *was* smiling.

Chapter 8

Outside the hospital Peach and Bella smoke underneath a no-smoking poster. Someone has drawn a massive cock and balls on the sad, bald cancer patient in the picture. As if he didn't already have enough problems.

An elderly couple are smoking too, the man's wheelchair parked over the no-smoking symbol painted on the tarmac. His wife removes his oxygen tube and lights him another Superking. Peach supposes you can't stop people indulging a habit which dulls the pain of terrible things in a place where they're most likely to be happening.

Peach's contact lenses have turned into salt and vinegar crisps in her eyes. She lights a second cigarette off the stub of her first. Bella paces and smokes like it is holding the sky up. She grinds out her cigarette under the vicious-looking heel of her ankle boot and holds out her hand for another.

'How's your love life?'

Peach passes her the lighter. 'Barren.'

'Like you.' Bella laughs.

Peach does too. 'Up yours. It's an ongoing choice rapidly becoming a foregone conclusion. What if Dad dies? Do you think Dad's going to die?'

'No.'

'You sound sure. We haven't even seen him yet and the doctor said—'

'He's not going to.' Bella huffs smoke through her nose and her voice is brave from fear, defiant because complying with the possibility of death might encourage it. 'You ever see Mark?'

'Mark? Never. What made you think of him? Doesn't cross my path, doesn't cross my mind.'

It's not true. Peach bumped into him a couple of months ago. She and Alex had started to talk again, pretending to want to be friends when really it was undeniable they were plodding out the hackneyed gavotte that was their way of initiating sex. Again.

They had been texting about how sick they were of London, saying they should both try harder to make the most of it, stop taking it for granted the way its inhabitants inevitably do. Galleries, museums, parks. It will all always be there. You could go any time and so you don't.

Because of that they'd met at Greenwich Observatory, pretending to want to talk when they just wanted to fuck, wondering why they'd met in a place so remote from their beds as to remove the opportunity.

Alex was a food photographer. He was hungover that afternoon: broody and uncommunicative. Peach recalled tricks of his trade he'd revealed over the years. Ronseal on roast chicken, baby oil brushed onto salmon, tampons soaked in boiling water and hidden under cold food to mimic appetising steam: yeah, she'd thought, that's about right.

Peach found herself talking until her voice sounded brash and inane as an ice-cream van braying chimes in chilly weather. It was all so pointless and demeaning that they doubled down, had an argument about whether or not the gender pay gap exists, then Alex had said #MeToo was making all the women he knew hysterical and she had called him the worst person in the world, bought a pack of cigarettes for the first time in two years, walked into the Gypsy Moth, and ordered a double gin and tonic.

She'd sat in the beer garden alone. Early autumn chill in the air. Gin not sinking her sadness but making it soggy, heavier. She had thought about how sadness used to come in so many different flavours: salty and spicy and sour, sweet even. Over the last few years it had grown tasteless and colourless, like her gut was perpetually bloated with plain bread and water.

As she was walking away, mouth ashy with failure, Mark had walked in. Bearded, balding at the temples, tubby satisfaction about him with a tiny baby strapped to his front. The baby's face was covered in both wet and dry snot. Its eyes were piggy in a way that reminded Peach of how Mark always looked when he was drunk. It grizzled and wriggled in the harness like a parachutist caught in a tree. Mark was carrying a pink scooter.

'Peach, wow, hey, how are you?'

'Yeah, good, you?' Gin had hit her hard, smudged her syllables.

Mark looked at her with judgemental concern. Poor Peach, predictably messy – self-inflicted but still deserving compassion.

'Yeah, great. This one here is three months old now and Charlotte's just started year two at schoo ...'

His wife and daughter flustered in, Charlotte wearing Mark's face in miniature, screeching 'No!' twisting away from her flush-faced mother who was spilling a tray of coffees.

'Well, nice to see you, Mark.'

'Are you okay, Peach?' Forcing his pity on her, like a representative of a political party she opposes trying to push a pamphlet into her hand.

'I am *great*. Have a *wonderful* Sunday with your *lovely* family.' Peach stuck her snoot in the air, stumbled slightly and walked off.

Behind her, Mark's daughter's voice, 'Who was that funny lady, Daddy? Why did she have all silly blue stripes in her hair?'

'Mark was too boring for you,' says Bella. 'Me and Greg used to call him Mogadon Mark behind your back.'

'You barely met him. Anyway, that's rich coming from Greg.'

'Are you saying our brother is dull?'

'Come on; he and Marcus wear identical cagoules. They finish each other's sentences. I can hardly tell them apart. They're like Gilbert and George in Gore-Tex, they're the Gilbert and George of boring.'

Bella looks shocked, then laughs. Laughs so hard, so long that Peach starts to worry.

'You okay there?'

'Shit, Peach, you can't say things that funny – my pelvic floor.' She wipes her eyes.

'I've seen your Instagram: you're always doing yoga and Pilates and bloody yogalates.'

'Yeah, makes no difference, have you seen the size of Octavia and Anais's heads?'

'They don't have particularly big heads.'

'Seven years old. Adult hats. That's all I'm saying.'

Then Peach laughs until she feels like laughter is trying

71

to suffocate her; her eyes feel like they are bulging out of her skull.

'You know, the other day I offered to take them for ice cream, as long as they promised not to tell Daddy, because obviously Douglas would worry that ice cream's off message for LightPlan. And you know what they said?'

'What?'

'No thanks, Mummy. Ice cream is bad for you and we want to do flute practice.'

'Wowser.'

'What have I done with my life?'

'Yeah. Well. What have I done with mine?'

'Fuck knows but at least you didn't marry Mogadon Mark.'

Peach and Bella snigger and blow smoke. It hovers about their heads – crowns them with clouds.

It seems so distant now: Mark. That life: two hollows in the pillows, two toothbrushes on a smeared glass shelf in the bathroom, two coats on the peg next to the front door. Home contents insurance. Dinner parties which ended in annoyance with people they knew would be annoying when they invited them. They bought grout and chose cushions, peed with the door open. They tolerated one another's parents and endured the smell of one another's farts – accommodations Peach discovered she was capable of once sex stopped being so important.

She experienced everything she assumed she was meant to. Compromise and tedium. Happiness and security. The frequent suppression of an overwhelming urge to scream.

She used to look at Mark, sitting on the couch in his pants, half a ball peeking out the leg hole, as he fiddled about with his mobile. With a mixture of disgust and satisfaction she would think: yes, this is it. This is my life. You are my person. She'd imagine getting fucked by some cheese-ball she'd exchanged pointy looks with on the tube and be glad it wasn't happening. Then she'd dive onto the couch beside Mark, feeling contented and restless.

Until the day of *the conversation* she assumed things would always be that way.

It started with Mark putting trousers on in the middle of a Sunday afternoon. Peach was sitting in the living room, unwashed and still in pyjamas. Christmas ones with a hole in the crotch.

Mark came into the living room, buckling his belt and asked, 'What do you want?'

'Watch a film? Maybe take another nap? Get a curry? Spice Palace do that Sunday special with all the poppadoms and dips and starters if you order before seven.'

'No. What do you actually want?'

She was aware of her stink, her pyjamas implying infirmity.

'What? You mean in a big life way?'

Mark sat in the chair only visitors used.

'Yeah. I do actually. I mean in a big life way.' He looked at her like he was trying to decipher the kind of abstract paintings she sometimes insisted they go and look at together. 'I've been thinking about it lately and I reckon it's time to make serious plans.'

'What kind of plans?' she asked. She wanted to get dressed.

'Marriage? Marriage,' he said. She wanted to get dressed.

'And kids. Marriage and kids,' he said to his fists in his lap and she wanted to get dressed and walk out of the house.

'Can this wait a second 'til I put some clothes on?'

'We need to talk about this.'

'I'm not dressed for this kind of conversation.'

'It doesn't matter.'

And it shouldn't have mattered. But it did.

It mattered that the imbecilic grins of the faded snowmen on her pyjamas had become sarcastic.

It mattered that she could smell the unwashed creases of her body.

It mattered that Mark being properly clothed made Peach feel like he was visiting her in hospital.

'I'll just be a minute.'

'Can you not?'

'Get dressed?'

'Yeah.'

'No. Look, I'd like to get married. I think I'd like to get married.' Peach tried to give Mark a winning/willing smile. All the right ingredients, but the recipe had gone wrong. She could feel it in her weird rictus skull-face, teeth biting each other.

Could see it in his face. Crestfallen, dawning realisation he would have to finish what he'd started, apparently on a whim.

'Are you proposing?'

'Why don't you go and get dressed?'

She moved through the house, experiencing Mark's belongings as the anticipation of his absence. One toothbrush standing in the plastic cup. Peg in the hall without his duffel coat, protruding like a naked erection. Sheets furrowed on one side, neat and smooth as a hotel bed on the other.

She'd had the sweaty, palpitating feeling of something life-changing and huge unfolding, but she remembers she kept thinking she was hungry. That she was hungry and maybe in an hour the house would smell of spices and she and Mark would be sprawled on the couch with mouths full of fire and heads full of nothing, just like any other Sunday night.

'I want to have a baby.'

'With anyone, Mark, or with me?'

'You. Obviously with you but—'

'But what?'

'But I *do* want a baby. So—'

'So what?'

'If you don't—'

'Then I can just piss off and you'll go straight out and find someone else to have a baby with?'

'Not straight out, but, I'd rather it was with you but—'

'So that's it? You want an imaginary baby more than me? I'm real and I'm here but you'd rather have an imaginary baby than real, now, right here me?'

'That's not what I said but—'

'The most important thing you are saying is *but*. The rest is noise. *But* is all I can hear.'

'No, listen to me; I love you. I love you, Peach, I really do but ...' Mark stopped and stared into the air in front of him, like this time he could see *but* hovering there in big red neon letters. The three-letter word that was at that moment ending their relationship.

Peach said, 'Yes, I love you, Mark. I *do*. But I don't want a baby, and I never will.'

And it hit her. Only her toothbrush would sit above the sink. Only her shape would be imprinted in the sheets. And that that was right. That Mark would have a baby and it wouldn't be with her. That there is no love in staying with a person because they have a great arse and correct opinions about books and they take the bare look off a place by coming home at night.

'So, that's it then, is it? You've decided you're just never going to grow up?'

'Don't be a prick. It's not about not wanting to grow up, it's about not wanting a baby. Anyway, not your problem now, is it?'

'Of course it's my problem – you're my girlfriend.'

'Am I?'

'No. Shit. No. I guess maybe you're not. I can't believe this is happening.'

Peach was devastated. Devastated to realise now they'd had *the conversation*, it was really, obviously, untenably crazy that it was the first time they had discussed these instrumental subjects in any serious way. Crazy in a very pedestrian way, which also devastated her: that even in its most dramatic moment for years, the story of her life was a film too tedious to shoot.

'So that's it then? You're going to throw away nearly five years together for a baby that might never exist?'

Mark rolled his eyes. 'So that's it then? You're going to throw away nearly five years together to go to parties and have hangovers forever?'

'That is not why I don't want a baby!'

'Then why not?' Mark came close to her, a pleading in his eyes she was ashamed to feel validated by.

'Why not, Peach? We could be happy. We *would* be happy, you'd be a lovely mum. You're great with kids. So why not?'

For a moment she mentally put Mark's toothbrush back, hung his coat up, placed a plastic step next to the sink, a potty, hung a tiny parka on the peg on top of his. She filled the house with tantrums, strawberry yogurts turning to pink stilton, skin-kind emollients. Her imagination tripped over blocks and buggies, teddies and sippy-cups, changing bags and board books with teeth marks in their covers.

Peach's body felt saggy and tired, the way it does now

anyway. 'Because I really don't want to. Not with you, not with anyone. Do you remember a couple of years ago when I was starting to feel a bit broody?'

'Yes.' Mark smiled.

'Well, that was terrifying. Having that bodily want. I used to think, right now I know that my rational feelings and this urge in my body are separate, like the reproductive equivalent of needing a shit, but what if I mix them up?'

'Gross, Peach. For god's sake.'

'Oh, give over, I just mean it felt purely biological. And I used to wonder, what if this physical urge overwhelms my certainty that I never want a baby? And you know what made me sure that that would never happen?'

Mark shook his head. He didn't look at her.

'Because every time I was out in public and I heard a baby crying or a toddler having a tantrum and I imagined that noise being my problem, imagined I was responsible for making it stop, it made my blood run cold. Actually made my blood run cold, and when I told myself that that noise would never be my problem I experienced joy. Proper, delighted, grinning joy.'

'But you love kids!'

'Yes! I do love children. Children are brilliant. Our friends' kids clench my heart. They make me laugh. I love holding a baby in my arms. I love the intense way kids play, I'm totally fascinated by the profound seriousness of their questions. But *I do not want one.*'

'But—'

'Don't waste your time, Mark. I lack that part. The drive is absent. I don't want a baby like I don't want an aquarium or a hang-glider or a horse or a caravan. They're life-affirming for other people but I don't want one.'

Peach remembers searching Mark's face to see if he was looking at her as though she was a monster. But he was just looking at her as if she was sad and pathetic. Sad and pathetic and misinformed like a zealot trying to convince him her UFO conspiracy cult had identified the secret truth under-pinning the universe.

And he didn't say 'You'll change your mind.'

He didn't say 'You wouldn't feel that way if it was your child.'

He didn't say 'Everyone feels like that until they have their own baby.'

He didn't say any of the things Peach got sick to death of hearing, any of the dismissive, incredulous things she was told all the time which people abruptly stopped saying about four or five years ago.

He simply said, 'Oh. Right then. What do we do now?'

And what they did was be kind to one another as they packed their lives into boxes, emptied their home of who they'd thought they were. Mark and Peach behaved like fellow competitors in a sport they had discovered they were not very good at – they commiserated with one another and went their separate ways.

Then Peach went to live with a depressed performance artist who had recently moved back to London from Berlin after a vicious divorce. And Mark went to live alone. Not for long though. While Peach grew a baby bump from lager and Domino's Two for Tuesday, Mark had a daughter with a fashion journalist from a magazine company he did graphic design for.

'We should go back in.' Peach sighs.

'We should. Ready?'

'Nope. You?'

'Absolutely not.'

'We can do this, we just need to stay calm and to not, you know . . .' Peach flounders.

'Fight? What? Are we going to nip into surgery for a quick personality transplant on the way up to see Dad?'

'I wish.'

'Bitch.'

'No! I meant for me. I wish that, sometimes, I wish that for me.'

'Me too.'

'Bitch.'

'No. Me too for me.'

'I know what you meant. You're fine as you are,' says Peach. Bella squeezes Peach's arm and gives her an inscrutable look, as if confiding something that cannot be spoken. Peach's organs feel ripe and bloody. Fat and crowded. Unspoken love and regret, years impossible to live differently plugging her heart like cholesterol.

'Bella?'

Sharply Bella says, 'Don't,' then softly, 'Come on. We better get up there, Greg's probably started a rave or something.'

Peach laughs and wonders whatever happened to Dominic who made such a thing as confiding, such a *simple* thing as confiding and laughing, so impossible between the two of them for all those years. Then she wishes sleeping with him was the only thing she did that made such things impossible in her family and hopes that Dominic is dead, or at the very least brutally unhappy in a life he deems beneath him.

Chapter 9

When Peach had finally ventured downstairs in the morning Dominic was gone: vanished apart from a slight smell of smoke and a head-shaped hollow on the sofa that was cold when she placed her hand in it.

Milk had been delivered. Solomon greeted Peach as if she'd been gone forever then nosed his bowl. It seemed miraculous. The sky wasn't falling. Living with a horrible mistake made it feel as though it was.

Three days later, Bella faced Peach across the breakfast table. Until then Peach had avoided her successfully. Bella had stayed two nights at Katie's house and had barely left her room since she came back.

Seeing her wasn't as bad as Peach anticipated. She'd resigned herself to carting shame through muggy days, weather like second-hand breath. Reading *The Bell Jar* in the garden and feeling like an intellectual heavyweight because of it. Listening to the Manic Street Preachers in Pamela's bedroom. Being amazed by *The Holy Bible*. Wishing she had reasons to be angrier. Forgetting as soon as the record ended, reverting to inconsequential chat about her life: safe enough to grow bored in.

She had found herself experimenting more and more with

taking pictures of herself, in the mirror, or using the timer. That strange transgressive thrill she'd experienced when she did it on a whim on the last day of school had lodged inside her like a spike. It felt sneaky and dirty in ways that compelled her to construct scenes and costumes.

An old net curtain pulled over her heavily lipsticked mouth. A matted blonde wig on her head that Mum used to wear in the sixties, neck heavily garlanded with beads. Mum's fur coat slithered from its plastic wrapper, stinking of naphthalene. She put it on, only her underwear underneath, twisted her body into gnarled shapes in front of a Persian carpet she'd retrieved from the attic. She had two rolls of film now. Two rolls of film she was eager to see, yet couldn't bring herself to have developed, in case she walked into Snappy Snaps to find the staff whispering and laughing.

Bella paddled her spoon round a bowl of cereal without eating. Solomon sauntered over. He huffed as he laid his head on Peach's thigh. She scratched behind his ear until his back leg thumped the floor and made his collar jingle.

'What?' asked Bella. 'What are you staring at?'

'Nothing – I just wondered if you were all right, after, you know, everything?'

'Everything what?' Bella's spoon drew zeros in milk.

'The other night.'

'Dominic?' asked Bella, halting the hundredth lap of spoon around bowl. 'Over him. Wanker. His loss. Hope the dirty shag was worth it.'

A graphic image of Dominic assailed Peach. Screwing her into the sofa. Repulsion tailed by a buzz.

'I hardly spoke to him but he seemed like a dick.'

Bella snorted. 'He is. That's all you need to know.'

She deposited her bowl on top of the leaning tower of dishes which had long outgrown the sink.

Peach wanted to crush her sister into an embrace. Instead she sat staring at a plate of toast crumbs as Bella receded down the hall to commune with ingenious Frenchmen who had beautiful ideas and could never let her down because they were dead.

Morning sun filtered through the frosted glass in the front door, diffusing her image until brightness swallowed her whole. She reminded Peach of someone – a sixties singer looking stunning and woebegone on the cover of a record no one had listened to for years. She reminded her of Patty Elder, until now only vaguely significant as her parents' dead friend, dead wife of the man Mum worked for. But now Peach could go to work for Ian and curiosity set her mind whirling.

Peach's memories of Patty were imprecise. An impression of conventional beauty seldom encountered in real life. An unaccountable conviction that Patty radiated remoteness which made her appear special. Perhaps it was simply that adults uninterested in children often provoke longing in a child to be noticed, but Peach remembered a glassy indifference about Patty which made her attention desirable.

Patty's car careered off a wet road, into a field and smashed into a tree. Just off the top road – almost home. She wasn't wearing her seatbelt. That was all Peach knew, that and the accident wasn't discovered until hours after it happened.

In the absence of facts, Peach constructed her own version of the scene. Seventies gothic, patinated in grainy film stock. Patty in a tight, black polo neck. Blonde hair, disarrayed in the collision, coiled over one of her open eyes. Her cheek resting against the steering wheel. She looked perfect, as if she might get up and walk away. Except for the uncanny angle of her neck, the rivulets of crimson blood coursing down her forehead, matching her lipstick. Rooks circled like undertakers come to help her soul escape. The tree's limbs spread in a shrug. Shiny sports car crumpled like a spent bullet against the trunk.

Peach killed Patty off so prettily, a lump of sadness bobbed in her throat.

A few years ago, Peach had walked up to the Elders' cavernous art-deco house to meet Mum. She remembered a huge framed photo of Patty. Time had made her clothes and hairstyle kitsch. Poor Patty, she thought. Poor Ian: Peach was glad her mother was his assistant and housekeeper. It meant he wasn't alone.

Peach wondered about working for him, doing Mum's dull-sounding job. It wasn't the thought of death still clinging to the house that put her off – it was the potential for dreariness.

Greg and Mitchell loped into the kitchen, scratching and yawning. Mitchell strode around topless. He stopped halfway across the room to release an extravagant belch. Greg, already dressed for sport, creased over with laughter. He looked at Mitchell like he was the coolest person in the world.

'Pathetic.' Peach stomped out of the room, down the hall, out of the front door into a day that already promised to be fiercely hot.

She drifted round to Pamela's house because she always did when there was nothing much to do. When she couldn't stand to be alone with her thoughts. Jade did too; she was already there.

Peach and Jade and Pamela lay on Pamela's bed like sailors becalmed on a raft. Pamela's bed was the place where they had congregated to listen to *Nevermind* and cry when they heard Kurt Cobain had shot himself. Where they'd studied for exams, complained about their sisters, eaten strawberry laces by the yard.

Waves of books and records and dirty laundry surrounded them. They had coasted hours away, the weather too stultifying to entice them out. Pamela's house always smelled unaccountably of ham. In her bedroom the smell mingled with incense, bad breath and sleep.

Pamela lay on her stomach, flipping through a copy of *Select*.

Jade was playing with her hair and wittering about whether or not she and Colin should *do it*. Lately that was all Jade talked about. 'We keep, like, so nearly *doing it*, you know, we've done everything else, but he is so paranoid about me getting pregnant, like even though I'm on the pill, he's mega-para about it.'

Peach realised that she hadn't considered *those* implications of the Dominic incident. Shock rolled her into a ball. She'd been so busy considering all the other ones that it hadn't even occurred to her. Fear made her gnaw the skin round her nails. Before she decided they were vapid, she'd pored over the problem pages in *Just Seventeen* and *More!* enough times to know the withdrawal method wasn't reliable.

Peach didn't know any teenage mothers. She had seen one or two on the high street, emerged from the council estate of which she and her friends understood nothing. Peach had never interrogated her glib, privileged judgement, only recoiled from poverty, shell suits and babies with pierced ears. She recognised them from warnings about slack conduct that teachers and parents issued into the cosy lives of children like her. Warnings they were convinced they didn't need, secure in the knowledge that girls their age pushing prams must deserve the lives they had.

Placing her hands on her stomach, Peach wondered if she should tell Pamela and Jade what she'd done. But Jade was busy talking about what *she* hadn't done yet and, looking at Pamela, Peach felt no connection.

She felt tired of them: begrudging their ignorance of things she hadn't told them. Hating them for not being the sort of friends Peach felt compelled to spill her secrets to.

'Let's go out,' Pamela said. She burped.

You're such a pig, thought Peach, pushing her head into a pillow. It smelled of unwashed hair. 'If you like.'

'Peach?' Pamela asked. 'Are you all right? You seem a bit funny.'

'Pam's right, you do seem weird,' chimed Jade.

Peach felt like an uninvited outsider: a third wheel. For so long she had taken for granted that she was an equal party in a three-way friendship, that her presence was welcome, since no one ever acted like it wasn't. Yet, when she thought about it, she couldn't remember the last time Pamela and Jade had actually invited her to hang out. And suddenly she could imagine them exchanging eye rolls behind her back, doing impressions of her after she left and mocking things she had said.

'Yeah, just hot and grumpy. Sorry.'

An easy laugh flopped out of Pamela. She looked childlike and pretty. 'Let's get cider and go to yours.'

They set off into the late afternoon. Cries from nearby circled them; Peach could not tell if the sound was being made by birds or children. The whole world had taken on the unreal quality of a dream.

Everything was saturated with bright light like an old Technicolor musical. Radios played songs of summer: the kind that stuck no matter how much you hated them – that soppy one by Wet Wet Wet that seemed to have hung around forever.

They met Ollie Watson outside the shops, kicking an empty bottle against the kerb.

'Do you want to come to Peach's house?' asked Pamela, looking down, tugging at her hair.

Ollie thought for a moment. Sun gleamed on his oily complexion as he searched his shorts pocket for cider money.

They peered round the door of Spar to see who was working. It was Blind Mo. Thick specs on a chain round her neck that she never put on her face. She'd serve alcohol to anyone who could see over the counter even if they had school uniform on.

Jade called Colin from the payphone and insisted they all had to hang around on the corner and wait for him. When he arrived, they were licking swirls of colour from Zaps, and Peach noticed Colin had started sneakily becoming attractive.

Something had snapped to fit behind his prominent jaw and square brow, turning him handsome where before he'd had a wonky primate look. She guessed he hadn't realised. He didn't seem to pay attention to anything or anyone except Jade with the auburn curls Peach coveted and the acned T-zone she didn't.

They walked down streets that all looked the same: comfortable people's comfortable houses. They rounded the cul-de-sac where Peach lived. Mr MacArthur was stabbing his flowerbed to death with a hoe while his wife carped at him between sips of Chardonnay. The cool poetry of the suburb where nothing, reassuringly, continued to happen was beautiful to Peach.

In the living room Peach's friends chatted over cider. Greg and Mitchell were doing wrestling moves on the sofa, already drunk off half a can of Kestrel each, while Solomon yipped and leapt.

Later Bella came in, tipsy from lunch with old school friends that had turned into drinks.

Peach readied herself for a scene, but Bella just winked and walked out. Returned swinging a vodka bottle. 'You wouldn't be embarrassed by your mouldy old sister having a drink with your mates, would you?'

'No! That would be great.'

Bella was sweet and entertaining. How strange to see her sister being so gregarious and pleasant. Like hearing her converse fluently in a foreign tongue Peach had no idea Bella spoke.

They put on records and danced in a circle: self-consciously trying out their best moves. Then rhythm and vodka and cider took hold. Bella dipped and swayed through 'Fool's Gold', arching her back in a way that made Ollie stare at his feet. Solomon slalomed between their legs. Peach moved among them with her camera held to her eye.

Bunching her hair away from her sweat-damp back, Bella took Peach's wrist and led her into the garden for a cigarette. Peach's insides knotted.

Patio slabs exhaled heat. A thin crescent moon picked through the sky like a fingernail. Moths dithered amorously round the porch light.

They sat side by side, in the downy dark, sipping cigarettes as night creatures serenaded each other among the plants. Watching smoke draw delicate calligraphy from their mouths to the dark, Peach noticed how similar they were becoming. They had come from opposite ends of the spectrum. Now they met in the middle.

Bella emerged from squashy cherub flesh to become tall

and lithe. Peach's appearance had always made nonsense of her name. She had been a twig, developing curves late in adolescence: so relieved when she finally did. She thought rude boys and mean girls would call her 'fried eggs' forever.

Only Bella kept getting thinner all the time, as if she was rubbing herself out. Peach had an unwelcome thought of Dominic knowing them both from the inside. Trapped guilt scuttled inside her. Bella looked so pretty. Bella was such a good sister really. Bella was so clever. Peach decided to tell her. It was only right.

Peach's voice was tremulous as the owl hoots quavering from the trees. 'I need to tell you something.' She watched Solomon fossicking around the compost heap, compelled by rotten tasty stinks.

'Yeah? No, because I wanna tell you somethin' first.' Bella's words all shapeless and slack with drink. 'I wan'd you t'come out here 'cos we need to talk 'bout something.'

Peach's heart punched and thumped: she already knows.

'I really want you to listen, s'important, yeah? Ready?'

'Ready,' Peach said, knowing she never would be. Anticipation snarled her gut like the endless second of waiting for a roller coaster to drop.

Bella's head nodded onto Peach's shoulder. It felt too light; those dark moods and unknowable thoughts ought to weigh more. Peach stroked her sister's satin hair; it felt expensive.

'I wanna tell you sorry. Sorry I'm such a bitch sometimes.'

'No, no, no,' Peach flailed. 'You're not a bitch at all.'

'I am – sometimes. Quite a lot a bitch. Uni's heavy. I get used to living away from home. An' like s'hard to come back and be part of the family again and I got, like, problems, like ...'

'What problems?'

'No problems, doesn't matter, anyway, blah, blah, blah. I feel bad about Dominic. I shouldn'ave dumped him on you. You were really cool about it.'

Peach felt like she had stolen something from her sister and sold it back to her for twice the price. A sour sparkle-burn behind her eyes.

'Wha'd you wanna tell me?' Bella hiccupped and sat up. Her face was innocent; unburdened. Filled with the relief of being drunk and free from everything feeling pointless.

'Oh,' Peach said in a small voice that seemed to come from someone else, 'I just wanted to tell you I'm glad to be hanging out with you tonight.' A tear glanced off Peach's cheekbone. She turned her head away.

'Sweet. Love you, baby sister.' Bella took Peach's hand, smashed it wetly against her lips.

Peach starts to cry.

Everyone stares at the broken mess, unable to believe it is Dad.

Peach does not believe it. Not really, not yet: she can't, so she is not crying for him. She's crying because she realises that night, in 1994, *twenty-five years ago*, was the last time Bella told Peach she loved her. Which means Peach is crying for herself and crying *because* she's crying for herself like she always swears she won't and then does anyway.

Dad is kept behind glass. Not that the thing in the bed is Dad. The thing in the bed is flesh. Flesh every colour but pink. Flesh and staples. Bandages and dressings. Cables and tubes spider from every corner of the pulped fragile thing which Peach cannot allow to mean Dad.

Maybe I have worked in galleries for too long, browsed too many exhibitions, she panics, I'm too acclimatised to strange sights displayed in cases, incapable of perceiving Dad as anything other than an object in a vitrine. Her brain scrabbles to penetrate the moment, get under the skin of it and experience the agony it deserves.

Greg starts to sob: gasps paced at intervals, even his distress is measured. But Peach hasn't seen him cry since Solomon died. It coaxes her into the moment, that in his own graph-paper way, Greg is losing control.

Bella is saying, 'Shit, shit, shit, shit, shit', deep breath, plaintively, 'shit, shit, shit, shit, shit.' Tears course down her face, pulling her make-up with them, like a candle burning down. The landslip of product reveals Bella's face: weary and ravaged. Her naked features shockingly private. Seeing her this way is as intrusive as catching her on the toilet.

Then Mum goes up to the glass, lips parted, buckling at the knees, so it appears as if she's genuflecting before an altarpiece, and says, 'Kevin. Oh, dear god! Poor Kevin. My poor boy.'

This too feels voyeuristic. Unexamined possibility exposed – three decades, three children. They grew up together, slept in the same bed, for so long comprising a single thing. A unit – parents, Mum and Dad, as impossible to separate one from the other as to identify the point where red becomes orange in a rainbow.

Peach is so used to Mum being with Peter, to Dad being with widows and divorcees who'd appear and disappear at intervals, that it has never occurred to her that, between them, there is love. Vestigial, a well-tended grave for a shared life sundered but no less deserving the definition.

Peach looks at Mum with her hands holding her head on and beyond her to the thing which is Dad. Which *is* Dad after all. Seeing Mum see Dad, properly *see* him, confronts Peach with reality, like a camera dragging her father into sharp focus. The centrifugal force of her family's despair collapses the distance between Peach and the frail, bruised human at the centre of the medical equipment.

Because *this is her father.* Her father who has Alzheimer's disease, her father who, even if he recovers from the accident, will always remain behind glass. Damaged, unreachable. Her father who is already like light returning to earth from a dead star – extinguished, only an illusion of remaining brightness.

Right now, Dad is alive. Tenuously, provisionally alive. Brutal wondering: if life sticks, if life struggles on, if his life has been saved tonight, then what for? To live at all costs because he can be made to? To stagger through some grey half-life together, bereaved of him in increments, and he of them as his neuron forest is razed. To attempt to explain what has happened to him, as if to a hurt child, scared and confused, as it hovers beyond his diminishing comprehension. To suffer his death again and again and again, each time he needs to be reminded of their names or his own. For there to be no such thing as love, once the collapsing folds of his brain uncouple language from its meaning until everyone is a stranger communicating in a foreign tongue. To watch disease rob him of dignity, rewriting their definition of compassion, of quality of life, one loss at a time in the depressing musk of the cared for. Wiping him, prodding him, making noises at him, pushing spoons into his mouth. Every act of care an assault.

Fate has written a cheque and all of them will have to honour the sum demanded, regardless of their means. This is no abstract wondering. Peach has helped her best friend Gwen through this. Held and consoled her at regular intervals throughout the last five years. Fed her wine, cooked

91

her meals. Listened to Gwen rail and weep as her mother devolved into babyhood just as her own children were beginning to emerge from it. Has watched Gwen's marriage, solid and happy, threatening to crumble under the onslaught of demands. Peach did all she could to help Gwen up off her knees once bereavement thrust her into afterwards, where the living, no matter how exhausted, are obliged to clear up mess inherited from the dead.

And in that way, Peach is almost glad she doesn't have anyone, because at least she will be spared the potential of another precious thing being bulldozed into the pit of dementia. Unlike Greg and Bella. Maybe even Mum: Peter hovers on the margin of the scene, he will not be spared but he may be remaindered.

Dad should have died. He should have been allowed to die tonight. Accommodating the certainty of that fact is an insufferable demand of love. One so enormous Peach feels she will split open right here like a dropped watermelon.

And finally, *finally*, Peach is crying for the things here which deserve to be cried for.

Chapter 10

For a while they take it in turns to go in. Peach takes Dad's hand and it is inert and unresponsive, like holding a steak. She lets her tears spill over his fingers as if she is watering a plant. The nurses come in, gently suggest they go home if they can, sleep if they can, come back in a few hours. Then they will lighten Dad's sedation. Then, he may begin to wake.

They all stand round. Seasick, reeling and useless. None of them live that nearby, none of them live that far away, and not one of them is capable of making a decision about where to go or what to do.

Behind the glass, a machine shunts Dad's breath back and forth. Behind the glass, Dad's body is a free fall of swelling and bruising, trying to protect him from traumas which have already occurred.

There is a dull slicing sound as the medical staff close the venetian blinds, concealing Dad behind the slats.

'What in heaven's name did your father think he was doing?' says Mum, not an enquiry, but incredulity.

'Wandering, I think. He wanders. I mean, he must have managed to get on a bus. He's quite capable of normal stuff sometimes.' Greg reverts to squeezing his hands together for comfort. 'But it seems like, we think maybe he thought he was going home.'

'Home?' asks Mum. Peter takes her elbow, but she shrugs him off.

'As in where we used to live,' says Bella, 'but one of the nurses said he was going on about Ian when he came in.'

'Bloody hell.' Mum massages her temples. Peter takes her elbow; again she shrugs him off.

'Doesn't mean anything,' Peach soothes. 'I think we have to start being realistic about Dad's condition, like not just this, not just now, tonight, what's happened I mean, but what was already wrong.'

Greg gives Peach a reproachful look, as if to say she doesn't know, hasn't been that involved in his care. She wants to say she understands that and is sorry. She wants to explain about Gwen, the intimacy at a remove she has, but it seems impertinent. Like a bereaved cat owner trying to tell a grieving parent they know how it feels to lose a child.

Greg is already talking anyway. 'Dad mentioned Ian to me a few times, said he'd been calling, I think, dunno, I think Ian's got bound up in some confusion of his or . . . '

Peter clears his throat. 'About that.'

Peter always has a slightly purple face, a red-wine drinker's florid cheeks, but as they all turn to look at him, Peach worries he might clutch his left arm and crash to the floor.

He says, 'Ah. Right. Ian did, uh, call the house, actually yesterday, uh yesterday and earlier, also last week, quite insistent, but I thought it was best just to, ah, send him on his way as it were. I didn't think you'd want . . . So I . . . '

Mum says, 'Oh Peter. It was obviously important. What did you do that for?' But she looks at him like she knows the answer: to protect you from whatever toxic spores the past was about to release. The ones which, it turns out, were already airborne and unstoppable.

Mum turns her back on Peter. 'What the hell does Ian think he's doing, calling us?'

Us, meaning she and Dad. Mum and Dad, Peach's parents. Together.

Memories curl up round the hurt.

Peach let a wounded moan escape, breathing the sand and feathers of too many cigarettes. Bolting to the toilet, she retched and spat slime into the water. She pulled her knickers to her knees and sat, head hung low. Dark drops of blood bloomed in the bowl. Crying with relief she showered, feeling, through the searing discomfort of her hangover, that it was time to forget the mistake with Dominic. She'd *tried* to tell. She'd *meant* to tell. It wasn't her fault Bella had usurped the moment of revelation. It was fate. It was right. Bella never needed to find out. It was a sign – time to move on. Peach let fault swirl away with the water and felt clean inside.

Bella was in the kitchen, cadaverously pale, scowling into a coffee cup. 'What are you smiling at? I feel like death.'

'Me too. Last night was really fun though.'

'Mum and Dad are coming home later, and the house is a bombsite.'

'Cleaning won't take long. We can all pitch in.'

Bella slammed her cup onto the table. 'Can't. Reading for my dissertation.'

'Get stuffed!' Peach laughed. 'It's your mess too.'

'I let you have your friends round last night, *and* I hung out with you.'

'You're kidding, right?'

'Nope.'

Peach searched her sister for any indication of the gregarious girl who had danced like mad and slobbered lovingly over her hand, but saw it was futile as digging for fire in a heap of ash.

'Fine, but I'm telling Mum.'

Bella shrugged and drooped out of the kitchen.

Cleaning made Peach miserable. Feeling lonely and irritable, she griped at Solomon who always seemed to be under her feet. She kept thinking the phone would ring – expecting Pamela to call for a post-mortem.

Last night, totally trashed, Pamela had got off with Ollie Watson, let him put his hand up her top in front of everyone. Ollie was nice, the sort of boy you talked to about The Smiths, or studied with, but he wasn't the sort of boy you wasted your last summer in town getting off with. She wondered how mortified Pamela was.

But the phone never rang, and once the cleaning was finished, empty time made Peach anxious.

From nowhere Peach remembered Mum's rose, the one she was meant to water. Guiltily she looked out of the kitchen window, then relief. It was a gush of blushing tissue, branches dressed in lace like a bride. Blooming. No thanks to Peach.

She drifted round the house, which had barely changed since they moved there. Fragments of her parents' art school past, all shades of umber, mud and Kelly green, fringed throws and stout pottery. Everything a bit tired. Stale and outmoded. G Plan sideboards and telephone tables: the tasteful non-taste of middle-class people trying not to say too much about themselves.

Menstrual cramps sent Peach distracted. She felt edgy: hankering after something nameless. She answered the hunger with food, although she suspected her appetite was for something vital and huge.

She made toast. It bunched into a wad she couldn't swallow. Spitting it into the bin, she admitted the starved feeling was wishing something exciting would happen while being simultaneously afraid of just that. Dread or trepidation or worry or one of the things she'd begun to feel all the time without quite understanding why. Something about the future. Something about the unknown. Or maybe, she hoped, just hormones and hangover.

She went into the front garden. Black clouds zoomed across the horizon, crazing sunshine into patches of white. Far towards town an ambulance siren announced the worst day of a stranger's life. On the scorched lawn no one had remembered to water, Peach scrunched herself into a ball.

Sometimes, lately, she thought, it feels like I have fallen down inside myself, and I don't know how to get up. The notion gave her vertigo.

Mrs MacArthur opened her front door and stepped out, pitching on the threshold; destabilised by afternoon wine. She sniffed the air, then disappeared back inside, shamed by daylight.

Mrs MacArthur's strange familiarity made Peach aware how hard she found it to think of everyone alive as really living, to hold in her head that everyone had an infinitely complex world inside them, no matter how boring they looked, or how old they were.

The hum of an engine advancing: Mum and Dad. As they rounded the corner Peach was relieved. The car parked up and she ran forward to greet them with a hug.

'Hey, hey!' said Peach's father, holding her tightly. 'Your heart's pounding, is everything okay?'

Peach burrowed into Dad's chest. She nodded vehemently. Without speaking, without looking at him, Peach stood there breathing his forever father scent and being glad that some things never change.

'I'm glad you're back.'

'We missed you.' Her mother's voice was light music. 'It's lovely to be home.'

In the garden with her parents, the friable feeling ebbed. Peach was simply standing in the sun with people she loved, listening to the pointless music of things. Insects, sprinklers, distant FM radio playing out on a loop until nothing was complicated.

'They're back!' Galloping into the house, Peach called to Greg and Bella, just to hear the words, weigh out their meaning in sound.

Mum trotted in behind her, buoyant and girlish.

Greg thundered down the stairs, awkward, ill at ease with his ever-expanding body.

'Mum!' he said, lifting her because he could.

'Careful!' Mum cried, caught off guard.

When Greg put her down, laughing, she was herself again, recognisably more Mum – not so carefree.

Dad struggled in with the rest of the luggage, shirt wide open, belly golden-brown from the sun. Mum looked all the paler and pinker in contrast.

It split them into sets. Greg wearing Dad's young face, body lean and tanned like Dad's had once been. Peach and Mum, pasty as something hauled from the sea – and the nose, of course the nose. Peach's hands crept up to it.

Bella appeared at the stair head. Pallid as Peach and Mum but much thinner. Lately Bella had a stripped look, as if she'd been filleted. It made her version of the accursed nose appear even more prominent.

'Parents,' she exhaled with ennui. 'How was the holiday?'

'Great!' said Dad. 'Lovely walks, good pubs, weather was excellent. How's you?'

Bella descended the steps with an invalid's caution.

'Yeah, fine. Great.'

'Have any wild parties?' Dad winked. 'Did the neighbours have to call the police?'

Bella halted, sighed some disgusted negative she couldn't be bothered to craft into a word, and hoisted herself back up, barely creaking the floorboards.

'Well,' chuckled Dad, 'that went well.'

Peach patted his back, felt the panniers of flab at the waist of his jeans. 'It's not you – she's pretty much been a cow the whole time.'

'Give your sister a break,' Dad said, crossly. 'She's going into her final year, it's very stressful.' Then too brightly and loudly, 'As you will find out this autumn when you go off to university, young Peach!'

He tried to draw Peach into a jokey wrestle, but she shouldered him off. 'Get a haircut, Dad.'

Peach realised Mum must be in the garden and rushed out. She wanted to see her face when she noticed the rose.

Mum was standing in front of the rosebush. Solomon was sitting, panting, his head against her leg.

'Look!' cried Peach. 'It's alive! Isn't it amazing?'

Mum didn't turn. As Peach got closer she saw that Mum was holding onto the bush. In her hand, a cluster of leaves in the vehement clasp of a nurse reassuring a patient.

'It's bolting,' she said.

'Bolting?'

'It's when ... at the end ... if it isn't going to produce any more ... when it's finished.' She sighed. 'Sometimes, when a plant is about to die it has one final flowering, one last chance to proliferate its genes.'

'Oh, but it looks—'

'Like it's doing really well? Yes. Doesn't it look like that?'

Finally, she turned to face Peach and the look on her face was one Peach later came to recognise. She sees it in stations and airports, on the faces of strangers. Difficult to interpret: the look of someone tolerating one of two kinds of sadness, opposite and alike. Anticipating the sad departure of someone they wish would never leave or the sad arrival of someone they wish would never appear.

Chapter 11

She wants to ask Mum: do you remember the rose? Was it really bolting, or did it survive? Almost inconceivable but Peach is about the same age now as Mum was then. She understands how easy it becomes to perceive nature as a series of crappily apposite metaphors for ageing. An ugly apophenia that can poison simple pleasures like russet leaves falling in October, eating a juicy nectarine on the last day of ripeness.

But before she can articulate any of it, Bella grabs her own long hair in her hand like she will use it to choke someone and says, 'Right then, I am going to find Ian Elder and find out what he's got to do with this.'

Peach knows she means it.

'No.' Greg looks at Bella like whatever is wrong with her is infectious. 'Just no.'

Peter looks at them like he is trying hard not to use the kind of language he strongly disapproves of. Peach puts a finger to her nose.

'It doesn't seem like a great idea, chaps,' Peter offers cautiously.

Chaps; what a Dad thing to say, Peach thinks. She has always regarded Peter as different to her father. Yet, she realises now he's the same brand of groovy grandad. Folk clubs and real ale, plays the mandolin, wears horrible waistcoats. He's also a retired art teacher and she's seen a couple of photos of him when he was young – balding with a ponytail. She can't believe she never noticed before: Peter is straight up Kevin analogue. Like Dad Quorn.

Bella looks like she'd happily behead Peter without the slightest remorse and hisses, 'I'd love it if you wouldn't mind staying out of this, actually, Peter, *thanks*.'

The words 'Dad Quorn' keep repeating in Peach's head, getting funnier and funnier. She laughs and tries too late to stifle it.

Greg puts his fist up to his mouth in exasperation. It looks as if he is holding an imaginary microphone and is about to sing a song.

Peach laughs louder. Her siblings glare at her with the dismayed contempt which enquires 'why must you always be *so* the *middle-child*?'

Mum holds on to Peter like someone grabbing the mast as they sail into a gale and says, 'This is ridiculous. *You are being ridiculous.*'

Peach can't disagree. She doesn't understand what they are doing, why they are doing it. Bella hasn't even asked Peach to go with her, yet intuitively she knows she is instrumental to Bella's reckoning. That it is Bella's will and Bella's will remains overpowering.

Already, Bella is holding the keys to her Mercedes in her fist. She looks prepared to gouge someone's eyes out with them.

'Peach.'

'Bella?'

'We're going.'

'But I don't think we—'

'Peach.'

'Okay, I'm going with Bella.'

Greg says, 'That's it then, is it? Unbelievable. It is *simply* staggering to me that you could leave with Dad in this state. It's like you're both still teenagers.'

Peter takes his life in his hands and offers, 'Maybe it would be good to take a minute to centre yourselves.'

Bella gives him the finger and tells Peter to 'centre himself on that'.

Mum asks Bella how she can be so childish and nasty at a time like this.

And Bella's eyes blaze. 'Do you really want to talk about this now, Mum? Shall we have it out right here?'

Greg puts his arms round Mum and Peter stands to one side, beetroot-hued with his lips puckered into a Frankie Howerd *how dare you*.

They walk away, Peach scuttling in Bella's wake, dismayed by her family's aptitude for introducing farce into moments deserving poignancy.

The corridor kaleidoscopes out in front of them, white fractals slosh around the shiny floor. Peach realises she has no idea what time it is. If it will be light or dark. She has simply forgotten there is such a place as outside. Time is suspended in the purgatorial null of the hospital: two minutes, hours or weeks could easily have passed, acting out the Godot repetition of her family dynamic. The only part that feels real is the realisation Dad will never be the same. That he might, perhaps, be better off dead.

The car park is the unhealthy orange of a fizzy drink. Small tornadoes of litter catch the migrainous light, gyrating in a way that makes Peach want to puke. Bella clicks the key. Her car chirps and clunks. Bella opens the door.

'This is not the right thing to do, Bella.'

'Get in the car, Peach. Bloody get in the bloody car. *Now.*'

Bluebottle thoughts blunder about Peach's skull; useless noise. Words composting in her mouth, tamped too tightly to swallow or spit out.

Half in half out of the car, Bella looks bleached and desiccated, fragile and pale as a leaf skeleton. Double exposure: Bella now superimposed onto Bella long ago. This moment interwoven with another in which she appeared exactly this way. Spectre and flesh, like an adult palm placed into a child's handprint on glass.

Then Bella and Peach are accelerating out of the car park in the direction of the place which was their home before Peach did the things she did in 1994 which meant they didn't have one any longer.

Chapter 12

Bella is driving like she is trying to kill them and smoking like she is trying to kill herself.

'Bella, don't you think you should slow—'

'Can you drive? No. You can't. So, don't tell me how to.'

'I just—'

'Go to sleep or something.'

Peach looks at Bella through half-closed eyes, like observing the blinding power of an eclipse through a pinhole camera. 'Bella, I just—'

'Go to sleep. Leave me alone.'

Peach wonders how Bella treats the staff at her company; she can imagine her being a tyrant, like her own boss Ben.

Ben Gardener spends the first hour of his day doing yoga and meditating and the next eight throwing tantrums a two-year-old would consider needlessly dickish.

He has the tuck-fed look of a public-school boy. Pudgy and spoilt and utterly used to the whole world existing for his satisfaction. His porcine face is permanently flushed with rage, usually at someone up a ladder holding a painting, doing exactly what Ben has told them to do with it.

The cowering gallery technician – Guy or Luke or Tom (they're all called Guy or Luke or Tom) – will spend the whole day fretting, while Ben forgets in favour of throwing a wobbly down the phone at someone junior minding their own business in a contemporary art museum in Amsterdam or New York. Unless Ben's trying to shag an intern or entertaining artists or collectors. Under those circumstances he is the living embodiment of upper-crust charm.

Once upon a time the Guy/Luke/Toms flirted with Peach. Now they look through her when she talks to them, as if she is a nice but slightly depressing teacher trying to show them how to do craft.

They are a brand of young man so ubiquitous in the art world that they are hard for Peach to properly think about, like lampposts or pedestrian crossings. They are always middle class and white. Handsome in an uninteresting way, serious in a faintly ridiculous way, averagely talented at whatever kind of painting or sculpting they do when they are not up a ladder being ripped a new arsehole by Ben Gardener. Which, of course, they are doing to fund a stellar art career which will likely not materialise. They may be privileged and complacent, but Peach loathes the way Ben perceives them as fleshy biros or post-it notes – handy, disposable, replaceable. She tries to help by parsing Ben's unfathomable displeasure for them, but half the time they still moon into the office at the end of the day asking to be paid cash in hand before riding away on fixies and vintage racers, never to be seen again.

Peach is appalled by the way she feels about her sister: having to allow the possibility that she too leaves her employees pricing up the cost of their dignity at the end of the night. Easier to think about the past than about Bella, about Ben, about the recent work situation that has left Peach's coat on a shaky nail with him for the first time in ten years. Easier to think about what she has already lost than what she might still be about to lose.

Peach let herself in to the still house, after an evening hyp-notised by MTV at Jade's. Peach's family didn't have satellite TV even though she and Greg often asked for it. Her mother never called things common but had a way of saying 'No, I don't think so' about stuff like that which made Peach suspect she harboured certain snobberies.

The living-room door was open. Watery TV light rippled across Dad's dozing profile. On the news, people her age were hacking other people her age to death with machetes, dying in the hot dust of a country she hadn't heard of until recently. She didn't have a frame of reference or a place inside herself to put it. Guiltily she switched the TV off, paused to watch Dad's snoring with affection. Feeling the theft of her spying, she tiptoed into the kitchen.

A whine came from the corner where Solomon was squat-ting, shaking with the force of defecating on the kitchen floor. He looked caught and abject as the stink assailed Peach. The lino was splattered with vomit and slicks of diarrhoea.

'Dad! There's something wrong with Solomon!' Peach dry-retched behind her hand.

Dad rushed in and he clapped his hand to his nose, exclaiming, 'Christ!'

'What's wrong with him, Dad?'

'God, I don't know. Eleanor! Come quickly!'

Solomon looked ashamed of the brown jet sluicing from his hindquarters.

Footsteps pounded down the stairs, Mum followed by Greg.

'Yuck!' gasped Greg, gurgles strangling his vowels.

'Right, I'll phone the vet. You two get out before you

throw up. Stay with the dog, Kevin,' said Mum, soap-scented in the folds of her dressing gown.

Greg and Peach shuffled into the hall.

'Do you think Solly's dying?' asked Greg, shivering in his underpants.

'I don't know. Come here,' she said, reaching for her brother.

They clung together: old, forgotten comfort.

Sobbing, Peach was shocked by the grown male substance of her little brother. Even making snuffling, small boy noises in her arms he felt alarmingly mature. Dormant power in his torso made her wonder how she had failed to notice the precise moment the scab-kneed brat had been swapped for someone recognisably masculine.

Only recently, it seemed to Peach, Greg was toddling round the garden – nappy bottom ducky fat, yawing on bandy legs like a tiny drunk, shouting 'Do!'

Do – his incantation, his demand, his question. 'Do?' he would say and poke his finger into the trumpet of a daffodil. 'Do!' he would say and punch a tulip in the face. Do. Pensively when he wanted Thomas on TV during *Newsround*, angrily when he wanted a broken banana mended. Do was a practical magic and one which often failed.

It made Peach feel like time was accelerating.

'Where's Bella?'

'Upstairs,' said Greg, blowing his nose on a long piece of toilet paper, produced from nowhere like an impoverished magic trick.

Greg let Peach take his hand and lead him upstairs. Apprehension froze them outside Bella's door like pupils awaiting punishment.

Greg opened the door to reveal Bella stretched out on her bed, eyes closed.

Stunted music hummed in her throat as she listened to a record through big headphones which cupped her face.

Candles guttered in a breeze which stirred the curtains like dancers' skirts. A record made endless smooth rotations.

Bella tipped her head back into the pillows, fragments of tuneless song tearing from her lips. She was solemnly murdering 'Pictures of You'.

Bella sat up; in an instant she was on her feet, tearing off the headphones. 'What are you doing in my room?'

'It's Solomon. He's sick, Bella. Really sick. Mum's getting the emergency vet and everything.'

Peach sat down, triggering an avalanche of books. 'I went into the kitchen and he'd crapped and puked everywhere.'

'Put some clothes on, Greg,' Bella said.

He looked at his body as if suddenly surprised, suddenly embarrassed to find himself undressed. He went to his room to dress.

Something thawed in Bella. She stroked Peach's hair. 'You've been crying.'

Peach leant her head against Bella's insubstantial thigh and felt like a faithful pet. Like Solomon. She began to caterwaul.

'I think he's dying, Bella. He's been all quiet and slow for weeks and he's our dog and I love him and he's dying.'

Candle flames blurred in Peach's tears.

Bella circled Peach, every inch the soft sister of their early years. Only the poke of her bones said otherwise.

'Let's find out what's going on.'

In the kitchen, fluorescent light hummed a headache frequency.

Bella and Peach entered nervously.

Mum had thrown on jogging bottoms and a shapeless cardigan. Solomon was whimpering in his basket. Mum was swaddling him in blankets, softly muttering comforting words.

'Dad and I are going to meet the vet at his surgery.'

'Can we come?' Peach asked.

'No.' Mum stood arthritically and put her hands on Peach's shoulders, as if measuring her, seeking something known and exact in the dimensions of her body.

They locked eyes. 'Peach,' said Mum, 'I know this is distressing, but stay here and Dad and I will let you know what's going on as soon as we can. Okay?'

Things were terrible enough already without Mum treating Peach as if she was five. She half expected her to say 'Be a big girl for Mummy'. Her palm tingled with the pent-up desire to slap Mum's face which reflected annoyance back at her.

'Okay.'

'Good girl.'

'Can you wait a second until I get my camera? I want to take a picture.'

'Darling, no.' Dad lifted Solomon from his basket with delicate solemnity. The dog sagged in his arms, tongue flopping, big sharp teeth exposed. Teeth he never used against anything but the penny floaters he burst by the dozen.

Peach reached under the blanket to stroke him. He opened his eyes a fraction. She hoped he saw her.

Dad buckled Solomon into the back seat of the car. He stood up and kissed Mum's forehead. They appeared to Peach as a couple, distinct from the people who were her parents.

Headlights swept the drive as they reversed away, leaving Peach to wonder why she kept feeling like she was snooping on her own life.

Back in the kitchen, Bella was making tea. Greg sat at the table shuffling a pack of cards.

'Thought we might as well play rummy,' said Bella, pouring water into the teapot. 'Tea?'

Greg dealt; each sibling tossing cards listlessly onto the table where normally they competed as if the future of the world depended on it. They made empty remarks about the game to try to feel normal. They gambled with matches. Probably a metaphor for something, thought Peach as their cups cooled, contents untouched.

Unbearable tension turned to torpor. The game was unfinished, but after a while no further hands were laid.

Greg paced between rooms, Bella fetched a book and Peach just sat, staring into space and wondering how she would feel if her parents came home without Solomon.

She kept thinking that she'd never experienced death before; but that was not true. Patty Elder had died. But Peach had been so young, Patty distant and inaccessible.

Mum's mum, Nana Hilda, had died a year or two after Patty. Peach's memories of her life and death were also gauzy and unobtainable.

Nana Hilda's life and death amounted to a handful of confusing recollections. Her visits foreshadowed by Mum becoming nervy and snappish. Issuing long lists of unfamiliar dos and don'ts that recast everyday conduct as forbidden transgression.

And then the old woman's unsettling presence. By turns kind and critical. A few lucid images: driving round a safari park with the windows rolled up. Everyone stuck to plastic seats, feigning enthusiasm for a buffalo showing off its dung-encrusted arse while lions hid in the shade. Sitting on Nana Hilda's knee: amazed by intricate lines inside her elbows and dark hairs poking like insect legs from her chin. But mainly a vague recollection of uncommon quiet in the house, Mum and Dad being edgy, Nana's unfamiliar smells imparting dim suspicions about cruel things time might do. Then one night, the phone ringing in the small hours. Light and sound announcing something wrong where dark and silence should be. Weeks of red eyes and distant relatives, a texture of strangeness that permeated the house like damp for a while.

More lucidly Peach recollected a weekend spent in the still of Nana Hilda's house, clearing her possessions. Tea sets and fish cutlery into boxes for charity shops, stubs of waxy lipstick and half-squeezed tubes of Germolene into the bin. She and Bella playing ladies in funny little hats and beady-eyed fox stoles they'd never seen Nana wear. She'd been struck by how strange it was that belongings remain after death. The old woman's wardrobe full of younger woman's clothes seemed indecent.

Peach wondered if her own children would ever recall *her* parents the way she remembered theirs: remote. Incapable of imagining what university might be like, Peach was unqualified to summon an impression of being somebody's mother, her own parents buckled by senescence.

That was back when she assumed mothering instinct would come. When she assumed her life would be a symphony instead of the sound of one hand clapping. When she took for granted that she'd leave offspring behind, as opposed to a load of old shit the Thames had spat out and a few boxes of photographs. Photographs she had once thought grandly of as 'her work', with all the pompous supposition of legacy that implied. Now Peach foresees that after her death, someone, probably her sister's children, will treat her art as the inconsequential equal of a chipped china kitten or Herb Alpert's Tijuana Brass on vinyl. It will end up in a car boot sale, or a charity shop. Or maybe it will be tossed straight into landfill.

And if it's true that people only truly die the last time their name is spoken, then Peach will truly be dead by the time Octavia and Anais reverse out of the crematorium car park on the day of her funeral.

The door opened. Her parents walked in, holding Solomon's collar. Dad had his hand on Mum's shoulder. 'I'm so sorry, guys,' he said.

Next morning, the carbon smell of burnt toast hung in the air. Greg chomped cereal. Bella read the same page of a book over and over then let it fall shut. Mum looked transparent with exhaustion as she breezed around trying to make breakfast time seem the same as it ever was.

Radio Four wittered significantly in the background, men with authoritative voices discussing a political situation Peach didn't understand and didn't want to. Something about the Labour Party, about the man with the crocodile smile who had taken over after the man with glasses died. Peach often thought she'd like to care about politics one day, thought she ought to if she wanted to be a worthwhile adult. Not today, though, not now.

Solomon's basket had been removed: an attempt to quieten his absence, which amplified it instead. Grief was like trying to breathe through a wet towel.

'Do you remember the day you got us Solomon?' Peach asked her father.

He shifted in his seat. 'You must have been three. Greg was only a baby.'

Dad and Mum exchanged an enigmatic look. It never ceased to amaze Peach how much information her parents could exchange with a glance while remaining unreadable to her.

'We were playing in the garden and you brought him round the side with that big ribbon tied round his neck. Someone was babysitting us while you went to get him, who was it?' Peach hoped everyone would knit themselves into the cosiness of remembering together.

'He got so excited by you and Bella playing with him that he peed on your mother's gardening gloves.' Dad took up the newspaper.

Peach laughed. 'Mum wasn't there though. We were terrified she'd make you take Solomon back when she came home.'

'Well, I didn't,' said Mum.

'Who was visiting?'

Her father rustled the *Guardian*. 'Haven't a clue.'

'Mum?'

'Haven't the foggiest.' Mum stood at the sink, staring out of the window with her hands plunged into the water, looking as if she was trying to see something very far away. Everything was normal yet so strange with Solomon missing.

The vet cremated him. The family held a little ceremony. They buried his ashes under the willow tree at the end of the garden.

The day was parched as everyone stared into the plant-pot-sized hole Dad had dug.

Each member of the family had spoken a few words. Mum read a poem. The only line Peach could remember was 'I am a thousand winds that blow'.

Greg had mumbled the rhyme 'Solomon Grundy'. They'd named their dog after the 'born on Monday' part since they *did* get him on a Monday – the names small children give pets at once straightforward and complicated.

Bella's choice of 'You Have Pissed Your Life' by William Carlos Williams seemed a wild card but they all knew better than to remark on it.

Dad had shambled through 'Who Knows Where the Time Goes?' on his knackered guitar, voice reedy as an adolescent choirboy. Distraught as Peach was, Dad's singing made her feel like her bum-hole was trying to crawl away from itself. She knew that if she and Bella looked at each other they would both burst out laughing. The moment passed unspoilt.

Afterwards they had a fractious barbecue in the fierce glare of the low sun.

Chewing a sausage her father had contrived to serve up charred on the outside while raw on the inside, Peach found her eyes drawn repeatedly back to the mound of freshly turned soil. She covertly dropped the sausage into the hydrangea bush behind her. Things change, she thought, things change no matter how much you liked them just as they were.

Chapter 13

Peach had been taking photographs of herself again. But they were beginning to scare her. They were driven by such huge impulses, swells of feeling. Outlandish imperatives that felt like they entered Peach from elsewhere.

They were getting so bizarre that it wasn't as straightforward as calling them photos any longer: fewer and fewer clothes, a parched palette of face paints rehydrated, streaked onto her skin. More props; a carved wooden mask with fangs she had been afraid of as a child. Swiped from its hook in her parents' bedroom and placed over her crotch, breasts painted and exposed, baring her teeth down the lens as the timer crunched the shutter. It was pointless: she never got them developed, so she'd stopped.

She'd been in the chemist trying out lipsticks she had no intention of buying on the back of her hand when she'd bumped into Alice from school. Alice had cropped her long hair and was wearing the t-shirt of a band Peach wouldn't have assumed Alice would like. She'd told Peach Ollie Watson was having a party and that she should come. Peach had guessed she must have missed a call from Jade or Pamela while she was out.

When Peach arrived at the party, she discovered Pamela and Ollie chewing each other like bubble gum.

'They're going out now,' said Jade before she resumed mauling Colin, leaving Peach to sit between two couples, feeling like a stale biscuit at the bottom of the tin.

She twisted her cardigan round her fingers and pulled at her necklace.

Unfocused agitation bristled in Peach. She drained her can, already drunker than she wanted to be, and went to the kitchen for another.

The kitchen was full of boys whose names she'd never bothered to learn; Colin's friends. They were talking about some game they'd been playing, something to do with the odd-shaped dice on the countertop.

Peach picked up someone else's can and drained it. The beer rushed to her head and sloshed into the ones she'd necked already.

'Hey,' said a gangly boy with a widow's peak, 'that was mine.'

Peach wiped her mouth with the back of her hand. Provocative, belligerent, deliberately letting her teeth show.

'We can share,' she said, shimmying up onto the countertop. 'Do you want to share with me?'

'Um,' the boy's Adam's apple bobbed, 'shall I open another?'

He was looking at his feet; grown man's feet in boy's shoes his mother had bought him. He worked at something in his pocket, like counting coins.

Peach perched on the counter in front of him. Parted her knees, leaned in close. 'Yeah. Let's drink a beer together.' The words and posing were cheap. Tacky acting coming straight out of a bad film, through her, into the kitchen, making the boys feel uncomfortable. They watched with the embarrassed curiosity of rubberneckers.

The boy took a breath in a way that made her feel bigger, in charge, but smaller and worse too.

He opened a beer. The pop fizz broke the silence. He was trying to stand straighter, jut his jaw and flex his thin arms.

Hooking her feet round his waist, Peach tugged him close, slipped the can from his palm and slugged. He had a greedy delighted look she recognised from other boys she had kissed just to be kissing someone. Peach wondered what stupidity she was conscripting him to; poor boy, poor me, she thought, and for a moment she felt far away.

In her head she saw Richey Manic, '4 Real' bleeding on his arm, and longed to be in a life where she only did things she meant to do, understanding exactly why she'd chosen to do them. She wanted to throw her body around to 'Motown Junk'. For music to lift her above an imagined wave of people, swimming in the air on top of the pulsing crowd as they carried her towards Richey and Nicky. But here she was instead. On a Formica countertop, in a town she'd never left, with a boy between her legs who looked like an Open University lecturer in training.

'So ... ' she rubbed her lip against the rim of the can, 'what's your name again?'

'Andy.' Half embarrassment, half anticipation.

She dangled the beer out to him like a prize. Like a trap.

'You're Peach, yeah?' He was trying out older, cooler gestures for size – they hung on him like a Halloween costume.

'Yup.' She ran her hand through her hair in an equally borrowed gesture. It made a plastic mannequin of her body. 'Peach.'

She didn't even know what her name meant, perched in someone's kitchen doing bad impressions of flirting with a boy who didn't interest her.

She could see his maths–club mind trying to calculate

probabilities, work the situation out as if it was composed of numbers. He swallowed hard and draped his arm over Peach's shoulders, like dungeon master Andy could be Johnny Depp in *Cry-Baby*.

He went in for a kiss. The kitchen was too light. Outside was too dark.

His tongue was like a slug. But he wanted her.

He squashed it up into her mouth and flapped it around. But he wanted her.

His nose whistled. Their teeth bumped. But he wanted her.

His friends stared. Looking and seeing Peach look back, they scattered out of the room, talking loudly.

Peach pulled away from Andy. She could feel him quaking under her hands. Thinking she was in charge. Waiting for her to do something. Peach was sorry for him.

All she wanted was for someone to hold her, to make her feel lovely. Not lovely even – just all right, a miracle of sufficiency.

He downed the rest of the beer and looked at Peach expectantly. If he was a dog he'd be on his back at my feet, she thought, offering me his belly to rub. She resolved to go home.

But when Andy made to take Peach upstairs, only empty resignation came.

Upstairs in Ollie's bedroom Peach shrugged off her camera and put it on the bedside table.

Outgrown little boy accoutrements everywhere: Panini stickers and Airfix planes. On top of a He-Man duvet cover, Andy went at Peach with incompetent vigour. He squeezed her breasts; first one, then the other, as if checking which was ripest, deciding what to buy in a fruit shop. She unbuttoned his fly. He groaned. Remembering what was his name? The boy from the other party: Dan. She took Andy's dick in her hand and hoped it might be enough.

It was clear she could stop this and make him feel like it was his fault she'd stopped. She let him carry on nuzzling her neck. Snotty noises. Smelly breath. *But he wanted her.* She kept her fingers curled. He humped her hand and groaned. Silence in her mouth where *no* and *stop* ought to be.

'Can we do it?' His voice was timid with hope.

'Yeah. Let's.' Her words sounded like they were coming back to her through a bad telephone line.

She goaded herself with thoughts of the couples below; seamlessly together – not missing her. From the bedside cabinet, peeling stickers of the Italia 90 squad spectated.

'Have you got a condom?' Please say no. I want to go home.

'Yep.' He breathed out the word – quick, greedy, like he could taste her uncertainty and his own.

She wondered why a shy boy like him had a condom. An optimistic, responsible father of course. Andy fumbled in his pocket, fingers useless with fright. Peach caught a smell that reminded her of the damp gloom in a dense wood.

He offered the condom and pulled his trousers down. Waning erection and skid-marked white pants.

Only the fear of looking foolish outweighed Peach's distaste for this boy who wasn't even grown up enough to wipe his bottom properly.

She tugged his limp dick. He pulled away, blushing.

'Can we just kiss for a bit?' He buried his words and shame in the pillow next to Skeletor's empty eye sockets.

Gary Lineker's faded green face leered judgementally from the bedside cabinet. Peach couldn't stop imagining everything that was not there: home, other places – anywhere clean with distance from this.

Andy lay tight with disgrace, trousers in a puddle at his ankles. She pitied him in a distant abstract way as if she was watching this happen on TV.

She reared up on the bed, struck an artsy pose, felt louche like someone from Warhol's Factory. 'Take a picture of me.' She picked up her camera, held it out to him.

'Why?'

'Just take a picture.' She bit her lip, pouted and straddled him.

'I don't want to, it's a bit . . . '

'What?'

'Dunno, weird or dirty or something.'

'Don't be so boring. Take a picture of me.'

Andy recoiled, then Ollie barged through the door: a rush of light. Ollie was porcelain white, livid cheeks. He looked like a puppet.

'You can't do it in my bed!' he shouted, his voice cracked high and girlish. 'You guys are sick!'

Peach sat up, trying to make words from the debris around her. Andy lay with his head pushed between the pillows like a mad bed ostrich, not pulling up his trousers. There was a sound: sniffling maybe, anyway, a sound. The forest-smell still dirty and sad. Ollie stood there yelling at them to get up and get out. The whole situation became irreversible – as if it wasn't already.

The person on the bed couldn't be Peach. Peach could not be looking out through her own eyes in her own face into a scene which was like something from a film too crass and idiotic to be real. But it was. Crass and idiotic and real, and laughter tore out of her as she lay drunkenly on the bed with her flies undone. It was not funny but Peach couldn't stop laughing. Unstoppable laughter felt like crying backwards.

Ollie was almost sobbing with the outrage of it all. Andy was pulling his trousers up with his head still sunk in the soft soil of the pillow like his dignity might grow back. An ugly noise filled the room and the sound was Peach screaming like the victim in a slasher movie. Peach letting go of something important which might never come back and not even caring.

She fumbled for her camera with hands that felt like oven gloves. Her feet didn't seem to belong on the end of her legs. Starting into the light; the corridor was full of people, awed and concerned as though attending a death. Barging them out the way Peach thought, I am killing summer. Her flies gaped like a mouth guffawing at something too raw and recent to be funny. She didn't even care that she was running laughing screaming half-undressed until she saw Pamela and Jade.

Catching Peach's wrist, Jade said, 'What is *wrong* with you?'

And Peach didn't know how to say everything that comes from nothing is wrong, so she let her body carry on. She pulled her wrist free with the sensation of a Chinese burn.

Out of the house, hurtling, purposeful and brainless as a missile; Peach's eyes filled with tears. The world melted into colours and shapes. She tripped and fell. The camera crunched between the ground and her body. She snatched at the pieces. Fragments of the broken lens cut her hands.

Grit and blood mixed in her palms like she was part of the ground. A thought came and went: Solomon at the bottom of the garden, things subtracted – a hole appearing underneath her.

Back on her feet she ran. Or did something like running. It was more the act of being mainly upright and falling towards home. Smashed camera punching her in the chest like a second heartbeat. Asphalt and glass niggled in her grazes.

Pain stuck fast in every part of her. Hurt so badly she could barely breathe. Being a public disaster was making it more bearable. The bloody mash of her hands and knees felt positive: an observable symptom – 4 Real.

At home the lights were still on, but why shouldn't they be? It was early.

She scraped her key down the door, failing to find the lock again and again. It seemed to go on forever. As the door opened Peach caved in with it. She fell on all fours and stayed there like an animal.

She heard Mum saying, 'My god,' asking what the hell happened, calling 'Kevin!' for Dad to come.

Suddenly, there were hands under Peach's armpits lifting her, air under her feet.

'Are you hurt? Has someone hurt you? Should we call the police?' asked Peach's father.

'You reek of alcohol, what have you been doing?' asked her mother.

No answers: Peach was limp as raw meat. Limp as a dog dying in her father's arms no matter how much she loved it.

Dad shook her. 'Peach, you need to tell us what's wrong.'

She stared into his ear. Her breath moved the tufts of hair that grew there like moss on a damp wall. 'You're getting old, Dad,' she slurred.

Her mother braced Peach's floppy head. 'Has something happened, darling, or are you just drunk?' Her voice wrong from being strangled with worry.

Peach was blank. She had cried herself hot and empty as a newly fired pot. She rummaged in her diaphragm for some sound she might make that would help. Instead she was sick over her father's shoulder. Greasy yellow vomit splashed her mother's sandals.

'I don't believe this,' said Dad from the other side of the world.

'For Christ's sake,' snorted Mum from some far reach of space, 'is my camera . . . have you broken the camera?'

Peach felt herself sinking, going down with her lights not quite out. The last thing she saw as she went under was the face of her sister. Bella appeared on the landing, jaunty as a pompom, pleased she was no longer the worst kind of trouble in the family.

Chapter 14

'Get up, please.' Mum snatched the curtains open. Sunlight cleaved Peach's head.

With daylight came flashes of last night. Peach moaned.

'You're coming to Ian's. You don't have a choice any more.'

'Don't want to.' Peach pulled the covers up over her eyes. The smell of her breath scrunched her stomach into her throat.

'I don't care. If you behave like a child, you'll be treated like one.'

Peach ran down the hall and spewed sour froth into the toilet.

She hugged the porcelain and felt bits of pavement and lens in her palms. She lay on the tiles.

Her mother's feet appeared. Her sandals were stained. 'You are almost an adult. You need to behave like one.' She paused, as if remembering the next part of her script while Peach gripped the floor. 'Your father and I treat you with trust and respect. You've thrown that back in our faces. We are so disappointed in you.'

The old 'I'm not angry, I'm disappointed'. Classic – always devastating. Peach snivelled.

'Now get up and get into a fit state for work.'

The feet stalked off, the door shut with a haughty snick.

In the kitchen Bella was by herself. She kissed a corner of dry toast between smirking lips but didn't put it in her mouth. 'Fancy a fry-up? A suppurating fried egg, a big fatty sausage?'

'Yes please. I'll have some black pudding and fried bread as well.'

Peach nearly threw up the sips of water she'd struggled down.

'What did you get up to last night?' Bella asked festively. 'Apart from leaving an impressive spew stain on the carpet.'

'Don't.' Peach folded her arms into a crash barrier for her brain and laid her head on them. 'Just 'cause it wasn't you causing havoc for once.'

'I don't remember ever puking on the parents.'

'Yeah, well, you never eat anything to puke up, do you?' Peach snapped from her helmet of pain. She felt sorry as soon as the words began to come but not quite sorry enough to stop. 'Or are we meant to keep pretending you haven't got a problem?'

Cold electricity sizzles through her; can that really be the closest she has ever come to a conversation with Bella about her anorexia, that hasty insult? Fuck. *Fuck*. It actually is. So distant from her all these years. So afraid of failing her by saying the wrong thing, she has failed her by saying nothing at all. There was never an opportunity and Peach was too cowardly to create one.

She didn't have to look up to know Bella had stormed off.

'Bella, we've never talked—'

'Don't you dare.'

'You don't even know what I'm—'

'Oh, I bet I do. I can hear the cogs grinding away, Peach, I know you. I know how your head works. I can just imagine all the sanctimonious little conversations you're having in there with your eyes shut and it's not your subject to broach.'

'No, but tonight I keep thinking about all the things we've never—'

'Don't bother, we all know what happens when you start having a think.'

'Come on, Bella, maybe it's time to confront—'

'Ian? Yes, that's exactly what we're—'

'I didn't mean—'

'Don't. Please don't.'

'The others were right: this is nuts, Bella. We should go back.'

Bella runs a red light. 'What for?'

'To be there. For Dad. If he, you know, what if he—'

'Dies? Just say it. That's always been your problem, Peach: you're squeamish about things that need to be said but you don't know when to leave things alone when you should.'

Peach thinks of Dad; he looked so small in the bed. Shorn and pulverised.

'You're the one who's making us do this. Dad is lying in hospital and—'

'Because of Ian.'

'We don't even know that. Where are we even going?'

'Ian's house.'

'Does he still live there?'

'Of course he does. He always loved living with ghosts. He'll die in that house.'

'Bella. Dad might die while we're arsing about playing police. Let's go back.'

Bella looks at Peach instead of the road even though she's doing ninety on the motorway.

'Dad is *not* going to die. We are going to get to the bottom of this and then we will go back. Dad isn't going anywhere. Ian might be though. God knows what he's up to.'

Standing, Peach's head floated alongside her like a helium balloon, shifting in the air, not quite belonging to her, the swing of it uncanny and nauseating. Mute on the heels of her mother, they stepped into a day which was already hot. A silver haze rose from the pavement, everything slick with light.

Mr MacArthur stood on the brink of his lawn with the mower idling at his feet: orange and shiny with inane purpose. He raised a hand in greeting with the air of a man waving to free souls from behind prison walls. The edge of his lawn seemed like the edge of his world.

'So,' said Mum as they turned onto the main road. 'Last night. That wasn't like you. What's wrong?'

How do I explain, Peach wondered, that the whole world keeps expanding and contracting? That it grows and shrinks and makes me feel like Alice in Wonderland. How to express that the world fills and empties like a pair of lungs, inhale, exhale, and I'm blown on the lips of it? Carried by updraughts, travelling without motive.

Peach did a vaudeville shuffle-hop to walk in step with her mother.

'Mum?' Peach wanted her mother to look at her. 'I feel funny. I can't really explain it, everything feels weird and I can't understand why. Every time I think I'm getting back to normal something else changes and I feel worse.'

Mum put her hand on Peach's back. In among the dusty

128

smell of the hedgerow and the liquorice tang of sun-softening tar Peach could identify the scent of her mother's body; a clean, sensible smell of home and okay and no more of this nonsense.

'I do understand,' Mum said. 'That was a silly mess you got into last night, but I can remember how strange it is to be your age. I mean, you're not quite an adult, but you *are* grown up and you're not sure what anyone expects of you, or what to expect from yourself, I suppose.'

'I think that's it. I'm not at school any more and I can't imagine what university will be like – I mean, I can kind of imagine that life but not really see me in it.'

Mum nodded, keeping her hand on Peach's shoulder.

Peach wanted to say she worried that it was something more than that, something worse. Bleak things she couldn't explain festered under the ones she could.

'I remember that.' Mum let her hand drop away. 'It feels like you wake up one day and realise things have changed around you. Like the world has started to turn faster.'

Not seeing her mother as being inclined to such poetry, Peach felt imprecisely unsettled instead of reassured.

Then Peach thought and said nothing as they left the clustered houses behind them. Leaned into her headache as they passed by gated mansions she used to fantasise about living in. She marched along quiet, familiar roads where woodlands and fields replaced housing estates and made other places seem further away than they were. She noticed a copse where she and Bella once made dens out of bracken, heard the tinkle of a stream she and Greg had dammed with stones. In the silence she was simply sick, sweaty, and surprised she had a job.

The Elder house stood out on its own on the crest of a

hill. It seemed isolated and remote even though it was only a fifteen-minute walk from home, another fifteen from the centre of town. It was set back from the road at the end of a sweeping drive. As they passed through imposing gateposts, Mum stopped. 'Wait a second.'

The house's leaded windows winked as the morning sun struck them. Mum folded Peach into an embrace. 'Don't do anything like that again. I'm here to talk to if you need me.'

'Thanks, Mum.'

They crunched across gravel together. Bees hummed drunkenly in the hollyhocks and snapdragons. And Peach allowed herself to hope that this job would return her to herself and make her feel like the calm, capable person she had always thought she was until something came unstuck on the last day of school.

Chapter 15

The garden was a rainbow blare; hectic and glossy with flowers. Like television with the brightness and contrast cranked too high. Gooey heat, the bees' plump drone as their thumb-fat bodies staggered into snapdragon hoods, woozed between lily folds. Stewed puce clouds knuckled into fists. Thunder swaggered about in the distance.

Peach stepped into the house, Mum's hand reassuring on her arm.

The contrast between interior and exterior was extreme.

The outside of the house was rendered white; hygienic-looking as clean teeth.

Strange, thought Peach – most places look smaller as you grow up, yet this building was far larger than she remembered. The drive longer and wider, the garden less a garden and more grounds. The house itself bigger, statelier. The architecture reminded Peach of old travel posters endorsing holidays in the British countryside – open-topped motor cars, ladies in cloche hats, men in cream slacks carrying wooden tennis racquets.

Inside was dark and still. Silence so dense it became noise. Dust motes milled in sails of sun. Into those, stained glass scattered jewels of colour. The gloomy, oak-panelled hall did not suggest the domestic; just the intimidating muteness of a sacred space. Velvet drapes, wainscoting, parquet floor; the portrait of Patty only increased the mausoleum atmosphere. She smiled out of the past into a future she never reached.

Peach's mother disappeared to look for Ian, consumed into a channel of darkness.

The house muttered generations of money. A wide staircase with carved banisters swept upwards to a gallery hall hung with big paintings: thick slashes of red on black, bombastic scribbles of grey on white. The canvases sat between strict doors like night-watchmen.

Downstairs the hall opened onto a vast living room where chesterfields grouped round an imposing inglenook. Every object, every piece of furniture looked expensive and grand, chosen long ago by people with refined taste in their genes. Slicked with the sweat and regret of last night, Peach felt like she radiated filth. Felt she might indelibly mark the priceless antiques if she so much as brushed a finger against them.

At the foot of the stairs, the top of a piano was crowded with framed photos. Peach tottered over to look at them. A stern old man in a stiff collar. A woman with the haughty look of a displeased duchess, never less sour at any of her ages. A little boy Peach supposed must be Ian. Here dressed like a miniature business tycoon, there in cricket whites. Then she spotted one of him as a young man, laughing with people she was astounded to recognise as actresses and musicians.

She was appalled by Ian's handsome youth. Intellect lifted out of the photograph, pulsing into the present. A smirk plucked his lip. Famous women looked at him in a hypnotised way, gawking with eyes full of a dog's dumb love.

Peach was reminded of Dominic. The look of a man who could make people want to do things they never intended to.

132

Down the hall, a clock hacked, mechanism grinding. Parliament chimes announced Ian's appearance at the top of the stairs, broad body framed by light.

Peach looked up at him, his image baffled by sun. He began to descend – stripped of dimension like a shadow walking without a man.

She tried her voice in the silence. 'Hello, Mr Elder.'

'Ian,' he said as if she'd insulted him.

His voice was deep. It rumbled up out of his wide chest. Brute was the word in Peach's mind. Brute because everything about him was outsize: hands that looked made to throw punches, big square head like a bull. Stubbled jaw. Threads of red in silver hair. Wearing a tatty jumper on a hot summer day, he seemed like a farmer. Like he must lug and plough even though she knew that, well – she didn't understand exactly how he spent his time, but she knew he didn't do that.

He paused to examine Peach with the idle curiosity of a rambler peering at a common but colourful flower, then sailed on into the voiceless recesses of his kingdom.

His after-image remained emblazoned on her retinae. Face composed of sharp features. If not handsome, distinguished. A mouth that had once been sensuous relaxed into sarcasm. His expression suggested he might start to laugh at any moment: only *at* you, never with you. A colossal beaky nose that made Peach's pale in comparison. She touched hers just to check and it felt dainty for once.

Voices rounded the corridor, announcing Mr Elder and Mum's return. He was softened in the presence of Peach's mother. He inclined towards her like a benign tree. His hand rested on her elbow with casual affection that made Peach seasick.

Peach had not seen Mr Elder in a long while. She supposed

he'd always been the oppressive presence before her. Previously she had dismissed it as awkwardness she always felt around adults. Now this capacity to create disquiet seemed like a singular quality of his.

Mum wore a private smile for Ian. One Peach didn't recognise. Its unfamiliarity shocked her. Oh, this job is such a bad idea, she thought.

'Ian's going to take you upstairs and show you what he would like you to do,' said Mum. Patting Peach on the shoulder, she slid away into the hush.

'After you,' said Mr Elder.

Peach stepped onto the staircase. She paused at the top.

'This way,' said Mr Elder with an irritable swat of his paw.

He opened a door. It creaked as they stepped inside. Dust caught Peach's nose. She sneezed. He glared as if he found it uncouth, indicative of bad character.

The room was the size of a large cupboard. The airless timbre of a place that had been closed up for a long time. Boxes lined the walls, so many there was barely room for both of them. Forcing them so close together, Peach could feel heat radiating out of Ian's body into her own. It felt intimate, inappropriate – her cheeks seared.

'Move these boxes.' Ian waved his hand dismissively.

'Where to? What are they?'

He sighed as if suffering. 'A load of boring old tat. Mine, my late wife's.' His accent was plummy with a slight Yorkshire edge.

'I remember her,' Peach blurted.

'And what do you remember about her?' Mr Elder's question was more taxing than any exam Peach had taken.

'Well ... she was ... nice?'

Ian's expression awarded Peach an F. 'Nice is a meaningless

word, implies lack of imagination. I'd suggest striking it from your vocabulary.'

Ian stared at her and Peach felt like he was x-raying her intellect.

'I don't remember Mrs Elder very well.'

'Better answer.'

Ian was close enough for Peach to smell sandalwood soap and stale log fire on his clothes, but his voice seemed to come from another room.

'What am I actually meant to be doing then?'

There was a thick, itchy silence.

Ian gazed out the window, across the fields towards town. 'Move these boxes. Eleanor's going to have to fish out some crap for this nosy bastard who's coming to write a load of puff for the papers. She can hardly do it in here, can she?'

It was shocking to hear Mum's Christian name; Peach rarely heard it spoken. She didn't like the way Ian said it either, like his tongue was too involved in pronouncing it.

'No.'

'Exactly. These bloody people. Poking their noses in. Raking up the past.'

'Why do you let them?'

He paused. Then he laughed – an untried sound. A brash noise that seemed as surprising to him as it did to Peach. A rasping sound: he sawed convulsively until tears ran down his cheeks.

'Oh,' he said. 'Oh,' wiping his eyes. 'You look so pissed off. I didn't realise how like Eleanor you are. Why do I let them? Good question.'

For the first time he looked Peach in the eye.

Peach jutted her chin. 'You don't have to, do you? Let people look through your stuff.'

'Seems that simple, doesn't it? Pity it's bloody not.' He became puckish, incongruous as green buds on a dead branch.

'Art's a minefield, see? Hardly anyone really wants to go and see it. Not if they're honest. They've a horrible feeling they *should*, though. Improving but not much fun. Like a dose of castor oil. So, you've got to tempt people in with stuff they actually are interested in,' he smirked. Peach chewed the inside of her cheek to arrest the spread of a smile.

'Misery, that's what they like!' he exclaimed mordantly, rubbing his hands together. 'It's a godsend for my gallery that I've got a dead pop star for a wife. Death and glamour – perfect for a glossy spread in the Sunday supplements, some guff in the *New Musical Express* apparently. That'll get people queuing up outside the Tate.'

'Was Mrs Elder quite famous then?'

'Much more famous than me. Proper famous – chart smash, top of the hit parade, whatever young people call it now. Not that?'

'Not that.'

'Of course, Patty wanted to be a serious artist, not some teeny bopper. Sent her a bit nuts; partly that, anyway.'

Peach had never considered the Elders' past as being so exciting. Or so intertwined with hers.

'What do you mean?'

'Nothing.' His bonhomie departed, cold reserve returned, like a medium deserted by a channelled spirit. 'I need to get on, I'm busy. I'm sure you can see what to do.'

Peach could not. His last few words were delivered quick and staccato as blows. He was gone before she could ask. Peach shut the door as carefully as she could and let fly a volley of sneezes.

Alone in the stuffy room, Peach was tired and confused.

Every exhalation stirred up dust. She had no idea what she was meant to do. Besides – she was still astonished she had a job.

Outside the storm began to churn, rumbling in the valley. Peach thought about last night. She thought about Dad and Bella and Greg at home, breathing and living in familiar ways.

Imagination failed her. There was nothing but now and alone. No tomorrow or even later, let alone university and adulthood. Introspection always seemed to turn into brooding these days, leaving her claustrophobic in her own head. She sat down on the floor.

She didn't know, then, how that feeling could set round you like wet cement and hold you there for decades. Had no idea how perfectly, horrifyingly possible it was to keep repeating yourself, to stay with your own mistakes like a sweaty gambler throwing loss on top of loss, unable to believe it would not come right, that the house would not pay out.

'We have to go back,' Peach says. 'I need to go back.'

'What, so we can look at Dad all smashed up and meditate on how he was already screwed and how he's even more screwed now and then not talk about it? So Greg can passive-aggressively imply he's the only decent person out of the three of us? So we can all pretend Peter isn't obviously Dad mark two and just gather round and have a lovely big Lewis family awkward silence and then maybe you and I can argue?'

'No, that's exactly why we should go back and try to be—'

'What? Better? Different?'

'Yes.'

'Too late. Forget it. We will only ever be who we already are.'

Peach thinks of her flat full of silence and tasteful crap

that she's chosen to prove how different she is to all the other people who bought the same tasteful crap. She imagines sweeping it all onto the floor.

All her stupid little installations dotted around. Her cameras gutted of film like opera singers with their tongues ripped out. The urge to make things that will not die, despite the fact her moment has been and gone and left her behind working for Ben bastard Gardener who doesn't even trust her any more.

There was a time, she can't even say exactly how long ago it was, because it feels like yesterday and another life, when she had exhibitions. Admiring mentions of Peach's work in the same breath as Cindy Sherman and Francesca Woodman. Canapés that only made her hungrier for a main course she was never served.

And it hurts so much that she can't even enjoy going to galleries any more because, these days, looking at art feels like watching someone fuck one of her lovers right in front of her.

It hurts so much she could smash herself to pieces just to kill her unsanctioned hope that one day she will feel like an artist again.

She imagines the car hitting Dad. She pictures shock registering on his face as his legs are swept out from underneath him and knows she and Bella should be in the hospital keeping vigil over his unrecognisable body. But Surprise! It turns out she and Bella are the kind of people to be vengefully tilting at windmills instead of holding his hand. Peach just can't take it. Not her life and not Dad's accident and not she and Bella and this *folie à deux*. She starts to kick the dashboard and hammer her fists against the door.

'Turn the car round. I want to see Dad.' Drumming and pounding.

Bella smirks. 'And I was always meant to be the psycho in our family. Even after you messed everything up, I was still meant to be the crazy one.'

'Turn the car round.' Peach can feel the blood bellowing in her temples, can feel it throbbing in her bruised hands and feet.

'No,' says Bella. 'This is what I need to do. And you owe me, Peach. You still owe me.'

Peach goes limp with her pulse howling and sprinting. Submits because she knows it's true. She will never shake the debt. Just like she'll never clear her credit cards or student loans or afford to buy a place of her own. As inevitably, as dispiritingly as that, she understands she will not be allowed to improve her credit rating with Bella. Not tonight. Or ever.

Besides: even if Bella *was* amenable, compensating her would still leave Peach unable to repay herself – the sum she owes is simply too great.

All because she was bored and nosey that first day at Ian's. All because she shook off her torpor like shrugging off a wet coat, hefted a box onto her hip without knowing where she should move it to and a photo fluttered free, insubstantial as a butterfly, with all the pent-up menace of a bomb.

She caught the falling photo in mid-air, between finger and thumb. Her parents and the Elders fixed in an instant of bliss. Peach wondered if they knew that one day it would be important to see what it was like: *there*, *then*, so their future selves might rely on the picture to endorse that – *yes* – they *were* happy.

It shocked Peach to see her father so striking, her mother so buoyant under mellow light. The kind that only seems to bless certain sorts of photographs of certain sorts of days.

Now three of them were old, one was dead, and their joy looked complacent.

Peach let the picture go. It spiralled to the floor like a sycamore key.

She turned the photograph over with her foot. She flipped it over to the Kodak, Kodak, Kodak side with a feeling like toothache in her heart.

And after all her false assessments about what set the dominos falling, she realises: that was really when the trouble started.

Chapter 16

Peach sat on the floor until Mum's head appeared around the door frame. Disembodied and cartoonlike.

'What are you doing?'

'Nothing. I started moving boxes and stuff fell out.'

'Then put it back. Would you like a sandwich?'

'I'd like to know what I'm doing here.'

'Didn't Ian explain?'

'Nope.'

'Typical. I knew I should have shown you myself. Come down to the kitchen.'

Peach was grateful for the coolness of the kitchen. For the stable quiet of Mum reading at the table, sandwich in her hand, a frill of lettuce peeking out between slices of bread. She placed her book down carefully. There was something precise and meditative about the way she navigated life, attentive to the small geometries of everyday things.

'How are you feeling?'

'Hungover. Wondering why I'm here.'

Mum rolled her eyes. 'I can't help the hangover. But I'll show you what to do once we've eaten. Then you really *must* get on with it. It's a job, Peach. You're being paid. Are you okay?'

Peach nodded; she wanted to tell Mum about the photo, the coursing feeling of her insides running while her body stood still. She wanted to give names to her fears in the hope they might be less forbidding with labels on them, but she couldn't cement contesting sentiments into words. Anyway, she was convinced they would be less real if she was the only one who knew they existed. Peach sat down. Met the chair like a full stop and kept quiet.

She watched her mother, who had begun to read again. Scrutinised her for signs of the flimsy sweetheart in the photo. Shapeless clothes, flat brown sandals good for your feet; plain grey hair pushed behind an unornamented lobe. She wondered how you got like that.

Peach has never been conventionally attractive. Striking, maybe, on a good day, when she was younger. Stylish perhaps, although she swithers now over whether her continued commitment to colourful hair and eyeliner gothic is defiant or pathetic.

Either way she feels like she has approached her innately unconventional looks with resourcefulness. Has understood for decades that maximising her potential and acknowledging her limitations is as close to good self-esteem as she can get. She thinks of herself as sexual kimchee – an acquired taste. Desirability contingent on giving the impression she'll be filthy in bed.

But now she feels too old for herself: the difficult middle age of the manic pixie dream girl. Too old for her unindividual uniqueness to be cute and too young for it to be eccentric. On her worst days it feels like she's stranded in the wasteland of the self, disappearing in fractions.

During slumps in the working day, if Ben is away, she

loses hours watching the Guy/Luke/Toms muck around like schoolboys on a free period. They include younger female staff in their horseplay. Peach is exiled: too senior to be involved. The quiet violence of erasure more wounding for being unintended.

The feeling of being ghosted is worse now the Guy/Luke/Toms dress in irono-nineties fashion. Nothing prepared her for her own past becoming retro. She never imagined being forty-three, surrounded by boys brutal with youth, doppelgänger of every indie-kid she had mediocre, post-club, pre-Y2K sex with.

If she had imagined it, she still would not have been prepared for the painful physical longing it stirs. Not between the legs, but in other soft, important places, equally fond of coming up with stupid ideas.

Growing older sometimes feels to Peach like communicating in a foreign language in which she has limited proficiency. Insufficient vocabulary to express nuance. Unable to explain who she is inside. Not that she'd go back.

With Mum in the kitchen back then, she had all these questions about how it felt to be ageing: is it like casting off in a boat? Pull up the anchor, wave goodbye to being conventionally desirable. Or a series of small shrugs and sighs. Little defeats, disregarded. Do you stop caring, when do you stop caring? Do you know the moment when it leaves you? A shudder of deep, brief horror – cold maybe, with nothing after. Is that how it is? Or just letting the rope slide through your hands because it is heavy and inevitable, and besides – you have better things to do than take the weight.

Peach questioned these things until her mother was flaccid and slight like a carrier bag blowing in the gutter.

'Let's get going then, shall we?' Mum said briskly to

143

Peach. She closed the book and rose from the table. As Peach watched her, the gutter thing was assembled again, face put right, outline restored to a body. All those things put together meant Mum and meant love.

She feels ashamed by that: the casual barbarism of pulling people apart to investigate how they work. Now she knows how easy it is to do. To herself.

Upset about the recent, awkward situation at work, she took two trains to her best friend Gwen's house in Crystal Palace.

She had believed her behaviour had been motivated by altruism, that she had done what she did on the girl's behalf, but was starting to worry it had been motivated by the easily dismissed spite of an ageing woman trying to assure herself of her relevance.

She had cued up a soundtrack to her sadness but thought better of it, put her headphones back in her pocket. The slightly festive air Saturdays in cities have had released her from introspection.

It was wanly warm. Summer's withering almost mistakeable for spring's promise. A thinness in the light forbade wistful error.

The London-ness of London lessened as the train slid away from Clapham Junction, giving way to tracts of suburbia. Green domestic places that felt a bit like home: narrow and secure, stifling and reassuring. Like family and roast dinners and time moving slowly. At least to people whose childhoods were secure enough to feel prosaic.

Gwen appeared at the door. Silver hair in a gamine crop, crisp white shirt. Gwen's unadorned attractiveness appears like sophistication. People assume she will be haughty and self-satisfied; her good-humoured friendliness surprises them.

In the past, Peach shared a series of happy, grotty flats with Gwen, so it is never a surprise to her.

Oscar, six, clung to Gwen's legs, but smiled a promise of play later on.

Martha, four, ran out, hugged Peach with such unconcealed joy that Peach almost burst into tears.

'Mummy did a big stinky poo today.' Martha gazed up at Peach's face, scrutinised it for a rewarding reaction.

'Mummy! You're disgusting!'

'Hello, love.' Gwen kissed Peach.

'How are you?' Peach kissed Gwen's cheek; she smelled of parenthood: fromage frais and lotion. 'So did Mummy do this poo in the toilet or in her pants?'

Oscar's reserve dissolved. He ran into the house. 'Daddy! Auntie Peach asked if Mummy pooed her pants!'

Huw, Gwen's husband, appeared, wild curls greying. Boxer-stocky, familiar white spikes of his *Unknown Pleasures* t-shirt stretched taut over his keg.

'*Did* you poo your pants, love? All right, Peach?' He kissed her cheek with the stubbly lightness of dads.

They carried Peach far from her own life into the antic heart of theirs. Paintings and ornaments Peach recognised from life before kids; jostled back by enough colourful play-tat to rival an atoll of plastic polluting the Pacific.

'Come and see my room, Auntie Peach!' shouted Oscar.

'Auntie Peach is coming to see my room first! She doesn't want to see boy toys,' yelled Martha.

'Bloody boy toys, gendered shit. She didn't learn that from me,' Gwen grumbled.

'We're going to the garden and you're going to play while Auntie Peach and I have a glass of wine.' She shooed the children towards the patio doors.

'You'll want a glass of wine, won't you, Peach?' Huw asked anxiously, corkscrew already deep into cork.

Five past twelve. The parents get to believe everyone is drinking because the childless person wants to. The childless person gets to believe everyone is drinking because the parents want to. Inevitable.

Briefly it chafed. But Peach decided not to mind: she thinks small children are best enjoyed through the haze of one or two large glasses of Pinot Grigio since their level of noise and disinhibition is roughly equivalent to that of drunks, their exuberance as likely to devolve into tears or fisticuffs.

Gwen and Peach sat on damp patio furniture while Oscar repeatedly threw himself off the compost heap. Martha did inept handstands, exposing the touching chubbiness of her legs. 'Watch me!'

'We are watching!' Gwen cried. She was actually looking out for Huw with the wine.

'They're so cute.' Peach smiled.

'Yeah, they make them like that so you don't strangle them or abandon them in Waitrose.' Gwen laughed. 'Fucking talk to me about books or sex or films or something. Remind me what they're like.' She pantomimed exasperation, but her voice was touched with love. Contentment shiny on her, like untold wealth spent discreetly.

'Yeah, I haven't read anything or shagged anyone or been to the cinema recently either and I don't even have kids to blame. But at least my chat might pass the Bechdel test for once.'

Huw appeared with glasses.

'Are you okay, love?' Gwen asked. 'Is it your dad, are you struggling with the dementia? Because that doesn't seem like you. You've always been the most sort of, *interested* person I know. Inquisitive. Voracious actually. It doesn't seem like you not to be … consuming. Books and films and exhibitions,' she giggled, 'and cock. *Are* you okay?'

Peach made a sound, the aural equivalent of shrugging.

'Peach?'

'I'm a bit lost. Worrying about Dad, some horrible bollocks going on at work. Not particularly loving being single, don't particularly want a relationship. The greatest hits.'

'Can I do anything?'

'Tell Huw to pour me a bigger glass of wine than this feeble effort?'

'Absolutely.'

They laughed. It scooped Peach into the easy contentment of being with Gwen, knowing she could tell her anything, trusting it so completely she lacked the inclination.

Gwen nipped indoors to the toilet. Huw sat down. 'Peach?'

'Huw?'

'Just wondering?'

'Yes?'

'Me and a few mates are going for a lads' weekend on a barge next month.'

'And you need someone to make up the numbers?'

'Hah, no, well, we fancied a bit of sniff, you know?'

'What?'

'A bit of coke. And I was wondering if you could get me some?'

'Why would I be able to get you coke, Huw?'

He squirmed. A middle-aged father trying to set up a drug deal for a barge trip with a group of other dads. Peach could see nothing had prepared Huw for the way he found himself appearing to both of them at that moment.

'Well, like, dunno, just thought, art world and parties and footloose and fancy free and all that, no?'

'I'm single and childless, Huw, I'm not Scarface.'

'No. Sure. Would you mind, uh, would it be okay if you don't tell Gwen about this?'

Peach minded. She minded everything about it. She is forty-three years old. And rejoining the endless empty pursuit of pleasure is the only thing that could induce in her a dimmer view of her life. She knows that's what people assume she must be doing and has become increasingly sick of it. Not that she really judges middle-aged party people any more than she judges parents, not really, it's just another set of things she doesn't want for herself. And in her opinion being talked at by an artist on coke is far duller than listening to a child describe the intricacies of the Pokemon universe.

'Yeah. Let's forget this conversation ever happened, Huw.'

'Cheers, Peach, sorry.'

Then Gwen came back. Her return inflected what had passed between Huw and Peach with glorious absurdity. Peach's dark thoughts blew through her head like bad weather.

The children demanded a game of hide and seek. They scattered around the house.

Oscar took Peach's hand and they hid together. He was pleased with her ingenious choice of squeezing under Huw's desk.

They could hear Martha and Gwen seeking. Booming voices, curtains being tugged back, wardrobe doors opening.

Oscar was hot as toast in Peach's arms, squirming and giggling. Milk had turned to cheese on his breath. It should have been such a bad smell, but it was just part of the fervent aliveness, the very now-ness of him. Whispering how much he hoped they wouldn't be found at a volume that ensured they would, Peach could feel Oscar's thrill at being safely scared thrumming through every fibre of him. And she hoped they wouldn't be found too quickly either.

Gwen and Martha stomped past the door. In the dark under the desk, Peach grew hot and sweaty. She was almost suffocated by her under-boobs racking up round her middle. Abruptly embodied: all pig leaden sag, Peach emptied of pleasure.

She had always refused to hate her body, but lately it didn't even feel like hers. Not since all her 'at leasts' began disappearing.

At least I don't have a beard has become hello Captain Birdseye. She has tweezers in the bathroom, tweezers in her bedroom, tweezers in her bag and tweezers in her desk at work. Sometimes she finds whiskers so wiry and long that she's sure they will soon enable her fillings to pick up Magic FM.

Her tits are still great buttressed by a bra. But now they unroll when she removes it. They're just about fine standing up. But when she bends down, they hang there looking like disappointed Wombles.

And they're not her only tits. Tits are growing all over her torso. Back tits, armpit tits, secondary, maybe even tertiary under-tits.

She always had a flat belly. Now a dough baby nestles in her lap when she sits. Aware of it, she imagines her friends with children losing their minds at bounce and rhyme, relentlessly winding the bobbin up, and thinks, I might as well have done that. I've got a toddler's worth of lager and cheese sitting on my knee, and no one to wipe my arse when I'm senile.

Her squishy places were smooth. Now cellulite makes her legs look like a pair of American Tans stuffed with cauliflower cheese.

Her jawline is pouching into jowls.

Her skin is dull and creased.

Her wintering lips, worsened by smoking. Greedy little feathers drink her lipstick and spread it all over her face as if she has been snogging like a teenager at a party.

She remembers the big self-portraits she used to exhibit. They confront her with how outdated her head's map of her body has become. Which, in turn, reveals the roadmap for her life to be an arcane curio: the blueprint for a utopia she never built.

With Oscar in her arms she felt the ground was crumbling underneath her. Falling, flailing for the life she meant to lead. *It was going to be beautiful.*

She recognised it. Truth: real and banal. Not the sad part of a story which makes redemption more beautiful but the unveiling of her regret, and it was just a bad thing like all the other meaningless bad things that happen on millions of days to millions of people between birth and death. Not a poem or a song. Not art. Just very sad and shit. Because Peach doesn't do anything any more except go to work feeling sad and come back feeling sadder.

Nothing winged will fly down and scoop her out of herself. No god, just or capricious, will mete out a fate more to her liking. The better angels of her nature are turning out to be just as much a bunch of cunts as the bitter, lesser ones anyway.

Her head was already a clamour of disasters until the world went fully fucked on top of it. Now she's got to try to sort out the inadequacies she already had *and* work out how to be a good human in an ever-worsening reality. She doesn't have the energy. She tried. At work last week she tried and look what happened. Forget trying again: she's old and exhausted and sick of going toe to toe with darkness. I'm becoming temperamentally unsuited to living, she thought.

Oscar gave hedgehog snuffles in her arms. He was starting to be afraid. The game had gone on too long. He sensed Peach's turbulence.

Peach held Oscar tight. So tight he squirmed.

'I want my mummy,' he wailed, twisting out of Peach's arms, running from the room, howling for Gwen.

Peach stayed still with her arms empty, her heart pounding and her head hating every beat. Her head hating her heart for not stopping. She pushed her face into her knees and sobbed into the folds of her skirt.

Little feet thudded across the carpet. Bigger ones gave chase.

'She's not in here,' Gwen said to Martha, 'Auntie Peach moved hiding places. I heard her go downstairs. *Go downstairs.*'

Footsteps cantered backwards. Gwen protecting Martha.

That made everything worse.

A hand appeared, like a love letter slipped under a door. It hooked itself round Peach's.

'Great hiding place,' Gwen said. 'I'm not going to fit in there, though, so you're going to have to come out.'

All this incoherent sorry bilged out of Peach.

'No, sorry, sweetheart. Just come out and we'll have a proper talk. We'll work out how to get you better.'

So habituated to *I*, Peach had forgotten what an embrace *we* could be. The profound solace of inclusion.

That was what she'd been trying to achieve. Including the intern in *we, us.* Securing the girl's exile in the process. And maybe her own.

Slowly, Peach crawled out from under the desk.

Gwen was waiting, deliberately looking away. Letting Peach complete the undignified slithering unobserved.

Gwen pulled Peach to her feet and listened. She made it smaller, she made it safer.

The shifting spotlight of her friend's perception: 'I don't know where you get this idea you're such a loser, Peach: you're single because you don't settle for less than you want. You're the only child-free person I know who is happy with their decision. You've got a responsible job in a blue-chip gallery.'

'Wasn't really deliberate, though, wasn't what I wanted.'

'Yeah, but it was like you didn't seem to think you had the right to keep pushing the art if people weren't pushing you to make it. Doubt crept in about what you were making, and you felt like you shouldn't make anything. Never bothers *some people*. But people like you question your work out of existence. Because you care about what you're saying, and you wonder whose expense you might be getting to say it at.'

Peach bridled. People being right about you hurts. Like a profound, psychological version of someone pointing out your skirt is tucked into your tights and you've been walking around with your arse out.

'But the fact you care is exactly why you're not a loser. Even if it's a real shame you don't feel entitled to start making art again. Because I do think you should. You're good enough.'

Peach wanted to tell Gwen her assessment of why she stopped making art was too generous. That she hadn't budged up and made room for new voices – she had given up in a huff since self-portraits had become something everyone made all the time so that her art felt irrelevant. And that, really, what she had done was dump art before it had a chance to break up with her.

And like the moment with her mother in Ian's kitchen: there was so much more Peach wanted to say, but she didn't know how to explain. And besides: she did feel better, about herself, her life, the incident with Ben and the intern and the arms dealer, so she didn't say any more. She recognised the difference between disquiet and tranquillity, like crossing an unmarked border between one place and another.

In Ian's kitchen, Mum had stood abruptly from the table and guided Peach upstairs.

'You need to move the boxes to my ... I've got a room here, a sort of, well, it's where I do my work ... my office? My office.'

Peach had found the idea of Mum having an office in Ian's house puzzling; not least from the hesitant way she described it as one. Once they entered the large bright room upstairs, Peach understood her reticence. She supposed it was an office of sorts – desk in one corner, pots of pens, typewriter, wall-planner – yet there was a rumpled day bed, a sludge green jumper of her mother's, slippers, a comb with strands of her hair in its teeth, much like her parents' room at home. It scandalised her.

'So I move the boxes from the little room into this one and then I'm done?' Peach wondered if she could move them all in a day and return to the lazy summer she meant to have.

Mum picked paperclips off the desk and plinked them one by one into a desk tidy.

'You move boxes today and tomorrow. Then you take over my day-to-day jobs for a week or so while I sort through them for this journalist.'

'Jobs like what?'

'Peach,' Mum sounded cross, 'I've *told* you. Housekeeping.

153

Preparing clay and plaster, clearing up Ian's studio. I'll make you a list. Just start with the boxes. I've got things to do.'

Peach turned out into the long, shady corridor that ran between the storeroom and her mother's ... place. She couldn't call it an office. It was barely that. But to call it a room? To accept Mum had her own room in Ian's house as if she shared herself equally between home and here? Too strange.

Mum's job was starting to seem superfluous and flimsy. And yet Mum came here most days and had done for almost as long as Peach could remember. Something brittle and precarious about everything it was founded on made Peach feel brittle and precarious herself. She began to understand that whatever strangeness she discovered in this house would be portable. Inevitably she would have to take it home.

In the storeroom the photograph of Mum and Dad and Patty and Ian lay on the floor, its image turned away. Peach scooped it back into the box. Being surrounded by history was oppressive: time seemed so big. Peach was too small inside it to really know how near or far she was from the past or the future. She swore she'd shunt the boxes as fast as she could without looking inside.

Later, grateful to be back at home, Peach watched her parents through the kitchen window. Dad was mowing the lawn. Mum was weeding in the near-dark, fingers mercilessly probing soft earth for interlopers. Low last sun illuminated portions of her at a time. A light wind made the flowers nod and curtsey in obedient beauty. Peach was glad of them living in careless, normal patterns, relieved they did not look like they had anything to do with the young couple in the photograph.

Scrappy leaves clung to the plates and cutlery, remnants

of the family's evening meal. Withering and drying, they reminded Peach of autumn, of the fact that this year, when it came, she would be gone, beginning a life she could not picture, in a city she had only visited for a single afternoon and agreed to live in for the next four years because it had seemed fine.

She swayed a little, tried to steady herself by concentrating on love for small normal things: terracotta tiles her feet had traversed daily, a dull silver ladle which had served every second meal she'd ever eaten. Mum's apron hanging on a hook. Fruit turning boozy and brown in a carved wooden bowl.

Chapter 17

The landscape has become familiar. Flats in boxy rows, squat industrial units. Edge-lands of the town Peach grew up in. She recognises the uniform houses. Huddled estates: potted bay trees standing sentry by double-glazed doors. Conservatories and hatchbacks, vertical blinds, tiny bikes overturned in the grass. Peach experiences a sense of home-coming so huge and dyspeptic it feels as though the streets have climbed inside her.

'All right?' Bella's driving is less suicidal. She crunches the gears at a roundabout.

'No. Yes. I don't know. Are you?'

Bella pulls over and puts her head on the steering wheel. The hazards craze their faces, strobe the pavement. 'No. I don't know where to go. Suddenly I can't remember where to go.'

Peach lights yet another cigarette, feels frail and pathetic. She has quit so many times. The desire for improvement and fear of its impossibility duke it out between draws.

'I can't remember either. Let's just go back.'

'We've come all this way.'

'Doesn't matter.' Peach strokes Bella's back. She is still so thin; so thin Peach experiences her sister's body as pain in her hand.

'That's *so* you.' Bella shrugs away from Peach. 'You never finish things. You hurtle into situations, drag everyone else along, then run away from the consequences.'

And this is *so* you, punishing me for being party to your weakness, thinks Peach. 'What about you, Bella? Aren't you running away? From Dad, from ... forget it.'

'From what?'

'You were right when you said it wasn't mine ... that I don't have a right—'

'This is you *respecting* that, is it?'

'It's me trying. Getting it wrong, obviously, but I want to try ... this, Dad, I wish we could try to—'

'No point.'

'But wouldn't it be nice if—'

'It would have been nice if our parents hadn't got divorced because of you.'

This is something Peach has told herself every day since that summer. She knows what Bella thinks. What everyone thinks. But Peach is wounded and winded by hearing it said. The first time she has heard it spoken by a voice not her own.

Bella sits up and holds the steering wheel like a little kid pretending to drive.

'Please can we go back, Bella? I don't want to see Ian. I don't think I can bear it.'

In answer Bella takes the handbrake off and presses the pedals.

Ian came stalking out of the dark.

'Good morning,' ventured Peach.

Ian replied with a raise of his brows that made good morning feel like the stupidest thing she'd ever said. Ian's heft and silence made him seem less human, more statue.

Peach assumed his head was full of clever thoughts she wouldn't understand. Talking seemed forbidden. Hush seemed to emanate from him, like a librarian's adamant silence. Mum motioned Peach upstairs, beetling after Ian as he walked.

The storeroom was stale as sleep and the boxes seemed to have multiplied overnight. Peach flipped up a lid: bills, contracts, typed correspondence on yellowing paper. She moved on to the next.

This one was filled with photographs of Patty. Here posing pensively in black and white, arms resting on the curve of her guitar. There on an outdoor stage, eyes closed, her skirt ballooned with air. Long-haired men whooped and cheered and fell more in love with every note she sang. Peach brushed a finger against the image of her cheek. Patty was blonde and beautiful in a straightforward way. Like a china doll that only exists to be looked at.

Peach searched her memory for a clear impression of what it had been like to be in Patty's presence, but only found scant scraps she'd already gnawed to the marrow. After that, absence. The blind clatter of a projector spinning with no film on the reel.

Mum popped in to say she and Ian had some errands to run, they'd be back in an hour or so. She looked around at the barely diminished quantity of boxes.

'Are you actually doing anything, Peach?'

'Yeah, obviously.'

She eyed Peach sceptically.

'I know this is boring, Peach, but get on with it. This needs to be finished today. The bloody journalist is arriving tomorrow.'

Peach flicked two fingers at her mother's back as she left.

When she was sure Mum and Ian were gone, she tiptoed to the door and peered up and down the corridor wondering why she was engaged in the furtive tics of wrongdoing.

Peeking behind doors, she discovered Ian's bedroom. A regal sleigh bed, red wine dregs scabbing a glass on top of a pile of books. A flamboyant satin robe puddled on the floor. She stepped in to look at the collection of photos arranged on the dresser. Ian as a small boy in black and white, sitting astride a baby elephant without appearing to take any pleasure in it, solemn in school uniform – knee socks and boater. Stiff family portraits. Every scenario bejewelled with affluence and yet no one looked happy. Peach couldn't see how it was possible to be that wealthy and that miserable at the same time.

She glanced into a room filled with furniture draped in dustsheets. They looked like monuments. They looked like graves. She shut the door.

Passing paintings on the landing, Peach prickled with the feeling there was somebody at her shoulder. A presence shimmering on the lip of her vision. She recognised the quality of light, her feet on that floor, running. The memory of a game; playing in this house with Bella when they were very young. Peach could almost hear laughter fetching back across the years. It felt like her own ghost slithering through her.

She discovered a bathroom tiled a bilious green. Air edged with Ian's musk of sandalwood soap, still humid from his morning shower. Yellow water in the toilet. She walked out.

Then shock: a room papered in pastel polka-dots. Empty apart from a rocking horse and a mobile – paper cut-out cats cavorting in the flat air.

A child's room. Confused, Peach felt impossibly huge. The

Elders must have had a baby. A baby that died. It sent a blast through her bones. Thoughts foundered in icy water. How insulting that rooms which contained the dead do not heal up round their absence. Perhaps that was why Ian was so chilly towards Peach. When he looked at her he was tormented by memories of his child who never grew up. Then Patty died too. Maybe he liked to delude himself that Mum was his wife and Peach being here disrupted the fantasy.

Only to focus on ordinary things, Peach went downstairs to eat.

In the kitchen, she noticed a snow of white footprints leading in and out of the back door into acid light and stewed air. She followed them across the gravelled courtyard. They led to a long, high-ceilinged barn with stone walls and wood roof. The door was unlocked, and she started as it creaked open.

The floor was thick with plaster, cement and clay. Vast drawings adorned the walls. Plans; obscure shapes sketched in charcoal, scribbled with measurements and annotations. There were books and papers everywhere, teetering in piles. Paint-spattered tools, stacks of wood, buckets of slip, jars of pencils and nails. Posters over a desk, advertising Ian's shows. The typography and design indicated most of them were ten years old at least. Yellowing reviews on a cork pin-board: peppered with laudatory adjectives.

There were several stainless-steel tables that looked like they were meant for autopsying bodies in a mortuary. On top of them loomed Ian's work. Sculptures four times the size of Peach at least. Curvaceous clay forms, like breasts and wombs, bottoms and hips mashed together, seductively luscious. Slashed in places, incised with metal plates in others. Vicious gouges torn out, pieces of wood forced in.

These are women, Peach thought. These shapes are women

and he's cut them up. Ian hates women. She was far more perturbed by the savagery of Ian's work than the room full of grief upstairs. Feeling cornered, Peach ran back through the courtyard, into the kitchen.

She sat at the kitchen table, breathing, trying to think and trying not to. Eating an orange, pungent citrus scent coated her fingers. She let the peel fall from her hand.

The sculptures looked so cruel and misogynistic: thrumming with spite and disgust.

Peach loved art, paintings and pictures and objects that told her stories, invited her to visit somewhere else. Fillips that blew her head off and stuck it back on a different angle. But, so far, she'd found abstraction impenetrable and dull. She knew there must be something to it because a lot of brainy people expended lots of effort on it. She understood shapes and shades were declaring something yet could only interpret it as so much throat clearing.

She knew art and galleries were all about sensitivity, beauty and progress. She must have misread Ian's work. They wouldn't display work that was callous or ugly. She must have failed to connect with some complex message, so intelligent and poetic it was beyond her mediocre comprehension.

She longs to reach into the past, shake that naïve child who did not think art could be glib, or ruthless or insensitive, wake her latent scepticism. To tell her: if you subordinate yourself before these things you will always be unequal to them. You will owe bad art the benefit of the doubt forever.

She aches to sit down at the table, wrap the young hand in her older one, urge her never to learn what art is meant to be, never to force the bridle and bit upon her wild impulses. To tell her: you will cry in front of Rothko's contusions of colour because you will understand they too are crying. Return repeatedly to Ophelia, whenever you need to remember that certain kinds of drowning always begin with love.

And that will be when you are still hamstrung by male orthodoxies of art. That's before you discover Tracey, Nan, Frida, Ana, Joan, Louise, Gillian. Before Adrienne, Claude, Sarah, Jenny, Cindy, Francesca, the Guerrilla Girls turn up, speaking to experiences you've had, illuminating ones you haven't in voices you recognise and want to mingle your own with.

It is the helpless saudade of longing to prevent an accident, the victim already bleeding out on the carriageway. As Bella steers the car into the sweep of its headlights, Peach wonders why, having sat through scenes from the past like a ponderous, harrowing film, untouched by the impulse to intervene, that moment is the one that javelins her with a cold bolt of regret. Inundates her with such yearning to turn the clock back that she has to sit upright to accommodate the sensation.

Peach heard voices and covered the peel with her hand as if it was a guilty secret. They carried the ditzy music of laughter with them.

'Thank Christ you came. I'd have bought that god-awful jacket if you hadn't stopped me.'

Mr Elder had his hand on Mum's arm, rested comfortably, so assured of the right to be there. Mum inclined herself towards him, scatty with amusement, looking so youthful and light it shocked Peach. They seemed oblivious to everything except each other.

'You looked like a vicar in it!'

They saw Peach and seemed caught.

'Oh,' said Mum. Mr Elder let go of her mother's arm.

'Hello, love,' said Mum with a peculiar shyness. 'We're back from town.' She put her hands up into her hair.

Mr Elder, still skittish in the doorway, thrust his hands into his pockets like a scoundrel schoolboy. Levity froze into imperious displeasure, the expression fixed to every face in his family photographs. He looked Peach up and down as if estimating what size of coffin she'd need.

'I ate an orange.' Peach revealed the peel as if evidence was needed.

'Clearly,' said Mr Elder in a tone so withering he might as well have just said *you're an idiot*.

'Tea?' enquired Mum. 'Tea, who wants tea?'

Mum fiddled with the kettle like she'd never seen one before.

'I'd better get on. I've been here a while.' Peach made to rise.

'No.' Ian took his hands out of his pockets and looked at them as though wondering what they might be about to do. 'No. Stay, have a cup of tea, wash down your orange. Tell us what else we missed.' He smirked.

Peach was beginning to think her clown-show of banality was the only incentive Ian had to tolerate her. It was so obvious he had agreed to give her a 'job' as a favour to Mum.

'Yes, stay?' said Mum, tender question rather than exhortation.

Peach sniffed her palm and smelled Christmas on her skin, a melancholy scent of misplaced celebration. I wish it was cold, she thought. I wish it was winter. Winter anywhere but here.

Dawn is breaking now. Softly, slowly, the world is revealing itself. Dark shapes become scout huts and civic buildings.

Shutters roll up on rows of shops. A stout old man drags a bail of newspapers into a branch of Spar where banks of fluorescent light are blinking on, one after the other. There are more cars on the road.

In taut silence, Peach misses her phone. She could check the news. She could browse winter coats she can't afford or books she's too depressed to concentrate on, anything to free her from looking at the road or her sister or her hands. She asks Bella if there's any way she can charge it.

'There's a socket in the dashboard.'

Muscles squealing, Peach began moving the boxes two or three at a time. She hated going into *that room*, where a comb brandished strands of Mum's hair and slippers waited for her to step into them as if she belonged here.

Thunder griped through the sky – headache weather. Jagged light crazy-paved the upstairs corridor as Peach went back and forth. She heard Mum and Ian chatting before she saw them step into his bedroom. Ian paused Mum mid-sentence with a touch to her wrist. Mum looked at Peach. And Peach noticed the precise second Mum chose not to see her. She looked but chose not to see – turned her head as Ian shut the door. Earthbound vertigo threatened to knock Peach off her feet.

Peach's phone lights into life and starts to ring.

'Oh Jesus,' says Bella. 'Jesus Christ.' She takes her hands off the wheel and the car drifts into the opposite lane. 'Is it Dad, Peach? Is it Dad? What's happened? Is it Dad?'

And it is Dad. Just not in the way that Bella means.

Chapter 18

Later, Peach and her mother ran down the drive of the Elder house with a coat tented over their heads. A collapsed sail, soaked in seconds. Torrential rain cowed the flowers, punching their petals off. Trees thrashed their limbs, bucking and rearing in steamy wind. Lightning cleaved the clouds.

'Hello?' Peach's voice trembles as she answers the phone.

'Is it Dad? Is Dad dead?' Bella is still driving on the wrong side of the road.

'One new message,' an automaton informs Peach.

A voicemail. Left hours ago, when everything was unremarkable. Back when the news headlines were telling Peach to sling back another glass of Rioja if she wanted her brain to shut up before midnight. God: her mobile has been dead all evening. She was so deep in shock she never questioned Bella calling the landline she never uses.

'Hello, love. Hi. It's me. Dad. Listen.'

Peach wants to lift Dad's stolen voice from the phone, carry it back to the hospital and put it into his throat.

Peach waves her hand at Bella to silence her. 'Work,' she lies, as all the blood in her body slides into her shoes. Bella sighs with relief and steers back into lane.

*

Dad tooted the car horn and waved. He appeared minute and isolated in his bubble of good cheer. He still fitted perfectly into the outline of him Peach had in her head. Unlike Mum who seemed so different, complicit in Ian's sullenness, never rebuking him, never so much as throwing a look to Peach that implied she didn't condone his disparaging attitude. Mum no longer conformed to Peach's idea of her.

She broke from Mum at the end of the drive so she could bag the passenger seat.

'Hello, loves! Rotten weather!' Dad chuckled. He smelled like soap, like toast. Like home.

Dad's voice in her phone is the flat, affectless one he has begun to develop. The one she can't get used to. He sounds like a worn cassette playing through a Dictaphone. Batteries running out. 'Hello, love. Hi. It's me. Dad. Listen.'

Mum huddled into the back seat. The urgent wetness of outside gusted in. She smelled like dust, like sandalwood soap. Like Ian.

'Are you there? It's your dad. I'm a bit lost. You know Ian? My friend Ian? Meant to be popping round to his but . . . where's this now? Park Street? Has he moved?'

'Darling,' Mum said, and it sounded to Peach as though she'd learnt that was what you ought to say to people you're meant to love. The mania of the storm permeated Peach's shivering body.

'Can't seem to get hold of your mother. And then I thought Peach'll know what Ian's up to.'

*

'Dad!' Peach threw her arms round her surprised father's neck. Mum sniffed.

'I think there's a bit of a situation. There was a bit of a situation, wasn't there?'

'Well,' laughed Dad, sounding more confused than pleased, 'this is nice.'

'Can you give me a bell back, love? I'm a bit stuck.'

'Thanks for the lift, we would have got soaked.' Mum put her seatbelt on.

'Give me a call when you get this and ... shit—'

And Dad says shit. Mildly, as if dismayed by a humdrum mishap like spilling tea and then there's this rush. A rush and a screech and a meaty, substantial thud that Peach's body recognises instinctively. A fizzy electrical wind then the line goes dead and the robotic voice starts offering Peach further voicemail options.

'There's nothing in for dinner.'

'I'll cook,' said Dad. 'I fancy making paella.'

'Lovely.'

They trundled down the drive. Peach twisted round to look at Mum who was playing with her wet hair, winding strands of it round her fingers. Peach turned back, looked at her own hands. They were just like her mother's. Mum's hands rested comfortably in Peach's own lap.

An image assaulted Peach – her fingers plunged into Dominic's hair. Pulling, grabbing. Peach thought that *she* would never have done such a thing. She was wrong.

Dominic made Peach understand that some people can unlock a secret self you didn't know you had. That the experience could be so intoxicating, so exciting that no love, no loyalties matter in the face of how good wanting and being wanted feels. That *could* happen to otherwise sensible people, that *did* happen. Peach was overtaken by the pale green sensation of nausea.

The more Peach thought, the angrier she felt. Peach kept seeing Ian closing his bedroom door. Mum turning away, looking and choosing not to see Peach as he did so.

Banal conversation chafed: the casual brutality of talking about shopping and dinner as if it wasn't all shit. The feeling she might vomit listed into certainty she would.

'I'm going to be sick.'

Peach is just a body with a pulse, with a heartbeat, with a skeleton and she can feel it all acutely: her body is all she is because she cannot think. She cannot be anything but a body made of thrashing heart and a dry mouth because if she tries she will have to consider the fact that another terrible thing has happened. Yet again, another terrible thing has happened to someone she loves because of her. Dad stepped out into the road because he was leaving her a voicemail.

How can she turn and say to her sister who already hates her, 'Oh actually that wasn't work, I don't know why I lied; and not only was it not work, it was Dad. And by the way I heard him being hit by the car because he was leaving me a voicemail when it happened. It happened *because* he was leaving me a voicemail.'

Dad slammed the brakes on. Peach opened the door and retched into the rain which chuckled in the gutters as if laughing at her.

The back door opened. Mum's sandal.

'No.' Peach spat a string of bubbly saliva onto the road. 'Don't get out. I'm all right.'

The other sandal, Mum's ankles, unbearably familiar.

'I said I'm all right.'

Peach pulled her body back inside. Dad patted her back.

'You look awful, love. We'll go straight home.'

'No!' Peach wasn't ready to take her horrible realisation home. 'No, I just, I'm okay, I just felt a bit funny.'

'Have you been feeling ill all day? You should have told me. You could have gone home hours ago.' Mum reached her hand out, put it on Peach's shoulder. Peach felt acutely aware of all the liquid in her body – blood, spit, piss coursing cold. Dad began to drive.

The car swishing down familiar roads felt like the spin of a fairground waltzer.

'It's a bit odd – I never thought about how the Elders are famous.' Peach's stomach was strangling her heart, nudging her lungs, crushing her throat so her mouth still swam with drool. Her voice sounded wet and strange.

'What do you mean?' Mum leant forward.

Peach had to hear Mum talk about Ian and Patty – a test. A test for her to pass, for her to fail. She needed Mum to say something wrong or right, to say something that would calm the chaos in her head, the riot in her body.

'Dunno, just, being at Ian's made me realise I only thought of the Elders the way we know them but they're actually quite famous. Strangers have heard of them – it's weird. It's nuts actually; I mean, Ian's meant to be some artistic genius and I'd never thought about that. Patty was special, and he *is*. They have *fans*. Journalists want to write about them and their lives. It's sort of huge.'

Dad gripped the steering wheel tighter than seemed necessary. Mum strained towards her, tensing the seatbelt.

'Hmm, well,' said Dad. Peach studied his face expectantly. 'Uh, well.' He drew in the air with his index finger to illustrate a point he wasn't making.

'Well,' said Mum, brittle-bright, 'they're just our friends, like Barbara and Laurence or Chris and Olivia. We don't think of them any differently. It just so happens Patty and Ian were successful in careers that brought them a bit of public attention. I mean, Barbara's a well-respected psychologist, and Laurence is a professor of molecular biology at Oxford – very renowned in his field, but I mean it's just, you don't get the same level of recognition for that, do you? Or take Olivia, she's—'

'All right, yeah, I get your point, there's no need to be patronising,' Peach interjected.

'Don't speak to your mother like that, please.' Dad's body was rigid in the car seat.

Mum stared at her knees with an absence of indignation which bothered Peach more than anything.

It was as though they were rehearsing a play about a family, actors running lines.

'Bella?'

Peach takes a breath that she hopes will push the truth out. About the voicemail. Knowing Dad never made it to Ian. But explanations turn to clay clots plugging her tongue.

'You know it doesn't matter, Bella. What Ian wanted with Dad. We don't need to know, we should go back.'

'You don't get to decide. I've had enough of your decisions to last me a lifetime, Peach. In fact, they already *have* lasted me a lifetime *thank you*.'

Bella gives a conceited little smile at having laid her ace and carries on driving. She keeps on going like she always does: chuntering forward like a combine harvester mowing down frail things while Peach drowns in what she knows. Dad speaking, the thud of his body meeting the car, knowing she's responsible.

The car sloshed down wet roads, where the houses were packed more densely. The downpour had emptied the streets, lending the town a post-apocalyptic air that chimed with the bombed-out, ruined feeling inside Peach.

'It's weird, though, isn't it? We know famous people. Isn't it crazy?' Peach pressed.

Dad pushed his palms against the steering wheel and sighed tersely. 'I had really never thought about it, Peach Lewis. Not for a long time anyway.'

Shit. Dad never used her first name and her surname unless she was making trouble.

Now she knew: her parents would never fit back inside their silhouettes. When Peach had drawn their shapes, she hadn't left room between the lines for the people they really were.

Chapter 19

Peach trailed through the surreal normality of the supermarket and tried to quell her panic.

Her parents were definitely acting weirdly. Not just Mum, Dad too. Yet outside the car, away from them, she felt sure that if there was something adulterous between Mum and Ian, they would never have offered her the job. That would be insane. Must be me freaking out again, she thought: absurd new messed-up me. She almost began to believe it.

'Peach?' A familiar voice said her name in a way that suggested Peach was only provisionally herself.

She drew Pamela into a limp hug. Pamela smelled like long days spent indoors; afternoon naps, fingering and kissing, the same clothes on a second day.

'Hey, what you up to?' Peach knotted her limbs into an impossible puzzle, studied her battered Docs.

'We're just going to hang out at Colin's, pig out, watch videos.'

Peach looked up. Jade and Colin, Pamela and Ollie.

A shared shopping basket: pizza and Coke, crisps and sweets.

A shared look: snugly snide.

A shared silence.

Peach swayed on glass legs, trying not to cry. Not just to refrain from crying but from weeping and sobbing and keening and lying down and pounding the floor and letting everything fly apart in the freezer aisle of the supermarket.

Pamela's green eyes bright as birthday candles on a plain sponge. Jade, poking a finger into the end of a perfect russet pigtail. Ollie like some cartoon professor. Hair wild, a shade too long to be short and too short to be long. Owlish glasses. Old-mannish apart from his spots. Colin lounging into the conventional adult handsomeness this summer had conferred on him: an abrupt coronation. Suddenly dressed like less of a scruff.

An unreadable glance bounced between the four of them. One that openly discussed Peach. Abrasive reminder of the way her parents had been behaving.

'Where's your camera?' Jade flourished a smirk at Pamela. Pamela crammed a giggle into her hand. Colin and Ollie snorted.

'Haven't got it on me.'

'That's not like you. Andy said you were trying to get him into photography. *The other night.*'

Colin choked back nasty laughter. Ollie and Pamela tittered.

Peach made a pantomime of yawning and stretching as though bored senseless.

'Have a good time, *the other night?*' Ollie challenged.

'Yup.' Peach shrugged, plastering over humiliation with insouciance.

'We better go,' Pamela said, biting at her thumbnail.

'Wait a sec, Pams. Hey Peach, do you like our necklaces?' Jade asked, proffering half a silver heart on a chain round her neck, broken down a zig-zag line.

Pamela was wearing the other half. She glanced up at Peach, telegraphing guilt.

173

Peach recognised this: a kangaroo court, just like the one convened against her four years ago. A thirteenth birthday party. A game of dare. A cupboard. Barry Jones.

In the dark of the cupboard, Barry's hand had shot up Peach's brand new ra-ra skirt. Shocking, adult and unwanted. Grabbing his wrist. Trying to pull it away as he parted her.

His hand was on top of her tights.

Her tights were on top of her pants.

Her pants were on top of her body.

Layers of cloth between Peach's skin and Barry's unsolicited fingers. But they burrowed at cleft flesh, so she *did* feel penetrated.

She'd whispered, 'Stop it.'

Barry's fingers had remained, invading a place she hadn't fully explored herself.

Not moving his fingers, but they *were there* – the furthest inside her anyone had been.

She hissed, '*Stop!*'

Barry wrestled his hand against Peach's hand which was trying to drag his away. Barry was automatic as a robot, wild as a wolf. She knew if she could see his eyes they would be glazed; full of nothing. '*Stop. It. Barry. Stop.*'

Suddenly he did, and she knew it wasn't because she told him to. Then he'd whispered, 'You're a tart anyway.' Tart: the trite, cakey word struck her as odd even then. At once old-womanly and childish.

He opened the door: a wordless awkwardness lunged into the party, out of the cupboard with Peach and Barry. Everyone waiting with eyes full of appetite, reporters outside a trial.

Peach's skirt rucked up, cheeks puce, eyes pricking. But it was dare. A game without rules: permission to try things.

Except that this time permission was revoked. Immediately Peach saw there had been rules after all, that everyone understood something had happened in the cupboard which broke them.

'What did you let him do?'

Peach opened her mouth.

It was full of truths as big and cold as stones. If she spat them out they would be thrown at her.

She closed her mouth around them.

'What did you let him do?'

Then Barry held up his fingers like a trophy and the room organised itself against Peach.

The party became a coven.

And Peach became a slut.

Something it was unsafe to be. Like being seen in town with your parents. Or having the wrong shoes. Or a sad jacket. Or going to church or tripping over. Like being fat or skinny or joining the badminton team or accidentally farting. Like having gone behind Spar with someone. Like having not gone behind Spar with anyone. Like being short or being tall. Like wearing glasses, like having braces, like having a stutter or asthma or acne. Like being ginger or Jewish or having moved from somewhere else. Like having a weird accent or a mum that taught at the school, like having a squint or wearing trousers too short or a skirt too long. Like being in the computer club, playing the trumpet or singing in the choir. Like being too clever or not clever enough. Like being black or Asian or lesbian or gay or poor or snobby or liking the wrong music or accidentally saying orgasm instead of organism in biology class. All these disparate things were equally criminal to the minds of Peach's peers. All these things, over which people had no control, were to be avoided, denied, disowned or lied about if all else failed. Everyone at the party, everyone standing in the supermarket, everyone Peach knew, unquestioningly existed in a tyrannical mass of white skin, affluence and complacency which perceived difference as a failing: part infectious disease, part goad.

Fuck that shit: school was over forever.

Fuck them, Peach said to herself.

Fuck Pamela and Jade and Colin and Ollie and their game of mummies and daddies.

Fuck Pamela and her faux-contrition, empty and plastic as a Care Bear's sentimental rainbow.

'Let's see your necklaces?'

Jade dangled the half-heart at Peach like a stupid boast. It had 'best' engraved on it. 'Like it?' Jade smiled sardonically.

Pamela held hers, engraved with 'friends', between thumb and forefinger.

'Nah. They're tacky as absolute shit.' Peach dashed her reply into their faces like a drink thrown in a bar brawl. Then she walked away.

Incredulous at what she'd just done, Peach hid behind a display of special-offer spaghetti, counted the money in her purse and stamped purposefully to the cosmetics aisle.

Chapter 20

'Bella, can we please stop?'

'What for?'

'A minute? A breather? A coffee? I don't know, but can we please just stop for a second?'

Bella taps on the steering wheel with her index finger; a physical version of the anxiety-inducing three dots that appear and reappear in a text conversation while the other person formulates their reply. Then she cuts up a Waitrose lorry, unleashes a stream of invective while honking the horn, performs some noisy zooming before screeching into a petrol station where she parks diagonally across two spaces. 'The coffee here is going to be filth. I'll have an Americano – there's no way they'll have oat milk.'

She sighs and tosses a twenty at Peach just like Ben Gardener does when he's sending Peach out for vegan sushi or plain steak cooked blue or whatever dietary extreme is temporarily instrumental to his wellbeing.

'Anything to eat?'

'Piss off.'

'That wasn't, I wasn't—'

'Hurry up.'

Inside, the petrol station is at once crepuscular and over-bright.

Peach presses buttons on a coffee machine. It splutters out something scalding and oily that smells like burnt Bovril.

At the counter, a wheezy man takes Bella's money from Peach. She is thinking about Dad, or, more accurately, feeling guilty about how adeptly she is avoiding thinking about Dad when the man says, 'Aren't you ... you've got a weird name – we went to school together.'

He is very large and bald, and Peach would have guessed he had a decade on her, but his face tugs a thread, a pull of indistinct recognition in her brain that feels oddly sore. 'Did we? Yeah, I sort of ... we did, sorry, what's your name?'

'Gary Martin.'

She knows she's seen him before, but he could be anyone. 'Oh right, yeah, of course. Nice to see you, Gary.'

'Peach! Is that it?'

'Yes.'

'What you up to these days?'

'Oh, just working, you know. You?'

Gary Martin who could be anyone looks at Peach as if she is unwell or mental or stupid or all of the above, which feels fair enough.

'I work here, yeah?' he says, gesturing at the Haribo and *Hustler*.

'Oh, right, sorry, tired, just drove up from London.'

'Live there now, do you?'

'Yeah.'

'Don't know how you can stand it,' Gary snorts, handing her a fistful of change. 'It's like a bloody foreign country there nowadays.'

'I remember you,' says Peach, stuffing the change into her jeans and picking up the cups, 'you were an arse at school, and I see you still are.'

178

As she walks out, with Gary berating her back, she thinks that she doesn't remember him, but that she does remember what it was like to be surrounded by people like him. What it was like to live in this town, and for the first time in months, or maybe years, London feels like a place of solace.

London has been Peach's home for two decades. When she first arrived, it felt like a Dick Whittington fantasy of gold-paved opportunity. So many parties and gigs and exhibitions, so many broke people finding ways to make art. So many places to discover herself and be discovered.

For a short while, it seemed like dreams and defiance were the only tools required to carve out a corner of it for herself. Every time tedious practicalities began to gain on her, some chance to outmanoeuvre them presented itself. Some rich old collector who fancied themselves a benefactor until she declined to give them a blowjob. Some decaying warehouse she could squat in with other artists and put on shows in, until prices rose and people who owned empty buildings started guarding them like gold bullion. Even when money ran out, hope had been abundant.

Now all she sees is hope pouring down the cracks in the pavements. Mad hopes and well-founded ones becoming the same as they trickle into the gutter. No dream too big and solid to be consumed by the city. No aspiration burns so fiercely that it cannot be extinguished, priced out of existence, or strangled at birth.

All over London there are shapes. Lumpy wet mounds Peach walks past all the time. And those shapes there are human.

There are obstacles at the top of escalators, slow-moving blobs cluttering up the pavement, impeding her progress.

Noisy objects making unbearable sounds when she is dying for peace. And those shapes there are human.

There are shapes on wheels and crutches, big shapes pushing small shapes, steering them haphazardly, catching her ankles, slowing her down. Some of the shapes have their hands out, some of the shapes ask for directions, cigarettes, spare change. And all those shapes are human.

All those shapes are human, and Peach can hardly stand it any more. She never used to have to remind herself that they were people as opposed to impediments to whatever she was trying to achieve. She used to know without having to stop and breathe and strong-arm it to the front of her brain.

She used to know those shapes were tourists whose excitement eclipsed awareness that the top of the escalator isn't a sensible place to stop.

She used to know those shapes were tired and sad and harassed and dying to get out of the rain, to go home to loved ones after long days in stressful jobs. That sadness and tiredness steered them inconsiderately.

But now they're all part of an obstacle course designed in hell, specifically to delete her empathy, test her patience and send her over the edge. It feels like quietly instrumental parts of her are dying and turning gangrenous all the time. Like some kind of intolerant zombie; instrumental chunks of her ability to be a decent human are rotting off faster than she can gather them up and stick them back on.

She has a checklist of forbidden dick moves:

Tutting at old people for being slow.

Getting impatient in a queue because the person at the front is trying to make themselves understood in their second language.

Eye rolling at noisy, excited teenagers being noisy and excited because they're teenagers.

Muttering fuck sake at someone for bumping into her in the street even though they apologised.

Almost every day she does everything on the list. Almost every day she is disappointed in herself before she even arrives at work where she will start being disappointed in other people.

Working in Mayfair is becoming too painful. Beggars and Bentleys, down-and-outs and diamond merchants. Glossy shops where dresses cost more than she makes in a month. The pittance she's paid that would be a fortune to people hunched like sacks in doorways. More to notice and un-notice. *Guardian* guilt and self-preservation arm-wrestle in her conscience. Her humanity and theirs eroded before nine a.m.

That's before she even sees them being moved on. If not by police, then by plastic police employed by boutiques to help customers forget what else their money could do. Everyone always being pushed out, priced out, displaced. Even outside the city centre, the smiling people pictured on hoardings wrapped round new housing developments look nothing like the ones who already live there.

The tube is torture. A cavalcade of dismay and self-rebuke: getting annoyed with strangers for conducting themselves in perfectly reasonable ways that make her unreasonably angry. The obligation to consider whether her misanthropy is more okay or less if she meta-critiques it at the same time as judging everyone and hating everyone and wondering if all apocalypses are necessarily bad.

She has begun to think London is the loneliness capital of the world. A Unesco centre of world excellence in abject isolation. Lit windows like a star map of human lives unfolding side by side without touching.

Recently, outside the ugly modern block she lives in, she saw two strangers through their bedroom windows. Neighbours she's never met. In separate apartments they sat, perfectly back to back against the party wall. A young woman reclining on her bed staring into space. An older man drinking a can of lager on his. Three and a half feet between solitude and company. Peach let herself into her own flat, aware of each person shouldering their own burdens and bedding down with them for another night, right across the hall from one another. Close enough to hear if somebody should cry out. If somebody called for help. Far enough away to imagine some selfless other would go to their rescue. In the distance an ambulance shrieked. Two streets away a dog barked and after that there was nothing.

Although Peach's capacity for joy feels like talent kept latent by lack of an instrument, sometimes, there are moments when euphoria startles her like St Pancras filling with sudden music as someone pauses to play a station piano. The disruption of beauty out of place: bliss comes to her that way when she sees a stranger conducting a telephone argument in two languages, slipping between two tongues because one is insufficient to express all their passion. It moves Peach to tears and reassures her that she is not dead inside after all.

It reminds her to smile at people. Demonstrates that if she does, then often they smile back, showing her how much warmth there can be in the essential act of people acknowledging one another's humanity. A vitamin shot of human connection. Nourishing in the moment, but alone at night it feels like a snack; delicious, inconsequential. No more capable of filling the void inside her than a pebble tossed into a black hole.

She was deep in the doldrums of such emptiness when she received a text from Per inviting her to dinner. As usual, there was a pulse of anticipation between her legs while nothing happened above the waist. Ever since they fucked in the toilet at an exhibition opening three years ago, Peach and Per had used one another's bodies like neighbours lending a lawnmower. Perfunctory pleasantries facilitating handy exchange: they'd eat out somewhere foodie and fashionable, give each other a couple of orgasms at his place then cease to exist for one another on any meaningful level for the next four to eight weeks.

They'd arranged to meet in some achingly current pasta place, which had a queuing system instead of reservations in order to prove to customers how irritating their desire to eat there was, and how fortunate they were to have their attempt to do so tolerated.

She was almost at the restaurant when she received a text from Per which said *in queue, don't freak out – had to bring a friend.*

She almost heard the rule book ripping: three years on, Peach and Per knew little more of one another than they did the first time they met. She knew he was Norwegian, that he was a theatre lighting designer and that he had a seven-year-old son with his ex-wife. A small, pale facsimile in miniature called Soren, who turned out to be the 'friend' in question when she arrived.

With both hands full, slopped coffee burning her skin, Peach headbutts the passenger window.

Bella has her face on the steering wheel. She sits up and opens the door, not taking the cups, allowing Peach to contort herself into the car while holding them.

'What's that smell?' Bella sniffs the air like a cadaver dog and wrinkles her nose. 'It's like gross beef, where the hell is it coming from?'

'In here.' Peach handed her a coffee.

Bella took a sip. 'Why does it taste like it's been in a fire?'

'How are Octavia and Anais?' Peach took a sip of her terrible drink. Gary Martin glowered at her through two layers of glass.

'What? Why are you asking?'

'They're my nieces. I want to know how they're getting on.'

'Why are you really asking?'

'I was thinking about … I've been seeing this guy who has a son.'

Bella looks shocked and delighted. 'Are you about to become a wicked stepmother?'

'Quite the opposite actually.'

Per had introduced Peach to Soren as Papa's friend then told her his ex-wife had been called away on business. Soren had shrugged acceptance of Peach's presence while she struggled to divine what could have possibly possessed his 'Papa' not to cancel their meeting given the outrageous flouting of unspoken rules the situation constituted.

Destabilised, she kept wondering why she was there when they clearly weren't going to have sex, discombobulated by the very fact that Per had incited her to wonder anything at all.

Halfway through the silkily perfect pasta, Peach inadvertently smacked herself across the face with a strand of tagliatelle and made Soren laugh. When he did, she was so charmed that she swung it around in her mouth, getting more and more sauce on her cheeks and chin, pretending not to understand what was so funny. Then Soren exclaimed that Peach was *so* funny. Unlike Papa's other *friends* he'd met recently. Then a second later he let slip that his Mama wasn't leaving for New York until the weekend.

Normally unrufflable, Per hunched his shoulders and stumbled over his words. Which confirmed to Peach that she was being interviewed for a promotion she had no wish to be considered a candidate for.

'I think you have a fan here, you know,' Per said.

Soren's little mouth was pursed, eyes downturned. His silver lashes like dandelion seed against his cheek as he tapped a fork on his glass. Already projecting adult individuality with his Ramones t-shirt and long hair. She could easily picture kissing his cheek in the glow of a dinosaur nightlight then going to the living room to drink a large glass of good wine with his father's arm round her shoulder. It moved her to a sentiment like a John Lewis Christmas advert, but just like one of those, it was slick promotional material for things she had no desire to possess.

'Soren – ikke gjør det,' Per said angrily, grabbing the boy's hand.

Per's Scandinavian silver-foxiness was transformed into seediness by the silence that followed. It revealed to Peach a bald patch she'd never noticed, jowls like flat tyres she hadn't clocked, little boobies starting to push against his plaid shirt.

They had waved away the offer of dessert and split the bill. Soren went to the toilet before they left.

'Hey Peach, look, I . . . ' Per had taken her hand.

'It's fine, he's a really lovely kid,' Peach had said.

Per let go of her hand. 'Okay.'

And when they left, it was obvious Soren understood exactly what had transpired. So that Peach wanted to offer to do it again next week just to see him brighten. But she knew inflicting a short-term unkindness on the boy was the only way to avoid inflicting a long-term one on all three of them.

She walked alone into the night, where the roads were gridlocked because someone was threatening to jump off London Bridge. An impulse she understood: what greater evidence could there be that a single human life is worth something than to bring London's traffic to a standstill?

'You know Octavia is so like you. She hardly sees you but she's *so like you* when you were little it's uncanny.' Coffee spills out the side of Bella's cup. 'Douglas is always telling me to stop giving her such a hard time.'

'I guess you probably should, remember how Mum always used to ... '

'I guess I'm trying to be fair to Anais. Mothers aren't meant to have a favourite.'

'Oh, Bella.' Peach reaches out to hug her sister, who demurs by snatching Peach's half-full coffee cup from her hand. She opens the driver's door, tosses both of their cups onto the forecourt and starts the car.

Gary Martin starts gesticulating angrily at them through the window and shouting over the Tannoy. Bella flicks him the vees as the engine roars into life.

'Bella?'

'Is that Martin Martin's little brother?'

'I guess – that was Gary Martin, but—'

'Who the fuck calls their kid Martin Martin?' Bella scoffs and they roar off down the road towards Ian's house.

Chapter 21

After the rain stopped, the car park was polished with moisture. The wistful scent of petrichor permeated the air. In the back seat of the car, Peach clutched a plastic bag and listened to the unmusical music of Dad humming tunelessly under his breath.

When the car stuttered to a halt on the drive daylight was starting to diffuse and soften. Peach looked across the street. Mrs MacArthur was pitching like a boat, bilging bitter recriminations as Mr MacArthur paced the living room, trying out places to stand or sit where whatever she was saying might not be the stupidest, most unreasonable thing he'd ever heard.

Inside, Bella was sitting on the hall floor, talking on the telephone. She stood as they walked in. 'Ugh, right, got to go.' She replaced the receiver.

Peach looked at the orange trimphone, anachronistic as a penny farthing. Her lip wobbled, realising she had no one to call now.

'You okay?' Bella asked.

Peach nodded half-heartedly.

'Sure?'

Wet eyes and another tepid nod.

'Bella, I was wondering if you could help me with something.' Peach tested a casual tone.

Bella's skin so white it was almost baby blue. Her lips painted maroon and of course her nose. 'What's up? You look miserable.'

'Am. Totally. You any good at doing hair?'

'Hair?'

Peach held out a box. Bleach. The packaging design was out-of-date Duran Duran cool that made her think twice. 'Do you know how to use this stuff?'

'Yeah, I do my flat-mate's roots all the time.'

Dad's plan to make paella had been scaled back to Mum making tomato salad. They ate quickly in silence. Bella took her full plate to the bin. Mum and Dad exchanged wordless worry.

'Peach, are you okay? Do you need to talk about anything?' Mum asked.

Peach shook her head, left the table and followed Bella up to her room. My Bloody Valentine roared and whispered in the background.

'Want this?' Bella gestured to a joint smouldering in a saucer.

'Yes!'

They smoked the joint together, sitting on the bed. Bella with her head on Peach's leg. Peach enjoyed the feeling of her sister's hair running through her palm over and over. She inhaled, letting sweet smoke insinuate its tendrils into her brain.

'Can we still do my hair?'

'Yeah. C'mon.'

They shut themselves in the bathroom with its beige and orange tiles, the ugly avocado suite. Bella put on latex gloves like a surgeon and mixed stinky blue paste while Peach sat on the lid of the toilet. She turned her head this way and that in a parody of a cosmetic advert, wondering what sort of a blonde she would make.

Pouting at her reflection, Peach realised that, to look like the version of herself she wanted to portray, she'd have to copy other people. Katie Jane Garside, Courtney Love, Kat Bjelland: a bad cover version. Explaining to Bella made her feel so pathetic she almost said forget it. But since Bella made no comment, Peach sat back and let her sister paint her hair with the fizzy, smelly mixture.

The laboratory stench of transformation, the featheriness of the pot, replaced doubt with thrill.

'She shouldn't have got me that stupid job,' she said.

Bella pulled the gloves off. 'What?'

On the cusp of confiding, Peach was afraid of making her worries into facts by speaking.

'It's just. The past. Mum and Dad's and ours, in some way ours, the Elders, it was the last thing I needed and now I genuinely feel a bit crazy.'

Bella clapped her hands together, a single unit of applause. 'I'm going to tell you something.'

Cold sweat pricked Peach's skin.

'When we were kids, something weird went on between our parents and the Elders. I don't know what, but they fell out.'

Peach's head buzzed like a broken fluorescent tube.

'I don't know why. But they were together all the time then suddenly everything was weird between them. Patty died, and Ian went to bits. Mum sorted him out and he gave her that job. And Peach, you *need* to understand that whatever it is, or was, isn't any of our business. Mum was mental to

189

get you that job, it's weird that Mum works for Ian at all, it's a weird job, right?'

Peach nodded. She felt suddenly certain her hair was going to look stupid. Bella continued.

'Like Mum is his housekeeper *and* his secretary *and* he hasn't even had an exhibition for years. She's like his nanny. He depends on her far more than is healthy. I try not to think about it because when I do, I'm like yuck, the whole thing's sad and creepy and where does all his money come from? Not art – inherited wealth. His dad had a tea planta-tion in India or some evil British empire shit. Anyway, Ian's loaded, and he keeps using his money to pay Mum to look after him. She should *not* have got you involved. Like you say, you were having a tiny normal crisis, totally understandably. I mean, you're getting shipped off to university, where are you even going?'

'Glasgow.'

'Right, and they picked it for you, like they were fright-ened of what would happen if they let you stop to think.'

'It feels like that. *I do* feel like that,' Peach said as relief breezed through her.

Bella put her arm around Peach. 'Crap, right? It's what they did to me. I'm making it work, but it's crap. I mean, not really – they're just doing what they think is right, but no one asked us. They didn't ask you. They're too busy being glad you're not me.'

'That's not true.'

'It is. Let's not pretend.'

'Well, who were they trying to get you not to be?'

'Them.'

Peach didn't really understand what Bella meant. But afraid of losing the moment she said, 'I wanted to go to art school, but Mum said you have to be really good, like *really good*, and it's practically impossible to get a job, too hard being an artist. So, I sort of negotiated her into History of Art because it was the least boring course out of all the degrees she would consider.'

Bella plaited her own hair idly, letting the weave slip out when she reached the end.

'And why do you think that is?'

'They want me to have a good job?'

'Because they went to art school and they're not artists. You could be an artist. There's no secret to it. There's no secret to anything. Life isn't like that. Some people always look like they know what they're doing. But no one really ever knows. Once you believe that it gets easier. Uni's just school anyway but more laid-back with a bar in it. You *will* be fine. But you'd be better off at art school.'

Peach felt ancient and deflated.

'Well, it's too late now.'

'Maybe, maybe not. But I'll tell you what you *should do* before it is too late. Get out of that job. Get out of this prissy, Tory, bore-fest of a town. There's nothing here for the kind of person you want to be. Anyway, let's rinse this bleach out.'

Then Peach leant forward over the bath. Saw steam rush upwards, smelled the pink scent of shampoo. Water rushed past her ears. A lock of perfect white blonde hair tumbled into the corner of her vision.

Bella wrapped a towel turban round it before Peach could look in the mirror. She giggled, 'Don't look until we're done. Hey, do you want to know a real secret?'

'Yeah?'

Bella turned, fumbled open the buttons on the back of her dress to reveal a big tattoo of a lotus flower on her back.

Peach was jealous and impressed. But unsettled too. Bella's flesh was embossed into her skeleton, bones on show more shocking than ink, although she'd never have guessed Bella would get a tattoo. It was starting to feel like her whole family contained hidden selves like Russian dolls.

'If you tell Mum and Dad I will actually kill you.'

Bella did up her dress and brandished the kitchen scissors. She snipped around Peach's forehead, cut a messy fringe.

'Sure you want a shaved bit? I'm pretty high – can't promise I won't do it wonky.'

'Sod it, you've got a tattoo. It'll grow back.'

Peach felt the zip, zipping of the razor. Watched fluff drift into her lap: a miracle of bleach blonde snow.

Bella kissed Peach lightly on the cheek. 'Right, finished. I'm going to tell you one more secret. Promise not to tell the 'rents?'

'Promise.'

'I'm out of here in a few days. Had enough, dying of boredom, losing my mind. I'm going travelling for a bit.'

'Where'd you get the money?'

'I work in the Marquee Club. See gigs for free and get paid. Meet some cool people. Get out of here and get a job like that; that's my advice.'

Wrench in the heart, Bella leaving. And yet, a world of possibility. Reminder of the vast world beyond 16 The Oaks, beyond the whole town.

Peach revolved the things her sister had said, tried to put a needle between the grooves but couldn't produce any music. She wanted to ask Bella to stay, keep talking, to prolong the moment of openness but knew that with Bella you always had to be careful not to ask her for anything she wasn't already handing over – she was halfway out the room already.

But then Peach's reflection in the oval mirror astonished her. A new self for a new life. Things are getting interesting, she thought, as she posed for herself. With her blonder hair and secrets, she looked like someone the world would have to give a fuck about. Peach was Courtney Love. She was Sylvia Plath, Laura Dern in *Wild at Heart*: too cool for those sneering prudes in the supermarket, too big for this suffocating little town.

Chapter 22

Bella slows the car to a crawl past the end of the cul-de-sac where they grew up and something inside Peach exclaims: home! This place she has had no claim on for decades fills her with melancholy gladness so huge and nameless it needs a German compound noun to describe it.

In spite of the front garden having been tarmacked for parking, in spite of the fancy front door, in spite of her grey roots and deepening crow's feet, Peach cannot shake the feeling that her family, as they were in the summer of 1994, are still inside. That her old life is just beyond the threshold: paused, waiting. That if she could only slip into the house, she might begin again.

In her head the decades contract; rush through themselves in a tide of undoing. Dad is plucked from the air and set safely back on his feet as a car disappears backwards. He steps back onto the kerb and puts his phone into his pocket. The moon sinks under the horizon, the sun hurtles into the sky. Peach slides into bed and the years stream in reverse: birthdays are unbirthdayed, the snow falls up, brown leaves spiral back onto the trees and turn green, blossoms burst into a froth of pink and white. Bella's pregnant belly flattens out. The buckling, darkening folds of Dad's brain plump and pale. He is restored to himself. Peter evaporates. Dad takes Mum in his arms and calls her sweetheart, she kisses him and smiles. Solomon runs through their legs in happy circles. There is a vibration: the mass murmuration of a million words unspeaking themselves, flocking back into their mouths. Their lips seal round the silence. As all the days which have passed blink out of existence, a bell rings insistently. The asphalt of the playground is warm on the last day of school which is only just beginning.

'Can we stop, Bella? Can we stop here for a second?'

Bella gives Peach a look which invites her to answer the question: have you been smoking crack? Then floors the accelerator towards Ian's house.

It reminds Peach of another car, another driver, back in 1994. *Him.* Far too often she dreams about *him.* His black eyes full of space and possibility. His hip bones peeping up above his waistband, smooth and carved as netsuke. A trail of dark hair, snaking into his jeans. Fuck. She jams her nails into her palm and is unequal to the pain. She isn't sure anyone has sent her demented with an ache that acute since.

Someone has come close – Simon with the brutal/beautiful, Egon Schiele drawing look *he* had. But as of last month, she and Simon are finally over. They had finished before, plenty of times, but their full stops inevitably grew into commas. This ending she grieves because it was different.

It happened on one of those days where barely perceptible thinning of the light becomes noticeable, meaning autumn taking hold. Hot on the heels of a long-distance word fuck that lasted for a fortnight, Simon casually announced he was in London recording a new album with his band, Holy Ghost Bulldozer: art noise favoured by the Guy/Luke/Toms.

On the train to meet him, Peach's brain was a multiplex,

screening imaginings: what she would say and what Simon would say. What they would do, or not do. Fretting over whether it would be one of the times when he is distant by the time she arrives, so that the lurid intimacy of their text conversations feels like a story Peach has told herself because she is lonely.

In some shiny serviced apartment in Shoreditch he was there. Real and Simon and a body in space. A body in her arms, briefly, before he dismissed her with a pat, the sort you'd give to a clumsy, enthusiastic dog.

'Tea?'

'Beer?'

'Sure, beer.'

He knelt in front of the fridge. Peach wanted to put her hand on him, to thaw the chilliness and melt into the intimate version of them that existed an hour ago when they were apart.

'When do you start recording?'

'Tomorrow.' He handed her a can of something small batch and trendy. Took one for himself.

'Excited?'

'Kind of.'

A flabby, disconnected silence made her feel like a spinster aunt trying to solicit conversation from a teenage nephew.

'Do you know exactly what the new album's going to be like, or is that something you discover as you're making it?'

'Yeah, both.'

'Well, that was a fascinating insight into your creative process.'

'Hah. Cheers.' Simon bumped his can against hers without looking at her, avoiding her eye like someone ignoring a mess they'd made that they couldn't be bothered to clear up.

'How are things then?' He sat on the bed and started to untie his shoelaces.

Hellish. I'm in hell. 'Pretty good. Nothing exciting to report. But all good.'

'Still living with that miserable performance guy?'

'Nope. Had my own place for a while now. You should come over.'

'Cool.' Simon looked at Peach. A silence gripped them, built itself steadily.

They watched one another like wildlife. Quiet took on the buzzy quality of a speaker waiting to transmit the first chord.

'Why are you all the way over there?' He tipped his head, a tiny inclination inviting Peach to sit beside him.

'Hi.' She sat, put on a pouty smile she knew he couldn't resist and watched desire accumulate and disperse behind his eyes like a time lapse film of fruit ripening and rotting. She pushed her face against his shoulder.

'You're like a cat.' He laughed. The brittle laugh of a dis-interested stranger introduced to a nuisance. Up above them in the air hung the story of Peach and Simon, like a net of balloons at a party.

'Do you like cats?' she asked. Jesus, Peach, what the hell? The balloons drifted sadly to the ground, released at the wrong moment.

'I like you.' Simon put his arm round her. 'I like you so much, Peach, but ... ' His eyes begged clemency.

She wished she was capable of allowing him not to spell it out, but her agony wouldn't tolerate the unspoken. 'But what?'

'It's not, we aren't, this isn't good, I mean it's lovely to see you and I know we were flirting earlier but this isn't ... '

'It isn't what?'

'A good idea. I mean, those texts were ridiculously hot but, like, look, now you're here I'm kind of thinking it's not a great idea.'

'You started it.'

'Did I? Maybe, look, I thought I could do this but I'm recording tomorrow, and I need a clear head. Please don't feel snubbed, or like I don't want you. But this can't happen.'

Soggy humiliation calcified into a sad hard rage Peach had no room for. It was impossible not to cry and she puked up a sob.

'Don't.' He pulled her close to him. 'Please don't. You're lovely but I'm a mess at the moment and I'm really not worth this.'

No, Peach thought, you're not. But I am. What I have done to myself with you, picked you up like the blunt instrument I know you are and coshed myself over the head – that's worth crying for.

She let herself cry.

Simon stopped holding her.

'Sorry.' He rubbed her arm like a parent scrubbing at a bumped spot on a hurt child. 'You understand, right? You know it's not you, right? Are you okay?'

She shook her head. She wanted to tell him he was making her want to be dead, but it seemed unfair – he made her want to be dead because the Venn diagram of things that made her want to be dead had become a circle. Because everything had been making her want to be dead lately and Simon was merely a subset of everything.

Instead of speaking she gagged up another sob so violent he recoiled. She could see he was annoyed. He had the audacity to be annoyed and the decency to be wrestling it back.

'Can you just hug me for a while?' She despised her

undignified clinging, hope consuming her from the inside like cancer. Worse than hopelessness: inability to shake the hunger for a reversal he was incapable of.

'Come here.' Simon gave Peach the laziest hug, like a pissed-off parent comforting a child who has begun to over-play their injury.

'It's getting late,' he said. It was half-past nine. 'Let me get you a cab.'

'I don't have any money.'

'It's cool. I'll get you an Uber. It's absolutely the minimum I can do.'

Which she knew meant: there is no amount of money I wouldn't pay to have you out of here.

For years Peach had supplied herself to Simon in hotel rooms and serviced apartments like some obsequious con-cierge. Every time he began to look at her as if she was the greasy remnants of a fast-food binge, she had cleared herself away.

'You know what, Simon?' She stood so he'd be small. 'Actually, up yours. Actually, fuck you forever, you utter piece of utter, utter shit. You text me for hours on end, that's just today. Actually, you text me for days and weeks and months and years, actually years on end, about eleven and counting on and off. You make me feel like there's something real between us, then I get here, and you act like I'm some stranger delivering a takeaway who's invited themselves in to eat it with you, as if I'm the one being weird. And this is about the hundredth time you've done it, so fuck you and fuck this.'

Simon looked afraid. Maybe of himself, maybe of her. She didn't know which. But she knew her distress permit-ted Simon to dismiss her as a psycho, a bullet he was smart to dodge. But he would find a way to think those things anyway – self-justification close at hand, like a breadknife under his pillow.

'Peach?'

In that moment Peach could see all Simon's goodness and badness, both equally true, equally him, none of it part of the story they told themselves outside that room and the burn went out of her. They were nothing but tired strangers who mistook a bedtime story for, not love, but something that sometimes felt powerfully real. Comfort, affection in the absence of anything more substantial. Like a dummy, or blankie or a stuffed bear. Something soft to hold tightly when loneliness and boredom bared their teeth, wrapped themselves round the hard hours and squeezed so tight it was difficult to breathe.

'What?'

'I *am* sorry.'

She left with Simon missing from her like a phantom limb; severed with the ache still attached. Stuffed full of trash and sleet, Peach caught sight of her reflection.

The callous glass of an empty office showed her exactly how she looked: a spiteful caricature of middle age. Eyeliner running into wrinkles, murky roots of her blonde hair like a calendar on her head showing her how quickly time was passing. How quickly she was growing old. Alone.

No more flirtations and friends with benefits to banish her loneliness. Not that they ever did, not really, but she could merrily have thrown herself in the Thames to drown the part of her that wished Simon would come after her and write a better ending to the pointless waste of – what?

Love? Probably not, no matter how many times the word appeared in her head.

Time, definitely. She could have volunteered in a night shelter, built matchstick replicas of all seven wonders of the world, been fluent in another language. Could have taken photos for exhibitions instead of sucking her belly in and sexting him pictures taken from angles contrived to stop her looking like herself.

All that time squandered on emotional tat – like money she should have invested wisely. Too late: the sexual equivalent of turning up at the bus stop to see the last bus disappearing, realising there's no alternative but to start trudging home in the rain. Knowing that at some point Simon will overtake her in a chauffeur-driven Bentley because that's the difference between being him and being her, between being a man and being a woman: between being Ben Gardener's flunky and being the lead singer of Holy Ghost Bulldozer.

And maybe her implicit understanding of that was the main reason she'd never put a stop to it before. Or maybe it was just because Simon reminded her so much of *him*.

Chapter 23

The morning after the haircut, Mum berated Peach, wielding words like ridiculous and unemployable and lobotomy. Humiliation reddened Peach's cheeks and brought tears to her eyes.

Suddenly Mum held out a finger and brushed it against the shaved part. 'Just a shock,' she said. 'I'm not meant to like it, am I? It's just hair. It'll grow. You're practically an adult.' Mum stood there telling herself the things Peach was meant to be yelling at her.

'I don't suppose it matters. Not in the scheme of things.' Peach could see it did. Could see Mum was appalled but that her disapproval had startled something in herself.

'You're seventeen,' Mum said as though confirming a surprising new fact. And just like that Peach had won.

Peach ran her hand against the stubbly, velvet nap, savouring the prickle as she walked to the Elder house to start work.

She kept summoning up imagined lives, adjusting them, fine-tuning pictures of herself at parties full of interesting people. She would have an exhibition of her photographs: hotly anticipated and glowingly reviewed.

Intent on possible futures, she walked past the gates of the

Elder house, only realising she had overshot when a battered green Mini tore up and screeched to a halt.

A beautiful man with dark shaggy hair and enormous brown eyes rolled down the window. A blast of loud music escaped. 'I'm looking for Ian Elder's house – do you know where it is?' he yelled over the noise without turning it down. Whatever he was listening to sounded like someone vomiting hammers into a metal bin.

Realising she'd have to tell the cool creature in the car that the house was back in the opposite direction and that she was going there too, Peach put her hand to the shorn part of her skull.

'Uh, yeah, I'm going there.'

'Get in then.'

Doomy public-service films cautioning against lifts from strangers played through Peach's mind. The man was improbably gorgeous: Manics gorgeous. She opened the door and hopped in.

'So where are we going?' he asked, flicking a cigarette from the packet on the dashboard.

'Reverse about a hundred yards that way,' Peach said truculently, daring him to ask why she had been going the wrong way.

He didn't. He pulled the car into a pitching turn. Peach's stomach lurched. 'I'm Nick.' Terrifyingly, he removed his hand from the steering wheel to shake Peach's.

'Peach. Up here, through these gateposts.'

'Peach? Cool name, mate.'

For the first time ever, she thought maybe it was. An unusual name for a remarkable person.

They hurtled up the drive sending gravel flying. Peach wished they were further from their destination. This felt like a moment from a life she wanted: speeding in cars with reckless men who looked like they could slot into the best band. The adventure was pathetically short.

'What you doing here?' he asked. The car skidded to a halt.

'I work for Mr Elder. I'm his assistant,' Peach said grandly. Nick smirked.

'Oh yeah.' He smashed out his half-smoked cigarette in among hundreds of stinking butts which flowed far beyond the ashtray and surrounded the gear stick. Some had lipstick on them.

'What are *you* doing here then?'

'I write for the *NME*: we're doing a piece on the Patty Elder re-releases. I'm actually doing a bit on Ian and Patty for the *Guardian* as well. I'm a huge fan.'

Holy fuck, Peach thought. A real *NME* journalist talking like she'd expect him to, smoking like she'd expect him to, crash-landed in her life like an alien spacecraft of a walking talking man. Of all the improbable, wonderful, terrible things which had happened in the last few weeks this one stunned Peach into a free-fall feeling of being more perfectly alive than she would ever have thought possible.

Peach sent up a silent prayer of thanks for her cool new hair, the impeccable timing of her makeover.

Now there was someone worth impressing, her boring job seemed interesting. She was glad Ian's life conjoined with hers; a life filled with the dark romance of untimely death, records, art and glamour. All of it had always been there – too close for her to notice before.

She paused on the step, turned on her heel. 'Just a head's up: Ian's kind of difficult. You'll need to play it cool.'

Nick shrugged and lit another cigarette. 'Yeah, cheers.' Smoke drawled off his lip. 'I heard he can be spiky, but you know, I was interviewing Morrissey one time and . . .'

Ian appeared in the doorway. Inside herself, Peach lifted and twisted like something from a dream of flight. She felt the slippage again, this time she felt scissored off the grey background of her life, collaged onto another painted in better bright new colours, until Ian spoke.

'Look at the tyre marks in my gravel! Who the hell are you?'

Nick and Peach stood stupid as a pair of posts until Nick proffered his free hand. 'Nick Young. *NME*. I thought you were expecting me.'

Ian kissed a tut off his teeth, a sound of pure disdain.

'Nick gave me a lift.'

'What a gentleman,' said Ian sarcastically. 'What happened to your head, Peach? Surgical procedure?' He laughed at his own joke.

Peach hated him.

Nick offered her a sympathetic look which felt humiliating, the sort that implied he was remembering what it was like to be Peach's age: embarrassed and embarrassing.

Peach stormed upstairs. She fulminated her way along the corridor, imagining that five years hence she would have an exhibition everyone was raving about which eclipsed any boring crap Ian (universally forgotten) had ever made. Five minutes hence Nick Young would come into the room and say he was sorry and explain that he was just nervous – shocked by finding such beauty here where he least expected it, then he'd try to get off with her and she'd say no.

Peach moved the last few boxes while injured rage steamed inside her until her head hurt.

She sold herself the lie of tea making and stomped down to the kitchen, slackening into an amble as she rounded the corner. Voices pulsed in the kitchen. Ian and Nick sat at the table, heads bowed together.

Peach listened outside. Nick spoke passionately of his admiration for Ian's art and love of Patty's music. Ian seemed to be receiving his words with pleasure.

Peach sailed into the kitchen on her wave of bitterness. 'I'm making tea.'

'I'll take another cup, mate,' said Nick. 'What you up to up there?'

'I've just finished moving the archive.'

Ian chortled derisively. 'Detritus more like,' he said. 'Mountain of crap.'

God, she hated him so much; his relentless casual contempt had been hard enough to bear before. Now in front of Nick it was intolerable.

She snapped, 'You're right. Why don't we just have a massive bonfire right now and Nick can go home?'

She waited for Ian to destroy her. Instead he leant back in his chair, put his hands behind his head and looked pleasantly surprised. As if discovering Peach had a bit more substance, a bit more spine than he'd thought. 'Great idea,' he smiled, 'a bonfire of boring.'

'Yeah.' Peach stretched exaggeratedly, pleased to see that Nick was looking at her; really looking. 'I pity you having to try to make this guy sound interesting.'

Nick laughed. His goofy giggle at odds with the spotless cool he projected.

'Probably just as well I'm mainly here to write about Patty then,' he said.

All three of them cackled and Peach felt entirely adult – confident and playful. At home with her shifting life of new moods, blonde hair and talking to artists and *NME* journalists who, of course, just happen to pitch up on any given day.

Her mother arrived, dumped a bag of shopping on the

counter and kissed Peach absent-mindedly. 'What the hell happened to the gravel?'

'I did. Sorry. Nick Young. We spoke on the phone.'

'Ah,' said Mum, amusement tickling the corner of her mouth.

Nick kissed Peach's mother on both cheeks like a Frenchman. Mum seemed perfectly at home with the gesture. Peach had a flash of her mother before mothering; cosmopolitan, sociable. She'd never thought her mother might have possessed exceptional qualities which had qualified her for friendship with exceptional people.

Slight regret shifted under Peach's sternum. It felt like her soul yawning as a new life healed over the top of her old one.

Peach decided she would get her nose pierced in the first week of university. She decided she would get a new camera, take more photos, watch more films (foreign ones), and read more books (difficult ones).

Then her mother said, 'Right you, come with me. I'm going to start on those boxes, so I've got a list of jobs for you as long as your arm. Ian isn't paying you four pounds an hour to drink tea.' And Peach was five years old again: a great big 'stop showing off because your friends are here' of the soul.

Later, Peach was mopping the upstairs corridor with some disinfectant that smelled like school. Mum passed by with a bundle of papers. Mum picked at her cuticle. Suddenly she was always poking and fiddling, pulling at dead bits of herself where normally she was poised.

Briefly, intensely, Peach missed the mouldy smell of poster paint drying. She missed the shrill sound of recorder practice drifting down corridors. She missed rain pattering on the prefabs next to the sports field. She missed being glad of double geography because it meant she wasn't outside playing hockey, discovering she did sort of care how oxbow lakes were formed after all. Then she was pleased it was all behind her; the smallness, the repetition. She swirled the mop around like a dance partner, humming under her breath – a run of notes her happiness composed.

Through the window a gust yanked open the door to Mum's room. Peach went to close it; the tune stumbled on her lip. But the scene beyond the threshold compelled her to step inside.

There were papers everywhere, boxes upended. Letters skidded across the desk, a blizzard of documents on the floor. Ransacked was the word that slammed into Peach's head.

On her mother's chair was a lumpy brown cushion. A corner of cream notepaper poked out from underneath, concealed like a bloodstained glove. Peach lifted the cushion and withdrew the letter.

She looked around, listened for footsteps. Almost put the letter back. Knew it had been hidden for a reason, unfolded it. Mum's handwriting.

Dearest Ian. I can't believe what has happened. Neither can you I expect. It doesn't feel real but I must remind myself that it is. I fear I will go mad without you. Such regret. Such deceit. We were so naïve to think we could put a stop to it so easily when it had already gone on for so long. I understand completely if you feel you have to stay away. But I do hope you will write or call. I hope we can find a way back from this dark place. My love, as ever, Eleanor.

The past smashed through the decades, landed in the now like a brick hurled through a window. Terrible cold rushed in.

Soap opera scenes readied in Peach's head; she waited to

cry but what came instead was stillness. Thrust into danger, Peach went slack. *My love. Such deceit.* She could scarcely believe it was possible to know this and still be alive.

Think, think, think, she pleaded with herself. But her head howled back, a shout echoing round a cave. Then worst of all she thought the thing she always did when her heart was crying for help. She thought: I want my mum.

I want my mum. Peach had never experienced pain to compare with that instinct; wanting Mum to come and make her safe from what Mum herself had done. Like depending on the kiss of life from a person who'd just tried to kill her. It was worse than Solomon dying, the torture of Mum just ceasing to exist. A replicant with the face and the body and the voice of her mother was downstairs pretending to *be* her, whoever *she* was. Peach wished Mum was dead so there would be no point in wanting her.

The pain was so big Peach didn't have space for it. This was like all the other conflicting feelings she had begun to experience this summer turned up to an unbearable volume. A frantic, impossible urge to evade things that lived inside her. Still, escape was all she could think of.

She jammed the letter into her pocket and ran downstairs, gasping into the barbarous heat. She remembered the urge that overtook her in the service station on their way back from the seaside – to walk. Recently she'd been fascinated by news footage of new age travellers: people who lived nowhere and everywhere, following sun and music. That was what she wanted. She made for the top of the drive. She'd walk and keep walking, getting further and further away from here, and she'd leave herself behind. Mum would find the letter gone and know why Peach had disappeared. And she would spend the rest of her life being sorry. Exactly as she deserved.

Except that Nick materialised in a cloud of cigarette smoke, wearing a leopard-print coat, looking like a cross between Richey Manic and Ted Hughes – a delicate lout. 'All right, mate.' He gave Peach a sweet lopsided smile.

'All right,' she smiled back – a real smile even in her sadness.

Nick: a journalist. Looking for a story that was in the house. In her pocket, in the boxes upstairs. Peach understood that she'd have to discover the whole story they told. Then she knew she was not leaving and the letter in her pocket was a burning ember against her leg. An ember that could burst into flames at any moment.

Chapter 24

Nick slouched against the house. His t-shirt rode up. Peach was assailed by the desire to lick the curve of his hip bone and the urge to punch him in the balls just to see the look on his face. He was so perfectly sculpted from the stuff of her fantasies that even the letter mattered less. Only for a moment, but still.

'How long are you going to be around?' she asked.

'Mate, yeah, look, I dunno, couple of days, maybe three. I've got to get back to London to review a gig Thursday so, you know, whatever works. As long as my articles are good.' He sniffed and didn't look half as attractive: the reality of people starts to betray the ideal of them with little things like sniffing, Peach thought, and felt too tired to be alive.

'You're so lucky.' Nick lit another cigarette. 'Smoke?'

She desperately wanted to. 'Nah, lucky how?'

'Growing up with Patty and Ian Elder. It's so ridiculously cool. Tell me what it was like.'

He drew near and gripped Peach's wrist as if it was precious. As Nick looked at Peach like he knew she was about to amaze him, she experienced her whole body as his fingers on her skin. She didn't know how to tell him she didn't remember that much about Patty and Ian. Certainly didn't want to think about them now.

And then it didn't matter because Peach could say any old crap. Nick wasn't listening. His attention was concentrated elsewhere; watching Bella and some sexy woman with a backpack walking up the drive, looking like something off a record cover. Damn it, Peach thought. Why does everyone keep appearing out of place like something from a lazy scene in a tawdry play?

Nick dropped her wrist. Peach cursed their arrival as Nick double-kissed Bella and the woman. Peach felt stupid in her haircut – she was so obviously a wannabe. A conservative version of the woman with her sister. The woman was an original: moving with absolute confidence. Carrying a camera.

'What are you doing here?' Peach asked Bella.

'Mum invited me. This is Magda, we met on the road and got talking.' Bella said this loftily to Peach like a grand visitor addressing a maid.

Comparing the way Nick looked at Bella and Magda to the way he looked at her, Peach revised the moments when she had been convinced he was checking her out. Deflated, she realised he had been checking her out to see *if* she would *do*, whereas now he was checking Bella and Magda out to see *who* he would do. Peach held Nick responsible for the pain of her own crass thought.

Then there was this other woman. Mum. Once, an actress from TV had come to open the school fete and Peach had found it so strange. Recognising the actress as her character, knowing that was just pretend, knowing she didn't know her even though she was so familiar. You could see the actress wasn't as nice as the lady she played. That was how it felt to see Mum.

'Are you the photographer?' the Mum-like woman asked Magda.

Magda pointed to her camera. Something so laid-back about her manner that it didn't seem like she was accusing Mum of being thick. 'Yes! I walked up from the station.'

'You should have called from the phone box. Nick or I could have come to get you.'

'I don't like to wait around. I love to walk. Such beautiful weather.' Magda's speech was accented: German or Dutch. She exuded latent sex, lust for life and wry humour. Her white mohawk was streaked with pink, blue and purple. A silver nose ring bobbed and gleamed on her nostril as she spoke.

New dreads bred on the mould of old ones as they walked inside, skins strafed with the house's coolness where it always felt like dusk.

Magda stopped in front of the picture of Patty in the hall. 'I love this photo!' she cried. 'It's from the cover of *The Pearl-Handled Revolver*, yeah?'

'Isn't it amazing? Really captures something about Patty and the beauty of her music.' Nick brandished a show-off smile to Magda.

'You know who took it?'

'I don't actually.' Nick looked like he was losing a game of Top Trumps.

'I did,' Mum said hesitantly, as if she was checking the facts against an encyclopaedia.

More shocking to Peach than the letter.

'Oh, you're a photographer too?' Magda grinned.

Mum looked sadder than Peach had ever seen her look before. 'No. Just did a few favours for friends back in the late sixties. Another lifetime.'

'This was the only one you did?'

'No, I did maybe five or six record covers for various bands, no one very famous. Not nowadays anyway. Publicity photos, gig pictures, press.'

'So, you *were* a photographer?' Magda said.

'Maybe, I don't know. I'm not any more. Had my kids so . . . actually gave my camera to Peach here.'

Magda looked heartbroken, as if the thought of life without art was unbearable. Then she turned to Peach and said, 'So *you're* the photographer in the family now.'

'No,' Peach said, 'no.' Because she wasn't, and Mum wasn't. Since neither of them were photographers and neither of them were special and both of them were just dirty bitches who couldn't keep their pants on.

'Drinks!' announced Mum like a chatelaine from a country house, and with that Peach felt like she was looking at her mother through a fractured lens, a camera that refused to focus.

'I'm tired. I might just go home and kick about with Dad,' Peach said.

'Nah, mate,' said Nick, 'come and have a drink.'

Ian came in and lit a fire; the house was draughty and filled with shade even in summer. Mum poured sherry. Peach sipped; it tasted of bottled cobwebs. Ian and Mum were like a couple. Peach downed it in one.

'Careful,' said her mother. Peach summoned her most evil look from the bowels of hell. Mum laughed and refilled her glass.

'So,' said Ian. 'A toast. To new friends and absent friends.' He sat down and rubbed his palms on his trousers. 'Well. I can barely remember the last time I saw you, Isabella.'

'No.' Bella barely cast a glance at Ian. 'Must be a long time ago.'

Ian looked reproached. 'How's university life?'

Peach hated how adults who knew you as a child carried on talking to you as if you remained a child.

Bella began to talk about her dissertation. Ian moved to sit beside her. He wasn't spiteful to Bella, Peach noticed; didn't treat her to his mockery. Ian's mammoth dimensions made Bella look more delicate and fragile than ever. Before long they were deep in conversation.

Mum and Nick talked; an improbable confluence of two kinds of newness. Nick and the secret world his arrival had imported. Mum and the secret world she'd been concealing all along.

Magda came to sit by Peach.

'So, you've come to take pictures of Ian?'

'Tomorrow, yes,' Magda smiled, 'then Amsterdam to see my girlfriend, meet some friends and go to Berlin, some clubbing, do a job there. Photos. Another artist for a different magazine.'

'Wow! But you've only got that tiny backpack.'

Magda laughed, a generous laugh, threw up her hands, covered in silver rings. 'I don't need so much stuff: camera, film, change of clothes.'

Amazing. It *is* possible to live like that, Peach thought, and felt the rest of her life approaching. She imagined herself in another country; standing on a railway platform waiting for the next train to who cares where. Comfortable in her own skin, like Magda, so at ease she'd look like a public health campaign for self-acceptance. With a camera round her neck.

'How do you become a photographer?' Peach asked shyly.

Magda fixed Peach with an inhumanly penetrating gaze. 'The thing is with photography . . .'

'Magda?' Nick swaggered over. 'Can we have a chat and plan tomorrow?'

'Actually, Peach and I were ...'

And then Mum beckoned them with a notebook in her hand. Nick and Mum and Magda talked and laughed together, leaving Peach feeling as though she was watching them from behind a pane of glass.

This time when she said she was going everyone simply said goodbye and no one tried to stop her as she'd meant them to. Peach left them to a snug world which had barely contained her.

Outside, on the drive, it was not the letter Peach found herself worrying about. It was the wisdom Magda was about to impart that she might never dispense. And it was Mum's stalled career as a photographer. An unpleasant sense the two things overlapped. Something Peach couldn't quite describe to herself.

Petals mushed into the gravel like spat gum. Smacked from the blooms by yesterday's storm. Occlusions of white cloud dripped lukewarm mizzle, turning the air to second-hand sadness.

As the car zips round the turns of the top road, they pass the tree Patty crashed her car into. It grasps at the sky like it always did, only now it is twenty-five years taller and broader, exuding malfeasance. Peach knows it is not. But everything is leaking foreboding as she prays for Dad to cling to life. Or for him not to. She cannot help feeling that he has already slipped beyond her reach in every way that matters.

As they near Ian's house, Peach wonders if what she could not articulate that evening as she walked alone, what frightened her about herself, about Mum, was the suspicion that

216

people filled with dreams are dangerous. Especially those whose dreams are broken. Living like a bag of smashed glass, always one wrong move away from hurt. The contortions they'll perform to avoid it. Nothing belonging to others that they won't demolish to preserve a safe corner in their own hearts. A hospital, a bunker, an asylum. The poisons people who feel invisible will consume to feed their hunger to be seen. Peach can't help but wonder if that is what moved her to put her job in danger. Pretending to shield the girl at work in order to make a scene.

But that night Peach understood nothing except that on any other night like this she would have lain on top of the bus stop with friends she no longer had. Instead she had pin-balled through dusty lanes, where soap opera sounds leaked from televisions and cooking smells drifted from kitchens. Slipped riskily down desire paths into thickets where crushed cans and dirty magazines mulched into the ground, the smell of private parts and dead things heavy on the darkness. Sometimes she still finds herself flirting with danger that way: drunken, late-night shortcuts across waste-ground with her phone on show. Not knowing quite what stupidity compels her, understanding it's something to do with the way disasters force normal life to pause, how crises solicit company and care.

Peach walked and walked until her thoughts were mince and her feet swelled into elephant pads. She saw a plastic bag caught in a hedge, tatted to lace by weather, so it looked like a shocked face straining in the blackthorn. She saw a pedal car, so long abandoned that foxgloves sprouted through the chassis. She wished she had her camera.

She tested a thousand different thoughts against the

contents of the letter, but they all slammed her up against the same brick wall. Mum and Ian having an affair. It filled her with such intense loneliness that it felt almost sublime and heroic. For a second she wanted to cry prettily for herself.

As she turned onto her cul-de-sac, the town closed in around her. Small, smug and suffocating. She felt other selves, other lives peeling off every step like a film strip. University and far from home shifted from possibility to imperative.

Bella and Mum rounded the corner, stumbling like disembarked sailors.

They cheered like football hooligans when they caught sight of Peach.

'We've had a little drink,' said her mother, head lolling. 'But we're all right. We're all right, aren't we, Bella?'

Peach had never seen Mum like this: two wines tipsy at Christmas – never anything more.

'I'm fuckin' 'ammered,' slurred Bella.

Peach's thoughts ran like a hamster in a wheel going urgently nowhere.

'Turned into a party at Ian's,' Bella burped. 'I feel a bit sick. Nick's a bad influence.'

'I like Nick,' said Mum.

'He's ridiculous,' Peach snarked.

'Heh. S'true. Guys like him're always crap in the sack.' Bella made to boop Peach on the nose with her index finger like Peach was a puppy, except she missed her nose and poked her cheek instead. Mum laughed a dirty laugh that didn't belong to her.

'Ian, though, nice to chat to him.' Bella nearly fell over.

Mum smiled at his name like a silly schoolgirl, all spongy with drink and affection.

Peach made a fist round her keys.

Dad rushed to the door as Peach unlocked it.

'Where have you been? I was worried.'

'I went for a walk. These lushes were having a party with Ian and some journalist from the *NME*.' Peach spat that, enjoying dismissing Nick. Repulsed by Mum – sentimental and unseemly.

Mum and Bella train-wrecked into the hall.

'We've had a little drink but we're all right,' said Mum.

Greg appeared in sweaty sports kit. Peach thought, sometimes I forget you exist, and longed to feel close to him.

'Are you drunk, Mum?' Greg looked aghast.

'We're all right,' hiccupped Bella, then tore off and was violently sick in the downstairs toilet.

'Oh my god,' squirmed Greg, 'I can't believe how pissed you are.'

'We've had a little drink . . .'

Greg snorted and stalked off.

'Teenage boys,' said Mum, prevailing on the chivalry of the wall to remain standing, 'sooo censorious.'

Dad looked at Mum like he hadn't seen her in a long time. 'Let's get you a glass of water and get you to bed.' He held out his hand.

She pushed his hand away. 'No,' Mum cried vehemently. 'I want my babies.'

'Mum.' Peach moved towards her as though trying not to startle a nervous animal. Her mother was crying. Her mother never cried, and she was crying. Her mother never drank, and she was plastered. Something was gaining momentum, winding itself in tighter circles around them all.

'You're all grown up. You're all complicated.' Mum put her face in her hands and sob-sighed.

'Mum,' Peach said, like her name was all she had to hand to her.

'I used to be a different person.' Mum coughed into her hands. 'You used to be little. Things used to be easy. Before.'

'Before what?' Peach was afraid the answer was in her pocket.

'Before everything.'

'Everything what?' Peach's heart kicked double drumbeats.

'Life,' wailed Mum dramatically.

Dad returned with a pint of water. 'Bed, love. Now, love.'

'What do you mean?' Peach asked in a child's voice.

Mum drifted sideways along the wall.

'It's all too much! Being all the me's for all the people.'

Her voice was squelchy with self-pity, her face sweaty and red.

'Eleanor,' said Dad tersely. 'Bed.'

'What do you mean, Mum?' Peach knew and it was strangling her.

Her mother opened her mouth to speak.

'She's just drunk and maudlin. Drink always made her maudlin. Didn't it, love.' Dad didn't pose it as a question. He issued it as a demand for compliance. Mum let herself be led away while Peach's world fell mutely, slowly apart in the hall to the desperate sound of her sister throwing up for what seemed like the millionth time.

Chapter 25

Lamps are ablaze in Ian's house. In dim overcast light, bright windows make the house appear astonished. As they swing up the drive Peach sees it has an uncared-for look. The render flaking. Weeds spill from gutters as if trying to escape the rot. A terracotta pot has fallen on its side spilling soil and it is clear this is a place where things that go awry have ceased to be set right.

Folded in silence, the car ticks and cools as they wait to see what has become of Ian. To find out what he wants. Cancer, thinks Peach, cancer or regret or both: things that eat people up from the inside and put time in short supply.

I don't want to do this, thinks Peach. I want to go back to my life, whatever that means. She doesn't know. Not since the intern. She is still so ashamed she can't even bring herself to say the girl's name inside her head.

The first time Peach saw her, she was surrounded. By Ben Gardener and Scott Fox: the human equivalents of an eggy fart deliberately released in a confined space. The sort of people who would knowingly throw a snowball with a stone in it and put an empty milk carton back in a communal fridge.

Scott was Ben's favourite of the artists he represented. The show pony of Capsule gallery. Peach arrived back from an errand to find him and Ben standing with an attractive blonde girl, a look on their faces like they were shopping.

They always looked like that; browsing the world and all the people in it with the acquisitive dispassion of spoilt children. That was how they were looking at the girl. Like they didn't even have to decide whether or not to consume her because, to them, she was like a watch or a coat or cognac; there to please, now, later or never depending on their whims.

'This is Grace – our new intern,' Ben said to Peach. 'Would you like a coffee, Grace? Peach will be going back out for coffees in a mo.'

Grace looked like a minor royal: imprecise, long-boned prettiness that inevitably turns horsey in middle age. 'Ooh, yes please, soy latte.'

She clapped her hands like a child and Peach felt sorry for her. Her skinless unpreparedness for what the internship would turn out to be. Pissing about under Peach's feet, being chosen to travel to art fairs over infinitely more proficient members of staff, until one day: gone. Ben would be extra insufferable for a fortnight. The next time his wife Julia popped in, she'd be wearing yet another diamond ring.

One day, Peach thought, Ben will have to go the whole hog and get her diamond gauntlets. Over the last few years, Julia has been running out of fingers as fast as Peach has been running through her will to live.

And that was all Peach thought about when she saw the girl. Resentment at having to get her coffee. Irritation that later she would have to issue her with pointless busy work. Assuming the girl was living out the lyrics of 'Common People' until she got bored. Just like all the other Sophies and Daisies and occasional Hugos who could afford to undertake unpaid internships in central London. Thinking of her as roughly equivalent to a lobster in a tank in a seafood restaurant. Only vaguely wondering what kind of monster that made her.

She didn't bank on the lobster tapping on the tank and asking Peach to save her a fortnight later. Her own fault she supposes. Back in the summer of 1994 Magda taught her that looking and seeing are not the same thing, and if Peach had held more tightly to that truism, perhaps she'd never have ended up in the messy predicament that had been hounding her thoughts and keeping her awake at night ever since.

'Peach. Love. Time to get up.' Mum's words came down like a kiss.

Peach woke to the gentle impact of her mother sitting down on the bed.

'Hangover?'

'Wish I was dead. Can't remember the last time I got drunk like that. I'm sorry.'

Peach stretched like a cat. 'You don't need to apologise.'

Mum patted her through the covers. Light beaded on the lip of the curtains. Outside Peach could hear the jubilant sound of little children playing.

'I'm still sorry. Your father was right. Alcohol has always made me melancholy. I said silly things. I didn't mean them. You shouldn't worry.'

'You seemed like you meant what you said, Mum. It was confusing.'

Mum put her face in her hands: a gesture ghosted from the night before.

'I just meant, well, yesterday, I was looking through all those

223

old pictures and letters – remembering being young then, thinking about you being young now. It's your last summer and I've made you do my job which I'm the first to admit isn't all that interesting and . . . I'm not explaining very well.'

She rubbed her face, shook her head.

'This time in your life: you're leaving home soon. I mean, I thought this job would be a good thing to keep you occupied. I was worried but now it seems . . . I don't know, like you're fine and you should just be enjoying yourself. Doing something, anything other than chores I could easily do myself.'

'You're busy. I like helping. I don't really know what else I would do.'

'Spend time with your friends?'

A stab of loneliness. 'They're busy with their boyfriends.'

'There's plenty of time for you to get a boyfriend.'

'I don't want a boyfriend,' Peach thundered. 'I just want a camera and for everything to stop feeling weird.'

'No,' said Mum, conciliatory. 'Of course. Growing up is strange. Particularly—'

Peach cut her off, newly awake, already irritated. She had to find a way to get back into those boxes. The things in there were incapable of telling the lies that people could.

'Everything is fine, Mum,' Peach said, although it wasn't.

'I'm not worried about anything,' she said, even though she was.

'You shouldn't be worried,' she said, even though she thought her mother probably ought to be very worried indeed.

At the house, Nick's Mini was still where he had parked it the day before. He and Ian were in the kitchen, talking over plates of congealing grease.

She could see Magda in the yard outside, sliding and snapping the legs of a tripod.

'Sensible decision to leave early last night, Peach,' Ian called out. 'Sore heads all round this morning.' That new friendliness again. A geniality Nick and Magda seemed to have woken in him.

'Speak for yourself,' said Nick. 'I feel great.' He leant way back on his chair. It made Peach horny and that made her hope to see him fall.

Mum issued her with another interminable list of chores. Peach wondered what was so special about Ian that he couldn't wash his own clothes. Even Greg did his own laundry. Peach supposed having money freed you from lots of obligations and hoped she would be rich one day.

Ian and Mum went off muttering conspiratorially. Mum's fingers were in her hair, making twists and snips as she spoke.

Nick lingered in the kitchen, did a yogic stretch with his arms. His shoulder popped. 'You know, I've been getting pretty into hanging out with Ian. He's a good guy. I haven't really got all the stuff on Patty I need for my articles, so I had a chat with him earlier and we worked out a plan.'

Peach made her body language lazy and disinterested as her anxiety rose. 'Oh yeah?'

'Ian and your ma are heading to London with Magda after the photo shoot, so he said I can stay here and do some work, then tomorrow—'

'London?'

'Yeah, staying overnight, then tomorrow—'

'What are they going to London for?'

'Something to do with his gallery.'

'Why does my mum need to go?'

'Dunno, mate – when I said we were getting on well I didn't mean he tells me everything. You okay?'

Peach tried to present a comatose level of detachment.

Magda was putting new film in her camera. Cut in half by the doorway, she clocked Peach watching; smiled, fired a test shot and turned her back.

'Yeah, yeah, no big deal, whatever works, you know? I was just thinking of heading to London myself, trying to work out if I could get a lift with them.'

Nick smiled. 'You fancy a night out in London then?'

Peach had never had a night out in London. It was flimsy in her head: postcards of tourist attractions.

Magda leant on her tripod, lit a cigarette.

'Yeah, London. Actually not sure if I can be hassled.' Badly forging a copy of Nick's stretches, she shammed another yawn. 'Yeah, don't reckon it'll work out.'

'I could give you a ride down tomorrow if you like, bring you back Friday morning. Got mates there? Where do you stay when you're in town?'

'With a few different people, but I better stay here. Got a mate who's having some problems and I should probably stick around in case she needs me.'

'That's really heavy,' said Nick, shaking his head as if it moved him profoundly. 'Sounds like you're a great mate.'

'I try, you know? I try to be good.'

They didn't even feel like fabrications: the friends in London, the friends at home. She wanted them so much, it felt less like telling a lie and more like making a wish.

Nick took Peach's wrist the way he had yesterday, held it like a fine thing. 'You do, mate. You're a cool little unit.'

They looked at each other, unflinchingly, in what felt like the extreme still and quiet before something falls, something crashes, the tense last second before pandemonium breaks out.

Nick made a snake move which was barely a move at all, a

slow undulation of all of him. 'So what are you going to do now?' he asked as if issuing a dare.

Peach rolled her head from side to side. 'What are *you* going to do?' Double dare.

Nick swallowed. Twin urges mugged her. Climb into his lap and suck his sexy tongue – slap his stupid, vain face. He let go of her wrist.

Magda was staring into the kitchen. She spat smoke and stubbed the cigarette out against the wall.

'Your mum found a stash of letters between Patty and Nick Drake,' he said, with the covetous air of a birthday boy about to unwrap presents. 'I'm going to read those. And there's some hand-written sheet music and unused photos from a cover shoot.'

'Sounds like there's a lot to look at.'

'Yeah, maybe enough for a book, so I'm coming back.' Nick scratched his wrist and his silver bracelets clanked. 'I'm going to head off tomorrow morning, but I'll be back the day after.'

'Oh yeah?' Peach remarked as if it barely piqued her interest let alone her desire. Nick looked sulky.

'That's cool though, isn't it?' he scowled. 'That I'm coming back?'

She couldn't think of Nick as some dumb guy any more than she could think of a rainbow as water bending light; yet his petulance reminded her of how boys her age behaved towards girls they liked.

'Nick?'

'Peach?'

'How old are you?'

'Why?'

'No reason, just wondering.'

He pouted and smirked. His mouth made Peach want to invent new swearwords. There weren't curses dirty enough to describe the things he made her want.

Magda was leaning in the doorway, looking sourly at her watch.

'I'm twenty-five,' said Nick.

He scratched his wrist again with his ringed fingers. Remnants of black nail polish scabbed his cuticles.

Peach put her finger to her nose. Impossibly grown up, she thought, impossibly beautiful. Impossibly cool.

Chapter 26

Ian comes to the door at once. 'Peach! Isabella! What a surprise.' He does not seem that surprised. He is unbearably diminished. Physical abundance shockingly abridged. He was always elegantly tatterdemalion. Now he appears threadbare and unloved – something of the mistreated animal about him.

His voice has the tremulous cadence old voices often do. As if habitually unused; throat tightening, words running out. But there's a sardonic inflection to his tone, implying a joke at their expense. He retains a sovereign manner indicating familiarity with visiting pilgrims.

He glances out to the car. 'Is Kevin with you?'

Bella goes straight at him. Even though Ian is so thin he looks like he has been gutted, even though his eyes are like half-cooked egg white, his knuckles painfully bunched, she just gets right into his face. 'He's in hospital.'

'Oh dear. Come in.' Ian is unperturbed. Food stains on his sweater. A musk of neglect clings to the air around him. Yet he still exudes emphatic vigour. His apparent enfeeblement seems like a prank. Mulched into a fraction of the space he used to occupy, he continues to project the intimidating aura of old.

Peach has never forgotten those first days in his house. His menacing physique. Ian towering over her as he wrong-footed her with acerbic remarks. It seemed to set a precedent. She often thinks of Ian when she is despising herself for feeling obliged to laugh at some unfunny joke about lady-art. His face appears in her head when she's loathing her complicit silence while Ben makes remarks about some female sculptor who has started looking old or fat.

Peach wonders if her whole life might have been different if that summer had schooled her in the power of speaking up, rather than teaching her how dangerous it could be.

The house retracts Ian, draws him into its dark, so that Peach and Bella have no choice but to follow him inside where the air smells of mildew and stale meals.

Years of breath and dust seem to have thickened the atmosphere. Peach feels entombed. Yet again she has that unheimlich sense of anticipation, as though her live self is the ghost, the haunting. As if her seventeen-year-old self will manifest on the stairs, trotting after Nick. Heart held out to him like a child's macaroni picture.

It feels as if those days in 1994 were the last time she was truly alive. The last in which she felt truly free. The last bastion of choice and chance before she had a past to drag around. She knows that is not quite right, but it feels like there's a line, a thread she can't help but track back to that summer where possible futures diverged, like rivers splitting into tributaries, taking separate paths to opposite coasts.

Like some hardboiled detective, Bella says, 'Let me take the lead on this, okay?'

And Peach just nods as they walk through the house, a prisoner going to the scaffold.

*

Peach went out into the courtyard. Magda was behind the camera in Ian's studio. Ian was in front of it standing proprietorially next to one of his sculptures as if the gouged mound was his meek wife.

It seemed crazy that Magda was the one taking pictures instead of having her picture taken. She seemed to draw all light towards her, burning in the centre of the room making Ian and his work appear irrelevant.

Peach spent a long time spying. Trying to figure out why Magda put the camera on the tripod when she did, why she took it off again. Why she asked Ian to move, why she moved around him. Observing Magda's subtle, deliberate movements, adjusting Ian, shifting her position, manipulating settings.

'I think I got what I need,' Magda said.

Peach made to scuttle away, but Magda saw her and called out. Peach entered the damp studio, trying not to look at the violated bodies of Ian's work. Ian slipped away into the house.

'Get good photos?'

Magda grimaced and leant on the tripod. 'Got Ian and his works, I think. Captured the relationship.'

'Is that what you should try to do?'

'The camera always reveals the truth.'

'You mean like the camera never lies?'

Magda made a spitting sound. 'Camera doesn't lie or tell the truth. Like a toaster doesn't make toast on its own, you know?'

Peach teetered uncertainly, not feeling like she understood.

'It's all relationships. Depends who's in front of the camera. Who's behind. If they agree or disagree on what the picture's meant to show. Conflict. Collaboration. If you know how to look – through the camera, at the photo – even the attempt to conceal reveals truth.'

Dejectedly Peach said she didn't get it.

'Come here, I'll show you.' Magda beckoned Peach towards her camera. 'Frame me up a shot.'

'What of?'

'Something that tells me what's important in this studio.'

'The sculptures?'

'Anything. A pencil, dirt on the floor. The sculptures or the tools or the view from the window. Just imagine you can make only one photo to tell someone who's never been here what it feels like inside this room. One photo to explain what happens here.'

'Can I take it off the tripod?'

'Sure.' Magda handed the camera to Peach. Her whole body remembered the feeling of her own camera crunching and shattering under her fallen weight. Magda's was heavy and priceless in Peach's hands, like she'd been given a newborn to hold.

'Maybe I shouldn't, I don't know what to, I'm not sure where to start . . . '

'Where does any photo start?'

'Looking?'

'Looking. Then?'

'Seeing?'

'Exactly.'

Magda squatted on the floor with the tripod in her hands, starting to slide the legs down. Even crouching on a dirty floor, she looked artful and composed.

Peach put the camera to her eye. Felt herself become the tripod: stable, dependable. She paced the studio scanning.

'Take your time, tell me when you find your shot.'

Steady, fluid scrutiny as Peach framed up the sculpture that perturbed her the most. A bulbous split form like parted thighs, squatting with a two by four shoved through the centre. But the viewfinder only confirmed the fact it existed. The malfeasant aura it oozed didn't translate. So, Peach stepped closer, focused the camera right on the point of penetration. Where the plank punctured the body, brutality entered the camera with the light.

'Here.'

Magda came over, substituted her eye for Peach's.

Magda burst out laughing and brought her finger down triggering the shutter. The shutter went crack and Magda laughed even harder. 'Got your shot.'

Peach felt her cheeks blaze shame. 'Oh, sorry, I just, I was being too experimental, it was silly, I . . .'

Magda slipped the camera out of Peach's hands and tapped beneath Peach's right eye with her index finger. She laughed, tapping, silver ring going off like a flash, dazzling Peach. 'You can't teach an eye like this one. I'm not laughing because it's silly. I'm laughing because it's so perfect it's almost ridiculous.'

'Oh I just, I just—'

'Don't say just, you never say *just* about what you see, or how you see it. You say *here*, you say *this*, you say *look*. You're a photographer: I knew you were.'

'I don't have a camera.'

'It's not about the camera. It's about the eyes behind. You can take a good picture with anything – disposables, a cheap point and shoot. Doesn't matter. What matters is you understand looking and seeing are not the same. When looking and seeing align then it's truth, it's power.'

She smiled at Peach. 'Like you see Ian and Nick, you see they are both such—'

'Hi girls, what are we up to?' It was Mum. She seemed unsettled. 'Ian said you were ready, Magda.'

'Ready to get on the road.' Magda gave the sculptures a disparaging glance.

What? Ian and Nick are what? Peach desperately wanted one more elemental moment of looking and seeing converging through the viewfinder of Magda, but Mum shepherded them inside, through the kitchen into the hall, where Ian and Nick stood. Waiting.

'I was just coming to say cheerio we're off to London.' Mum went to put her arms round Peach. Peach shifted beyond her reach.

'None of my business.'

Ian was frozen; half in half out of his coat. Watchful.

Mum was wearing an unfamiliar scent, powdery and old-ladyish. She couldn't work out if her mother would think the perfume was sexy. Mum had given up on fashion, her clothes favoured utility over beauty. Rifling her parents' attic for costumes recently, Peach had discovered that in the past Mum teetered on platforms, sparkled in lamé, floated in winged concoctions of chiffon.

'It's work. It's just work,' Mum said. A weird thing to say. Why did she have to say it? The shiver and burn of flu raced through Peach. 'See you tomorrow, love.'

Magda shared a smile with Peach, tapped beneath her eye, winked.

Peach returned the smile, the tap, the wink.

'See you anon,' boomed Ian with a wave that was part salute.

Ian steered Mum without touching her, palm cupped round air next to her elbow, a gesture of enduring companionship.

Peach kept the image in her head: all of them standing in the hall. She looked, and she saw: Magda champing at the bit to be away. Nick looking at Magda, looking at Peach as if he wanted to be seen. Mum and Ian not looking at anyone but each other. Just like a couple.

'Why have you been trying to contact our parents?' Bella demands.

'Trying to do them a favour.' Ian walks, speaking to Peach and Bella over his shoulder as if conducting a guided tour.

'I find that hard to believe,' Bella rejoins.

He ushers them into the living room. Fire quakes in the grate. Frail light comes from a standard lamp, shade squint like a tipsy aunt with her hat askew at a wedding.

'Let me stoke up the fire and put the kettle on.'

'There's no time for that. Dad's in hospital.' Bella is shrill. Bella is frightening.

'Sorry to hear that.' Ian keeps feeding small logs into the fireplace as if she poses no threat.

'Because of you. He was on his way to see you when the accident happened.' Bella paces the room like something wild in a zoo enclosure.

'My apologies.' Ian turns meekly towards Bella. Under the veneer of submissiveness Peach identifies mischievous intent.

'You don't seem interested, let alone apologetic.' Ian should be worried: this is Bella turning the key in herself, winding herself up.

Ian massages the arthritic bulges at his knuckles. 'I really am very sorry, but the fact remains that Kevin and I urgently need to have a conversation.'

'Well, I've got some bad news, Ian,' says Bella. 'Not only has Dad had an accident but he's got dementia so you're going to have to deal with us.'

'Oh.' Ian crumples onto the sofa. 'That is awful news, how completely *horrifying*.' His knees creak like a wet towel being wrung, and he seems profoundly moved, tearful even. Peach thinks there is always something unbearable about old people's tears: they should be permitted to retire from crying. Ian's ravaged diminution makes his distress particularly intolerable.

Bella is suddenly fluid – soft; empathy cancels her rage and she sits down beside Ian and takes his hand. Both so thin – bones on bones. Peach watches the unguarded gesture of compassion and experiences it as a grinding in her skeleton.

Ian rubs his palms together as though he is applying Bella's touch like hand cream.

'Poor Kevin. What terrible news, although—'

Ian smiles. Too quickly he smiles. A grin that materialises so efficiently it appears like a shark attack. And where his eyes looked tearful, now they seem to sparkle blankly like light on ice. 'It could work in our favour.'

'In *our* favour? What, how? Ours? There's no ours, there's no us,' Peach says.

'Oh, there is, whether you like it or not. I'm working on a project, all to your family's advantage. A counter-project you might call it, with an old pal, an . . . *acquaintance* of yours actually. He's staying here.'

And before the air of the room even stirs with his arrival Peach knows. By the pure white trembling look of her so does Bella.

Nick. Nick Young.

Chapter 27

Nick paced the living room muttering into a Dictaphone. He clicked it off and enclosed Peach's arm with his fingers. 'Mate, do you fancy cracking a bottle of wine?'

'I thought you were staying here to work.'

'Do my best work after dark. What is it now, like two or three?'

It was three: three on a Wednesday afternoon. At this moment, people were working in offices, performing tasks whose functions were instrumental to the world but obscured to Peach. All the shops in town were open, with vegetables organised in inviting lines outside the grocers, people were queuing in the bank, drinking tea and pushing forks through the rich flock of cake crumbs in the café, curls of hair were falling to the floor in the hairdressers. Life carried on being tenaciously normal.

'Wine it is!'

Nick sloped off to the kitchen. He moved with smug looseness. Peach watched him go. She put her fingers to the shaved part of her head and massaged curlicues against the stubble. He came back with wine and glasses and a crooked smile.

'You should listen to *The Pearl-Handled Revolver*.' He went over to the large clunky hi-fi system. 'You into it? Get a feel for Patty's music?'

'I can't believe I've never heard it.'

'Most people haven't.' Nick slipped the vinyl from its sleeve. 'But that's going to change. She's going to be redis-covered in a big way, you know. This record's going to be as massive as it should have been first time round.' There was a fizz as the needle kissed the vinyl.

He said Patty should have been our Joni Mitchell. Peach nodded wisely as Nick uncorked a bottle. She didn't know who that was.

'You were little, right? When she died?'

Peach watched wine bleed into the glasses. Twenty past three, Patty's beautiful voice ached on the still air of the big room and the world outside the house was boring and far away.

He handed Peach a glass.

'I was four.'

'I'm sorry.' He took a drink and fixed her with a look so serious it was comic. 'Must've been rough.'

'I don't really remember her, to be honest. Is that bad?'

He thought a while.

'Nah, mate: that's kids, isn't it? You don't think. Nothing is complicated.'

'I miss that.' Peach took a bigger gulp of wine than was sensible.

'I know. I mean, I like thinking, I love thinking. I love it when you're aware of thinking, you know? When you're joining things up, really seeing the world, but sometimes that's tiring. Sometimes that's sad. That's why it's good to get wasted, slip into just *being*. Or listening to good music – that's the best of both worlds. You get into yourself *and* out of yourself.' Sprawled on the couch, his body was art.

'I think too much these days. I don't know what anything means.' Peach hugged her knees.

'But mate.' Nick turned on his side. His hand slipped off the couch like someone dipping their fingers into the water off the side of a boat. 'Your life's work isn't to know things – it's to find things out. Or maybe I just think so because I'm a journo. That's why I wanted to be a journo anyway. I like finding things out.' He smiled like his own self-knowledge was warm and satisfying to him.

The record moved loops on the turntable. Patty sang about birds and leaves and winter: the poetry of cold weather.

'You're so nice.' Peach finished her wine in a second careless gulp.

Nick refilled her glass then his own.

'Mate, you're nice. You're cool. You're going to be unstoppable when you get a chance to get in the world and set about it. I know a cool person when I meet one. I write for the *NME*. Sorry. Sometimes I like saying it out loud, you know – I can't really believe it's actually happened. I feel like an impostor, right? I'm just a kid from Stevenage who loves art and words and music – *I* can't be writing for the *NME*. It's too much of a dream to be real. But it *is real*. Probably seems stupid to you, like, you grew up around people like Patty and Ian. I mean, it's nice here, how none of you give a fuck about my job.'

Peach shrugged to emphasise his point.

'People get an idea of me because my job is kind of impressive and for some reason it makes them want to impress me. They start acting all weird, showing off. But they also want to hear stories about famous people I've met and stuff. Sometimes I'm in the mood for that, don't get me wrong, but often I'm not. Often I want to just hang like we're hanging. Listen to good music. How good *is* this record by the way?'

Patty's voice soared over lyrics about flying.

'Yes, so complicated. I can hear her heart bleeding in the grooves of the vinyl.'

Nick sat up. 'That's it, mate, that's it. You've got a pretty way with words. I'm going to pinch that for one of my articles. Is that okay with you?'

Peach aimed for the insouciance Nick claimed to like but was ecstatic at the thought of her off-the-cuff comment solidified in the ink of the *NME*.

Footsteps in the hall froze them.

Bella's voice disappointed Peach. She swept into the room in a long cream dress with her black hair plaited and looped like a noose. Nick looked at Bella like he wanted her between his teeth. 'Ian said he'd look out a book for me to borrow.' Her eyes went to the coffee table. 'Great. There it is. He remembered. Where is he?'

'London,' said Peach flatly, 'London with Mum.'

'Right.' Bella hoisted the book into her arms and held it like a baby. She stood there looking at Peach as if she was trying to work out where she'd seen her before.

Don't, don't, don't, Peach thought. Don't *what* she didn't exactly know. Don't say something which will make me look stupid, don't look at me like I'm immature. *Don't stay.*

The moment was already broken. Compelling Peach to say: 'We're having a glass of wine, want one?'

Bella hesitated. A look in her eyes as though she was counting small change she'd been saving to buy something important.

'Yes please.' Bella sat down beside Peach.

'I'll get you a glass.' Nick loped off.

Bella stroked Peach's head. 'You look so grown up lately.'

Her fingers tickled her scalp like little wings. 'Don't grow up too quickly though.'

Where the meaning of a foreign word for love may be understood by the intonation of its speaker, Peach heard this as love. She pushed her skull against her sister's hand and said, 'I won't.'

Nick came back, poured wine and turned the record over. He asked what Bella thought of Patty's music. She was idly flipping through the massive book Ian had left for her.

'The music is stunning. Patty was a bit of a bitch though.' Bella laid the book in her lap. Her body was so small inside her dress that it hurt to look at her.

'How was she a bitch?' Nick bristled.

'Aw,' Bella smirked. 'You're a bit in love with her.'

'I'm pretty in love with her music,' he parried sulkily.

'In what way though?' Peach asked, gripped by intrigue.

'She always seemed pretty in love with herself. Self-involved. As if other people didn't really register.'

'Aren't all creative people like that?' Nick countered.

'Not all.' Bella put the book on the floor. 'But Patty always seemed like she was owed something she never got.'

'Well, she was, mate – she should have been a star. I mean, just listen to this music.' Nick looked triumphant.

'It's gorgeous. But Patty was mean. She was vain. And she was bitter.'

'You were only little,' Peach said, battling on Nick's side. 'We can't really remember *that* much about Patty.'

'I remember quite a lot about her actually.' A bead of wine fell on Bella's dress. She tutted and licked a finger to rub on the spot.

'I only really remember her in our garden this one time when we were small. Do you?' Peach asked.

Bella kept rubbing the stain. 'I remember her sitting in a deckchair, smoking cigarettes. She smoked like a chimney.'

Nick leant forward and drank. 'I always thought her voice changed tone between the two albums. Cigarettes. Of course.'

'Shitloads.' Bella peered at the wet spot on her dress.

'I think maybe it was even the day we got Solly,' said Peach.

'Unlikely.'

Nick's interest piqued. 'What's this?'

'Absolutely nothing.' Bella's tone stuck the words up against Peach's throat like a shiv.

'Boring family stuff.' Peach downed a whole glass of wine in one. Nick filled it again without her noticing.

Peach listened to Patty in the past sing the exact notes of her own hurt in the present.

Nick persevered. 'Don't you think that the way things played out must have been hard on Patty though? Nearly making it big, having that huge hit, then nothing?'

Bella regarded him glacially. 'I think it was probably crap having a successful husband while no one gave a toss about her. It was probably miserable being little wifey to a big-name artist. I imagine she felt even worse once she was a one-hit wonder. But my honest memory of her is that she was up her own arse, didn't like anyone who didn't have a penis or who wasn't drooling all over her. She was basically a bit of a dick who made some pretty music.'

Peach understands now that Bella didn't know those things. That Bella had interpreted something from the way their parents behaved, things she'd overheard them saying. Perhaps Patty represented something Bella disliked about other women or was jealous of: the way she'd demanded to be taken seriously and paid attention to, something personal at any rate. Or maybe, in the moment, Bella was simply enjoying the authority her 'knowledge' exerted over Nick. But at the time it felt like disparity between the sisters' memories, insight Bella possessed which troubled Peach imprecisely.

Nick looked downcast. 'I hear you. It's disappointingly common. I've met some of my heroes through work and wished I hadn't.'

Bella handed him the booby prize of a sweet smile. 'I could be wrong. I mean, I'm not. But draw your own conclusions. She's not around to argue. I guess you're really just writing about her music.'

'For the *NME*, yeah, but the *Guardian* magazine spread is more her life story, her and Ian's to kind of tie in the re-releases of her records with his big retrospective.'

'You want to do a Plath/Hughes on them?' Bella asked. 'Because Ian's a bit of a sleaze and Patty's dead?' Her pupils disappeared into the back of her head.

'That's not fair – Ian's a great guy,' said Nick.

'I bet people were saying that about Ted while Sylvia had her head in the oven,' snapped Bella.

Nick changed the record. He replaced Patty's yearning soprano with languid, smoky soul and opened another bottle.

'We should go,' Bella said.

'That is the last thing you ladies should do.' Nick grinned wolfishly.

'Ladies? Are you a cruise-ship entertainer?' Bella stood up.

'If you want me to be.' Nick started to snap his fingers, bopping stupidly round the room. He picked up the wine.

'Laydeez . . .' He bowed low. 'Can I offer you some fine French wine?'

Bella and Peach giggled.

'That's Rioja – it's from Spain, you prick.'

Nick went down on one knee before Bella.

'Forgive my ignorance. I'm just a cruise-ship entertainer.' Bella held out her glass. He filled it.

'I demand a cigarette!' Peach exclaimed with a dramatic swoon.

'But of course.' He placed one between Peach's lips, lit it and kissed her cheek. Her skin tingled where his lips had touched her.

'How dare you kiss my sister?' Bella cried in mock outrage.

'I have never seen such beautiful ladies. I'm carried away.' Nick boogied over to Bella.

She astonished Nick with a slap; a real one, whip crack like a starting pistol. Nick grabbed Bella's wrist with impulsive violence. Everything in the room froze and melted like a frame of celluloid jamming and burning on the reel. Nick and Bella stared each other out. He pulled Bella's palm to his lips and licked it slowly, like he was writing his name on her skin with his tongue.

The ash on Peach's cigarette grew long and fell to the carpet as she watched them. Jealous, perplexed and utterly turned on.

'Now me!' Peach cried.

Nick let go of Bella's hand. 'Mate,' he said to Peach, with the red print of her sister's quick right hand on his face while Bella closed her fingers round whatever was written between them in spit.

'I'm going.' Bella tripped over nothing.

Nick tried to steady her. She pulled away. Peach could read the climate of her sister's moods. As she stood to follow Bella home, she sensed a gathering storm and was docile in the face of it.

'See you next week?' Nick enquired.

'Yep,' Peach smiled weakly.

'Good.' Nick's smile was hangdog.

Bella tutted, and her clogs made the clop-scrape of coconut horse hooves as she lurched away.

Outside, early evening felt like high day.

'It feels like it should be night,' Peach said.

Bella's dress kept sliding off her shoulder. Peach pulled it up.

'Don't touch me.'

'Why are you being like this? Is it because N—'

'Don't speak to me.'

'Bella.'

'What?' Bella turned. Her face was florid with anger.

'I don't know, I don't like—'

'I don't care.'

Bella stared at Peach as if she was a turd.

'I'm frightened.'

'Don't be melodramatic.'

'There's something really wrong.'

'With me?'

'With everything. With all of us. With Mum and Dad and—'

'Grow up,' Bella spat. She threw this over her shoulder like she was getting rid of litter.

'What is up with you?' Peach shouted.

Bella stopped. 'Everything apparently, wah, wah, wah.'

Peach grabbed Bella and pulled her into an enraged tango.

'Why do you have to be such a bitch?'

Bella got into Peach's face, right in.

'You think you've got this big universe in you but you're barely even alive. You're pathetic and naïve and self-absorbed with your fanny all wet for that dickhead. He'd ruin you, and you'd thank him for it. You want to suffer because you want to matter. You think your thoughts are so special and important? They're not. Go and shag Nick if you want to find out how little you matter. He *will* fuck you.'

Bella tore her hand from Peach's grip.

'I don't want to.' Peach sobbed violently. It felt like she was throwing up her soul.

'Don't try to manipulate me.'

'I'm frightened, I think Mum and Ian—'

'Don't. Do. Not. I warned you to cut and run.'

'But Mum and Ian seem so close—'

'Stop seeing sex everywhere. The world isn't made entirely out of sex because *you're* horny. Get away from Mum and Ian and do something with *your* life that *you've* chosen.'

Bella grabbed Peach's upper arms, her hands like bird's feet, sharp and vicious. She shook her.

'Don't you understand? When Nick's done with Ian and Patty people are going to care about their lives, and that means our parents' lives and you shouldn't want that. I realise it's all *NME* journalists and fame and glamour to you but for god's sake don't be seduced by what you think this means. Let the past be the past.'

Peach's teeth resonated with ghost vibrations of her sister's violence. Bella's mad bird hands spiked Peach's flesh.

'So there is something?'

'Just the kind of interest that turns real life into gossip, so strangers have something to read about. You shouldn't work for Ian. Mum shouldn't work for Ian. The whole thing is incestuous.'

Bella let Peach go and laughed; the sound was hysteric derangement. She began to walk. Peach didn't move. Witch-thin in her creamy swirl of garments and long black hair,

Bella was like a storybook madwoman. The illness of her laughter drifted back to Peach like the sound of something being killed in the distance.

Peach's tears spilt like ink on the dusty pavement. Dominic tore through her mind and it didn't seem any wonder to Peach that he'd screwed her in revenge. Bella left people with nowhere to go but down into darkness. And so Peach turned and went back to the Elder house. She looked at her watch. The time was five past six all smeared in the madness of midnight.

Peach pushed the door. No one ever seemed to lock up. The strains of Patty's voice pulsed through the rooms, that song again about birds and winter. It moved in Peach like a familiar disease.

She called Nick's name. He came into the hall. His feet were bare. He looked annoyed – Peach knew she shouldn't have come, it triggered more sobbing. Irritation went from his eyes.

'Mate.' He led her to the living room. He held her.

She tipped her chin up, made her mouth available.

'Mate,' he said: his placeholder for not possessing enough words. Or being unwilling to find them.

Peach moved towards him.

'Don't,' he said quietly.

'Why not?'

'Because I'm not a cunt.'

'Please?'

He cupped Peach's face in his hands. His rings were cold against her cheeks. This was the paused last second of before. She parted her lips.

'Mate, you are lovely,' he sighed. 'A total sweetheart. And your sister is a nightmare. I've met girls like her before.'

Peach slumped down inside herself with disappointment, and a stupid kind of hope she wished would die.

'I could see she was working up to a scene. Don't let it upset you. It's not even about you. I could see her getting it ready in her head. People like her are like bombs. They don't care who gets their face blown off once they're ready to detonate. I saw it. I was going to say you should stay but . . . ' He spread his hands in a wide shrug, like he was checking for rain.

'But you thought I might—'

'Mate, honestly. *I* thought *I* might. I'm not going to though.'

Peach rested her head on his chest. She could hear his heartbeat: softly important and near far.

'Don't you want me?'

He kissed the top of her head. Kind and brotherly.

'Of course I want you. You're adorable. Ridiculously cute. Sexy because you don't know it.'

'Then take me to bed.'

'No way, mate. You're a cool little unit but you're seventeen and I'm twenty-five and honestly: I would intend to be good to you, I would absolutely mean not to mess you about, but I absolutely would.'

'I wouldn't let you.'

'You would, kid.'

'Don't call me a kid. This is already so humiliating.'

'Don't feel humiliated. I'm kicking myself already. I mean look at you. I could eat you.'

'Do.'

Nick hugged Peach tightly and his warm arms were full of a friend's good intention.

'No. I'm sick of feeling like a bastard. Back in London I've got all sorts of situations going on. I really want to feel like a good guy this time.'

'So you want to shag Bella?' Peach sulked. Nick didn't say no. She felt like throwing up with jealousy but she was glad he was honest. At least someone was treating her like an adult for once.

'I want to shag everyone. That is basically my problem, but I came here though – listen to me, mate, I need you to really listen to me because this is important, okay?'

Peach wove her fingers into his. It felt like something nice from a long time ago which had never actually happened before.

'When this job came up, I was over the moon. I've been listening to Patty for years and it seriously *killed me* that no one had heard of her when she was such a genius. Ian's work is interesting, but Patty? She's something else. The whole thing felt honourable, really decent. A chance to get out of London, calm it on the partying and the drama with girls like your sister and just write something true and from the heart to bring Patty's music the attention it deserves. Pure. I didn't expect Ian's house to be full of hot girls and for him and me to get on so well. Like look at this now: he's hardly met me, and he's left me alone in his amazing big house with his sexy assistant to drink his wine. I'm in Patty and Ian Elder's house. The whole thing is a beautiful gift and I don't want to taint it.'

'And if we went to bed it would.'

'*I* would. You wouldn't but *I* would. I like you. You're part of the gift. You're my little mate now. Yeah?'

'Yes.' Peach kissed him on the left cheek. Nick kissed her back on the right cheek.

'Now go home before I change my mind.'

'That's like a shit line from a shit film.'

'I feel like a shit guy from a shit film right now. Like some kind of cowboy dickhead.'

'You'd make a terrible cowboy.' Peach stood up.

He lay back on the couch. He smiled. He winked.

Peach walked. Just walked in a mist of the saddest happiness or the happiest sadness, it didn't matter which, having stumbled upon some adult pleasure in learning how to meet something complex with simple joy. To accept contentedly only what Nick offered her without regretting, or at least only regretting a little, what he did not.

Chapter 28

It's not like she hasn't seen him since. Because it's not like she never gets three glasses stupid in the bleak hours and types his name into the search bar. Reading gig reviews and articles, looking at pictures; sticky-beaking on his Twitter and Instagram so she knows he has a son with his ex-partner. The singer from a band Peach used to love. But she could disappear him at a click.

Now Nick is standing in front of Peach, laying his hand over his heart. The sound of it beating comes back to her. No rings on his fingers these days. Tattoos on his knuckles instead. Love on his right hand. Love on his left.

Black hair only just frosted, touched with the lightest dusting of snow, bushy beard where he was clean-shaven, but still Nick Young. Still swiping the breath from Peach's lungs, still dropping her whole being into her pelvis, still making her feel seventeen and full of scorching, humiliating desire, as he stands there with bare feet, looking like he's just woken up.

He says, 'Shit.'

He says, 'Mate.'

And looks at Peach with some soft happy shock that she wishes she could enjoy. Her seventeen-year-old self wears her adult face like a latex mask. She pulls at her jaw and for the second time in twenty-four hours or maybe the third, or the fourth, or the thousandth: things which should be apart are crumpled together. Things which should be solid are broken.

They never should have left the hospital. Death is coming. She wonders what it will be like to be bereaved of Dad. Wonders what it will be like to find that she is wearing a black dress in a crematorium, shaking hands with people she vaguely recognises from childhood.

Nick feels known in Peach's bones. But he is only the past made flesh. The flat disquiet of hoping to write a better ending to something which has already ended the way it has. Peach knows the desire he ignites is the longing to start things again at the point where they began to go wrong.

Peach's whole life has felt like grieving for a better person she never became. Someone contented and secure she suspects she once might have been capable of turning into. Just as art can transform an unmade bed into a sculpture, it can turn a person into an artist. Being bereaved of that identity will always hurt, if not replaced with another. Peach never wanted to be called wife, she never wanted to be called Mum; but she always wanted to be called important.

That is why she followed Bella here: it made her feel necessary, part of something. In the hospital there was nothing to do but to stand around with Greg and Mum in whose presence she can't see love past guilt and shame.

It's why she fiddled in the margins of her dalliances for so long. Temporary answers to the slippery, unresolved sadness that appeared to be permanent: someone, somewhere, thinking of Peach. The domino-topple of endings stranded her with nothing but her own insignificance for company.

And she can no longer delude herself that it was anything more noble, less despicable than that which motivated her involvement with the girl.

Grace. Her name was Grace. Not *the girl*. Not *the blonde*. Not *the intern*. *Grace*. And one Sunday morning, when Peach had grudgingly agreed to man the gallery, Grace appeared and asked for her help.

It was the day after Peach's catastrophic meeting with Simon. Grace rapped on the glass before the gallery opened and Peach let her in.

Grace looked tired and worried. Purple under her eyes, chapped lips. Pretty face looking old beyond her years so that perversely she appeared younger still.

'I came early because I was hoping we might have a chat.'

'Oh?' Peach nodded. 'Coffee?'

The gallery was dead on Sundays. She could afford to open late.

'Yeah.'

'You okay?'

'Not really.' Grace looked like she might cry.

Peach sent her to sit down in Ben's office, in his chair that cost more than a car.

Approaching the glass-fronted office Peach noted Grace's fists stuffed into her pockets, shoulders hunched up like a duck against the cold. With her clean hair scraped back in an elastic, Grace moved Peach like a dog or a baby or any unsullied thing.

'What's wrong?'

'I'm worried, I'm not … I know I don't really know you … I don't know if I'm speaking out of turn, I don't want to put you in an awkward position, you seem really nice

253

but I'm not sure ...' Tears filled her eyes as equivocations streamed out. 'Sorry, sorry, I'm just, it's just ...'

'You can talk to me.' Peach put her hand on Grace's, the skin on it smooth with youth. She imagined Grace learning an instrument, practising drawing. School: she imagined her in school.

'It's just, Ben's so pervy, Peach, is he always pervy or is it me? Should I say something, or put up with it or leave?'

'Oh Grace. *Grace.*'

Oh shit. This had never happened before.

Peach wondered what compassion Grace could possibly have perceived in her. She hadn't offered her so much as a crumb. Then she realised that when everyone is monstrous, desperation casts the least bad person as an ally.

'Shit, Grace. No. You shouldn't leave. It's not you, but I don't know what to say, he ...'

'Always does this?'

'Always.'

'And what do you usually do?'

'I'm ashamed to have to tell you I do nothing. I'm too busy trying not to lose my mind.'

'He doesn't behave like that towards you. Did he used to?'

'Nope; I'm not his type – it's the main reason I've managed to keep my job for so long.'

'But *I'm* his type?'

'Completely.'

'Wow. I've been lying awake at night, worrying and all the time I knew. *I just knew* it wasn't even happening because I'm special. This place is some kind of sleazy sausage machine.'

'Yeah. Sorry.'

'God. What should I do?'

'I'm not sure why you're asking me. You should ask someone better than you for advice, not someone worse.'

'What do you mean?'

'You're the first person to act like you don't deserve this crap. And you don't, and none of them did, but I've been turning a blind eye for so long. Burying bodies on Ben's behalf like it's a normal thing to do.' Peach pushed her face into her hands because there was nowhere else to hide.

'I guess it's not as bad as all that, not really.'

'Oh, *it is* though, Grace; the only person worse than a bully is their sidekick.'

'But Ben's ... powerful, he's overpowering. He seems to make everyone miserable. I shouldn't have added to your burden.'

'Don't apologise. Please.'

'What are we going to do?'

'I don't know, Grace. But I promise you something – for once in his life Ben Gardener isn't going to win. And I'm not sure how we're going to get one over on him yet, but we are. Stick with me. I'm going to make it up to you.'

Listening back to it in her head, Peach hears her declaration as cheap cinematic bluster. Sees that in the moment, she was so seduced by the thought of redeeming herself, she didn't consider that redemption and damnation might be two edges on one blade. Or that a blade inexpertly wielded doesn't care who it harms. She'd been so exhilarated by her not-all-heroes-wear-capes fantasy of a kick-ass showdown where the good guys always win, she forgot that in real life, sometimes, the good guys have too much at stake to risk everything. Or that sometimes, they just don't turn out to be all that good.

Chapter 29

The alarm clock buzzed at seven thirty. Peach sprang from the bed with purpose and started trying on outfits. Nothing was right. Everything too effortful or too slovenly. She settled on a diaphanous floral dress – soft, pale, old and pretty. An impetuous jumble-sale purchase she'd never worn. It reminded Peach of something Courtney Love might wear. She put on red lipstick she'd dismissed before as slutty. Painting her lips, the wax of it tasted like the future.

She dripped White Musk on her wrist. She looked in the mirror – she was dressed like the person she was finally ready to be.

It was another blistering day and the MacArthurs were having a fight for breakfast. The distance from her front step to the house across the street used to be an ocean wide, the end of the cul-de-sac another country. Now Peach felt like she could touch both sides of the road if she opened her arms wide enough.

She scurried to Ian's house, praying Nick would still be there. He was; standing blearily in the hall, wearing his leopard print coat even though it was boiling. Too cool to swelter, not a bead of sweat on him. Peach felt herself get wet.

'You're here early, mate, I'm just about to head. Shame. You look great.'

Peach bit the inside of a cheek to stop herself grinning too maniacally.

'Got a bit of lipstick on your tooth,' Nick remarked. And a small important part of Peach died forever. These are the sorts of humiliations people remember on their deathbed.

'Looks good though. Lippy suits you. Better go, gi's a cuddle.'

He threw his arms round Peach. She crushed her body against him, arched her back, and pushed out her chest. Words blundered around in her mouth.

Nick pressed his thumb onto her bottom lip, so she felt like clay, as if his imprint would remain and from now on, whenever she thought of her own mouth, she'd think about him touching it.

He said, 'You.' *You* as if it meant she was important in good ways and bad ones.

Peach wanted to say, 'What about *me*?' What about me; lately she wanted to ask that of everyone about everything. The thought of hearing her voice enforced silence.

Nick looked like he was waiting – maybe for a magic word, maybe for a magic silence.

She began to move her lips against his thumb, letting it slip between her lips. He made this feral sound: a gasp, a moan, urgently soft, and pushed his index finger into her mouth as well. She mouthed at his fingers like a puppy. He said, 'Don't,' and pushed his fingers further in.

She let her tongue brush against them and felt the rush of air as Nick exhaled. 'We've got to stop,' he said and crumpled his body into hers, pushing her up against the banister.

'We can't do this,' he said and grabbed a handful of her.

His collarbone swooped into his t-shirt, so perfect it looked sculpted. Peach pulled the fabric down. There were two purple marks on his chest, so close together they almost formed a figure eight. Fading love bites.

Nick lifted Peach's dress up, opened her legs with his and she understood the passionate violence of that other mouth biting down. She covered the stranger's shape with her lips just to see if she could still want Nick with his skin tagged by someone else.

He was muttering stop and all the time showing Peach's hips how to move with his hands, moving her hips so the bulge in his jeans rubbed her body's doubts into silence.

He smudged his lips against hers, so they were breathing one another. Not kissing. Just breathing. He was breathing and pulling her underwear to the side, unbuckling his belt.

Peach wanted to hold on to the thinking part of herself which cautioned her not to go any further and equally to let the feeling between her legs colonise the rest of her.

'Oh, baby girl,' he said, 'no,' as he slid against her, stroking her open. His hands didn't need to tell her how to move, Peach knew the tiny adjustment she had to make to change nearly to definitely. And as she did, as he helped her to find him, just as they were as close as it was possible to be, he whispered, 'We can't, baby girl, we can't.'

Enough. She was sick of his shit.

Suddenly sick of him and whatever game he was playing. Suddenly sick of not understanding what anyone was doing, least of all herself. Let him go back to London and work someone else like a puppet. 'Yeah,' she said, 'you're right – we can't.' The hunger where his body met hers still demanded to carry on.

But right then she hated how men seemed to be allowed to

tell women what their bodies could be. How they could draft and redraft the rules to suit themselves. Write their names all over you and wipe them off whenever it suited them. How they could afford to say no and mean yes. Could reposition your sexiness as sluttishness while they stayed in exactly the same spot: the driving seat.

Now she knows she didn't articulate her feelings to herself like that. She was just horny, annoyed and aware Nick was being unfair to her. Adult understanding has overwritten memory with a feminist polemic that wouldn't have occurred to her at the time; those ideas hadn't entered her head yet. They didn't for a larger number of years than she's comfortable admitting.

It's hard for Peach to know what she does remember correctly, all these decades later, with Nick right here, looking at her like she's important, holding her eye as if they're bonded by something ancient and kind. Behind it, Peach sees emptiness. Nick pinning a win on making her yearn, just to see if he still can. As an adult she knows availability is the most unattractive quality a woman like her can reveal to a man like him.

But what she does recall with perfect fidelity about that day in 1994 is that, thwarted and panting and in Nick's arms, she found herself thinking about the strangest thing. She found herself remembering sunlight blinking and flinching on the surface of the local swimming pool a few years before. Happy voices rising and reverberating.

She had hauled herself out of the water. Tiny crystal globes gathered on her skin. Trembling and falling as she breathed. Collecting on the tiles at her feet.

Peach was thinking of nothing but how cold it was, how

259

delicious and sudden it would feel when she plunged back into the warm pool.

A group of boys from school were jostling and jeering at the shallow end, so busy showing off to one another that Peach had escaped their notice. They slipped her mind with the heavy ease of a dropped coin.

She prepared her body to dive.

She had to enter the water precisely as a knife. She put her hands together as if praying. Raised them above her head.

When the lifeguard's whistle tooted rebuke she knew it wasn't for her. Legs thrummed with latent dive. Arms taut as a bow. She was meticulously prepared, when, from the corner of her eye, she saw Grant Biddle from her class.

He was running along the edge of the pool. His swimming trunks were the colour of Tizer. His head was oily wet like a seal's.

As time shrieked and skidded to a standstill, Peach's arms fell limply to her sides. An unfeasible quantity of minutes seemed to pass between the realisation of what was going to happen to Peach and the moment when it began to.

Grant Biddle grabbed the straps of her swimming costume. He pulled it down to her waist and shouted 'Bare boobs!' into Peach's face.

His breath smelled of cheese-and-onion crisps. Peach flopped into the pool like a dropped sack. The last thing she heard as she entered the water was laughter and the lifeguard shouting 'No running.'

Water roared into every open part of her.

Underwater was dumb, blue peace. Skeins of sun bent and flexed. The fluid world impossibly solid. It held Peach as she wrestled her swimming costume back up like an escapologist twisting in chains.

She punched through the meniscus, mouth clawing air. Shouts collected in the high ceiling and bounced off the plate-glass windows. Light burst like fireworks against the ripples.

Peach expected ridicule or concern or both, but none came. Nothing and no one came.

The lifeguard was watching a girl in a red bikini descend the ladder into the deep end.

Children were smashing the water with happy hands. Adults trudged lengths.

It seemed the moment had healed up over Peach's head; indifferent and seamless as water.

Then she realised Grant Biddle and his friends *were* looking at her. They were watching Peach as if she was a bag of dog shit they had set alight for fun. Waiting to see what would happen.

What happened was Peach swam. With the fragile dignity of a small ship embarking on a long voyage, she pushed off the side and swam until her body was elaborately stiff and cold as a crystal chandelier. Until it felt like it would break beneath her. Until *finally*, the boys scuttled off, glancing back and whispering.

In the water Peach had still been herself. When she climbed out of the pool, she discovered she had become someone else. Her body would never belong to her again. It felt public and thumbed as a library book. A smutty novelty, like a pornographic playing card. She was twelve and a half years old.

'Sorry,' Nick said. 'Just, you're so young. And Ian and your mum must be on their way back, and I really need to go . . .' He didn't move away, didn't release her.

'Yeah, you're right,' Peach said. Nick let go; she brushed her skirt down.

'Sorry mate,' Nick said as if Peach was a stranger whose elbow he'd jogged in a bar.

'Do you want a coffee before you go?' she asked.

He buckled his belt. 'Yeah, amazing, thanks. I'll just go and grab my stuff.'

In the kitchen, Peach put the kettle on. Two minutes later, she heard Nick's car start, heard him depart in an ostentatious spray of gravel and Ministry.

'Wanker. Fucking absolute fucking wanker,' she shouted and kicked the skirting board until her toes hurt.

She made toast because certain types of misery feel like being hungry. Standing by the window, she watched the sun bend the house's shadow across the lawn like a gnomon and remembered Nick had not been her only reason for arriving at Ian's so early.

The door to her mother's office didn't give. She pushed and pulled: locked. A huge unhappiness flexed its muscles – everyone knows what a locked door means about the things behind it.

She had to get inside. She ran downstairs. She sprinted outdoors and looked up: the window was open. Peach remembered climbing the ropes in gym and only ever making it halfway up while Miss Linton shouted 'Don't look down, girl! Keep going up!' as Peach shimmied back to earth, limbs trembling.

The drainpipe was hot as a cooking pot, but she hauled herself up. Her body recalled the movements of knees and elbows needed. She made the first few feet okay. The next few were accomplished more shakily, muttering don't look down under her breath. But Peach ignored herself and the world below whirled sickeningly as she saw how high up she was.

Fear of Mum and Ian arriving back to find Peach shinning

up the drainpipe like a burglar spurred her on. Panic stilled her just below the window. She couldn't go up or down. Stuck, she imagined her broken body being found on the gravel. Her hands were slimy on the sheer pipe. 'What was she doing?' people would say and weep round Peach's coffin. Mum would suspect.

Something crunched on the gravel below. Grabbing the window ledge Peach pulled herself up, muscles shrieking, and swung her body inside. Panting she looked out. A fat ginger tom was chasing a cabbage white across the drive. She thanked him for scaring courage into her.

Mum had neatened the papers. Peach searched and searched, trying not to make a mess that would give her away.

Churning through bills, newspaper clippings, enigmatic reels of magnetic tape she lacked the wherewithal to play, she found a document – Patty's death certificate.

It made the particulars of death seem banal, a mere administrative concern until Peach saw that the column headed cause of death held a revelation. In hard, icy type: *suicide*.

She looked at the quivering paper again and again as if the words might rearrange themselves into something more innocuous.

Patty was more remote than ever. Peach remembered her smoking cigarettes in a deckchair in their back garden when Solomon was just a puppy. How much time must have elapsed between that day and Patty's death?

She tried to lay out the huge creased map of time, tried to place her memories on it where they might make sense, make them represent days she'd lived, places she'd been, but a blur of moments flowed together in colours and temperatures. Trying to remember more clearly felt like attempting to gather in mist.

Peach delved back into the papers like a diver undertaking a plunge to the bottom on a single breath.

There was a letter on headed paper from a therapist. A man called David Eve had been treating Patty for what he described as *depressive disturbance of mind*. He said Patty had described *recurrent thoughts of death*, had been *trying to resist suicidal impulses* and had *desperately wanted to make her marriage work despite the obvious issues*. Yet he questioned the coroner's verdict of suicide, said there were *possibly grounds to appeal the verdict on the basis that Patty was excited about her pregnancy*. Saying that, *as her therapist, I think it unlikely that she would have taken her life, as she appeared to be looking forward to the future and the birth of her child*.

Confusion boiled under Peach's bones. She was shocked by sympathy for Ian. He was meant to be a father. He must have felt like one for a while. Maybe he still did.

She thought of the room upstairs with the rocking horse and mobile. A nursery, waiting for a baby, like a pot full of soil waiting for a seed. Somewhere in the process of dismantling it, he must have given up – unable to strip it of those last few objects. Unable to remove the remnants of the life he was meant to lead.

That must be what his work meant. Not that he hated women. The sculptures were the crashing car, the dying wife and disappearing future. He was reliving the loss as he forced planks through fleshy clay. As though he could remake his present by reliving the past.

Digging in substrates of paper, Peach's fingers bumped against a thick shape. A small black notebook which felt as solid as the other contents felt insubstantial.

The book was tied with frayed ribbon. Undoing the knot felt invasive. It belonged to Patty. With a child's possessiveness she'd written her name inside the cover.

There were spiralling doodles: the kind people make during tedious telephone calls. Jotted times and dates. There were poems, lyrics; fragments of thought captured and re-drafted. Peach skipped over metaphors for nature to the ones which spoke of love and pain.

She found the words she knew meant the most to Patty and the most to her:

> *I thought you were the kindest one*
> *My friend, my dearest love*
> *I trusted you to nurse my heart*
> *And hold it like a dove*
> *I thought you were the one who would*
> *Protect my interests*
> *Instead betrayed, my world has swayed*
> *You both destroyed our nests*

Patty's pen had carved into the paper. She knew the violence in the carving, understood it told the same truth about her mother and Ian that the photograph did.

Then recollected pain appeared: raised voices from the living room. Her parents shouting downstairs while Peach and Bella sat on the floor upstairs and Greg cried in a Moses basket. Mum had gone away for a while.

Peach scrabbled through the boxes, plucking out pictures of Ian with an unkempt beard and hands dripping cement. Documentation of his shows: sixties and seventies hipsters smoking over plinths in black and white. Patty and Dad and Ian and Mum.

Patty and Dad, barely looking at one another. Ian and Mum in close-up, laughing mouths in the shameless proximity of kissers parting or advancing. Mum's face like an advert for absolute happiness. Just like Magda had said: *the camera captures the truth of relationships.*

Peach felt like there wasn't enough air in the room for her and what she had discovered. It was as if Patty was right there, whispering; *your mum, my best friend. She killed me and my baby.*

Peach wanted to talk to Mum, but she was someone else now: a stranger wearing her face.

She wanted to talk to Bella. But she would say 'I told you so.' Bella had clearly known, or suspected, some half-haze of the truth. 'What did you expect?' She'd leave Peach even more alone with it.

She wanted to talk to her father. But doing so would destroy him.

And Greg? She didn't consider talking to Greg. Or she did so only for the second it took to dismiss him. Simultaneously, wondering in some insipid way if she would ever know him better than she did now. Then she envied the uncompli- cated life he would enjoy while Peach protected him from what she knew.

Peach felt banished. She said the word 'No' over and over, like a spell to take time back which refused to perform any magic. She kept filling back up with misery as she tried to empty it out.

The fabric of Peach's life was unravelling around her, yet she was aware of time passing, the hazard of Ian and Mum on their way back from London.

She went to the window and looked out. Sun still blazed in the blue sky over the garden, the weather of uncomplicated happiness. The view left Peach incredulous that she'd ever made the climb.

Think, she told herself aloud. Think. She grouped together all she had found. Evidence of the lie festering under her life:

the notebook, the death certificate, the letter from her mother to Ian which she had once hidden in her pocket, the letter to Ian from Patty's therapist.

She took them down to the floor and unscrewed the brass heating grate with a letter opener. In a panic of scrabbling, she pushed the wad of paper inside and secured the cover.

Trembling, she began to ransack the drawers. Paperclips, staplers, multiple rolls of indigestion tablets; she crunched a couple just to feel like there was medicine for what was wrong. Then spare keys – two large bunches. With shaking hands Peach tried six before the door came free. She locked it behind her and fled as if there was any way to leave what she knew behind her.

Chapter 30

Nick and Bella don't even look at one another. Bella stares into the fire as if she reserves special contempt for him even though she hasn't seen him since the drunken day he licked her palm.

An insect chirruping begins. They all jump. Bella scrabbles in her bag which exudes blue light. Her phone is the newest, the swankiest. Peach's heart clenches like a fist. Dad has died. They were not there.

'Soon,' says Bella.

'No,' says Bella. 'No change. All right.'

'Soon, I said. God's *sake*, Greg. I said *soon*.'

Dad is just the same, and Peach is horrified by how little consolation the news provides.

'Is Kevin going to be okay?' asks Ian.

'No,' rails Bella, 'he's been knocked down *and* he's got *dementia* anyway, like I already told you, so get that into your thick skull and understand that whatever we, whatever *you* wanted to talk to him about, it won't happen.'

'This is tricky,' says Nick, '*very* delicate.'

'Could be useful though, strategically speaking.' Something turns over on itself behind Ian's eyes, his dynamic old self.

'Oh, I don't think, now's not ... Ian, mate. I hope your dad gets better.' Nick looks at his feet.

There is something here, lurking, something diseased.

Peach says, 'I think now *is* the time. Tell us what we're actually talking about here, so Bella and I can get back to the hospital.'

Nick makes a gesture towards Ian as if ushering him through a door ahead of him and Ian clears his throat. 'I know it must seem distasteful in these circumstances, but Nick and I are writing my memoirs,' he declares.

A Bikini Atoll of anger detonates across Bella's face. '*Of course*. Of *course* you are; you never cared about Mum or Dad. You only ever cared about yourself. Never thought better of dragging up the past because you can't resist an opportunity to talk about yourself,' Bella rants. 'Or are you *so* bitter about the fact people care far more about Patty nowadays than they do about your big boring blobs? Or—'

Ian cuts her off. 'Forgive me, *Isabella*, if I find it hard to believe *you* care *so very* much about your parents, or indeed that Kevin is as grievously ill as you'd have me believe. If his condition's critical, why aren't you at his bedside? Why are you here, behaving like the witchfinder general?'

There's no answer to that. However vain and despicable Ian is, Peach and Bella are no less callous or narcissistic for having come.

'I would think twice,' Bella looms over Ian, 'before dragging my family into whatever self-serving version of history you and *Nicholas* are planning to write. Because I'm pretty rich nowadays and I have a *great* lawyer. You'll be hearing from him.'

'It's my right,' thunders Ian, '*my* story, *my* past. Besides, the whole filthy business is *her* fault.'

Of course, thinks Peach – it always comes back to that. To this haunted house.

'It's not,' Bella turns to Peach, 'it's not your fault.'

'Oh, not Peach,' says Nick, 'Magda. Remember her? She's making a documentary about Patty, and Ian's just trying to redress—'

'Sorry, what?' The ghosts just keep on materialising. Bella sits down, and Peach starts shaking.

'That bitch never liked me,' gripes Ian, 'from the first moment she arrived here she was judging me, *in my own house*, and she took that photo that keeps turning up. The one that makes me look a right . . . ' Frothy white spit accretes at the corner of Ian's mouth, lending him a rabid air.

Like a son, like a good and caring son, Nick touches Ian's elbow. 'Yeah, Ian, let me—'

But Ian won't be restrained. 'Now she's got Patty's ancient mother on board – ninety-seven the woman is! She's probably senile, and *she* never liked me either. *Plus*, she's got hold of tapes of Patty talking to that fly-by-night David Eve – therapist my foot, he was a charlatan. He's given his tapes to Magda, tapes of Patty saying *things*. About me – but they were different times. You can't judge the past by present standards, and now she's coaxed all sorts of silly . . . women out of the woodwork with their flaming torches.'

Nick says, 'Maybe calm down a bit, Ian, this isn't helping. Look, we – Ian and I just think a bit of balance would be—'

'Balance?' Bella stands. 'Don't insult my intelligence. You want to control the truth because you're afraid of it.' She gives a mirthless chuckle and runs Nick through with a stare so vicious Peach expects to see blood start blooming across his shirt.

'And so should you be,' smirks Ian. 'This memoir will be going ahead, with your family's collaboration or without it. I think I'm being very generous by offering you some input after what your family did to mine, so I'd think long and hard before rejecting it. Now be sensible, take a moment to decide, then tell me what you want to do.'

Peach waits for Bella's big go-fuck-yourself-Ian monologue. But it doesn't come. Instead Bella gazes at Peach as if she expects her to have the answer.

But the first time since 1994 Peach thought she knew what do in a situation like this was only a month ago. And she is still feeling the reverberations of it.

Days had passed in a blur of purpose. Peach and Grace took their lunches to Green Park and ate among tourists and pigeons, watching men in overalls stack the deckchairs onto a truck.

In the course of those hours, Peach discovered Grace was funny, smart and ambitious, aware of her privilege like all her predecessors probably were. Sometimes Peach could hardly force food past the carcinoma of guilt constricting her windpipe. She'd insist on buying Grace a coffee or some chocolate on the way back to Capsule.

Back in the gallery, Ben snuffled around Grace like a pig hunting for truffles. Every time he went near her, Peach inserted herself between them. Every chance she got, Peach sent Grace out on errands. In response Ben was grumpier than ever, more tyrannical to the Guy/Luke/Toms. He fired one on the spot for dropping a hammer.

It occurred to Peach that finding ways to enforce restraint on Ben instead of teaching him to restrain himself was no solution at all. But powerlessness made small acts of resistance mistakeable for power.

A show was opening: expressionistic splashes, fleshy and saturated with erotic longing. Painted by an obscure older woman, suddenly in demand now Ben and his kind judged her sufficiently sexless to be permitted a last-minute career. Peach should have been delighted to see an artist like that garnering attention. But she knew if the paintings had been done by a younger woman Ben would have dismissed them with a comment about how the artist was obviously dying for a good seeing to. And all week, Peach had watched Ben treat the painter like something between a mascot and a maiden aunt. The worst thing was, she hadn't seemed to mind. In fact, she'd appeared grateful. Peach couldn't judge her for that. But she couldn't stand to watch it either.

As Peach printed out gallery maps, she'd reflected on how quickly time had passed, how rare it was to have lived so many days in a row where she wasn't constantly straining against the leash of time passing. How much more present she was now she felt responsible for something outside herself.

Grace was polishing wine glasses while Ben stood beside her with the look of a glutton selecting steak.

Peach walked over. Ben sent her sharply back behind the desk with a remark about how he hoped she was planning on getting changed before the opening, that she wouldn't be wearing *that*. She was being punished.

For so long Peach had felt like a stick insect. So inconsequential, no one ever shook her jar to check she hadn't died. If Ben was noticing her, she must be pissing him off. If she was pissing him off, she must be doing something right.

The gallery had begun to fill with the usual mixture of expensive-looking older people whose restaurant bills could pay a month's rent for the younger ones, there seeking free drinks, sex and careers. All of them behaved like hummingbirds, hovering in conversations, throwing anxious glances

272

over one another's shoulders in case there was someone more important or useful or cooler on the horizon.

Once, these occasions were important to Peach. Drenched in potential sex, thrumming with possible shows. Now she was no longer part of them, they appeared vicious and silly as a Punch and Judy show.

I used to love this place, she thought. Working at Capsule used to feel like being part of a club instead of being complicit in something wrong. It seemed to Peach a damning indictment of her character that she had no idea when the shift occurred. She only knew it happened a long time ago.

Someone had been pressing an empty champagne glass into Peach's hand with no more regard for her than if she was a table, when she saw that Ben had Grace cornered.

Ben had his arm round Grace in front of Ivan Rook, an arms dealer who bought hundreds of thousands of pounds' worth of art from the gallery. They were laughing with their teeth bared and Peach thought: none of this can happen.

Feeling sick, she took a deep breath, walked over. Inserted herself rudely into the situation with Ben and Grace and Ivan Rook, pushing herself into the centre of the group with no regard for delicacy or hierarchy or any of the boundaries that usually penned her in.

'Can Peach get you another drink, Ivan?' Ben asked.

'I'll get it,' said Grace.

'How's business, Ivan?' asked Peach, and she'd felt like a heifer realising the electric fence around her pasture had been switched off once she took the first jolt.

Silence. Ivan Rook glared at Peach. You don't ask Ivan Rook how business is. You accept that he is a leading global provider of transport and logistical services and you ask if you can get him anything.

'I'll have another glass of red,' he said, eyeing Peach nastily.

And Peach had kept standing there. Not saying anything. Just looking at Ben and Ivan like shit on her shoe. Silence and stillness more disturbing to them than any word or action because it refused to be disrupted or dismissed.

'Ivan has an amazing yacht, Grace,' sputtered Ben, 'he throws the most fantastic parties on it during the Venice Biennale; you should come along next year. Peach, get Ivan a drink.'

How fragile it all is, Peach thought, how pathetic these people are, that me standing between them uninvited, asking a perfectly polite question with a look on my face they don't like, is intimidating. The eerie silence gathering up around the four of them was so deafening that people nearby had begun to notice.

Peach made plenty of scenes in her life. Crying at parties, drinking until she blacked out, swearing or shouting or stripping. Because she was drunk. Because she was heart-broken. Because she thought that artists were too free-spirited to be constrained by manners. Because she was buying into a tissue-thin self-mythology. But this time she was caus-ing a scene because something real was wrong and had to be stopped.

'I see there's a new gallery named after you in Paris, Ivan, how wonderful! I was reading about it just the other day.'

The opening event had been ruined by protesters smeared in fake blood who had smuggled themselves in disguised as caterers. Ivan had been rushed out of a back entrance by security.

'You don't seem well, Peach,' hissed Ben. 'I think you should go home, have the evening off.'

'Actually,' she replied, 'now you mention it, Grace and I have both been feeling a bit peaky. I think we should both go.'

'Grace is fine.' Ben put his arm round her. 'Aren't you?' Ben held her like a knife to a throat.

'No, I think Grace and I are going to leave.'

Grace was frozen: such a cliché – animal in the headlights, but she was composed of pure trembling survival instinct as the moment unfolded. Peach wondered if she was any better than Ben, any less in this for herself as the two of them squabbled over Grace like two brats pulling the limbs of a teddy. She was cold with doubt.

But then Grace said, 'I don't feel well, Peach.' A squeak, a strangled squeak.

'Well, *ladies*, you'd better leave then.'

'Ivan, let me get you another drink. Peach. My office. Ten tomorrow.'

Peach gave a whatever shrug, then she and Grace pushed their way through the opening, out past the throng of smokers who had spilt from the opening into the street and were performing themselves very loudly.

Chapter 31

Peach walked home, nursing her unhappiness, in air so filthily humid she could feel the exact margin where it ended and her body began.

Greg was in the kitchen, wearing pyjama bottoms with a little-boy pattern of jolly footballs. He stood beside the fridge posting slices of ham into his mouth like floppy pink love letters to his stomach.

'How are you doing?' she asked him.

He looked disquieted. 'Uh, yeah, fine.'

'What's going on with you?'

'Why are you asking?' He opened a yogurt and tipped out the pot into his mouth.

'Just fancied a chat.'

Greg looked suspiciously at Peach, like he thought she was setting up a practical joke.

He lobbed the yogurt pot in the bin. 'Yeah, gonna play basketball with Mitchell,' he said and walked out.

Dad was in the garden, poised at an inadvisable angle on top of a ladder, barbering the hedge with the electric trimmer.

He had been an artist once, played guitar in a band. Love and sex must have ebbed once babies and boredom came — after the endless possibilities of youth proved dismayingly finite. She expected Mum turned to Ian when the lustre went off Dad, when he forfeited his dreams to teacher training. It was so unjust. The sight of him was unbearable. He was the best, most straightforward person in Peach's life.

She went to her room and lay on top of the bedclothes.

Downstairs the telephone rang; sound floundered around in the air for a long time until someone answered, or the caller rang off.

Peach manoeuvred thoughts round her head like pieces on a gameboard.

Confront Mum, break the news to Dad or tell Nick? If Peach told him about Mum and Ian, Dad would know the truth, and no one would need to know she was responsible. She'd tell Nick in exchange for anonymity. He'd understand.

All the previous decors scrolled through Peach's head: animals, then rainbows, now cornflower-coloured paint. She itched to run a nail down the seam, peel it back, as if glimpsing the old paper would confirm life had been simple and reassure her it would be again.

Footsteps came up the stairs. Peach heard Bella moving round her bedroom, drawers scraping, the wardrobe doors opening and shutting.

Peach looked at her wall of photographs; she got off the bed and began to take down the ones of her friends. Ex-friends.

So many rectangles of paint exposed, so many gaps. She was rolling Blu-Tack into a ball when Bella came into her room.

'What are you doing?'

'Having a clear-out.'

'Talking of which, I'm going to head to the station shortly. I'm going.'

'Where?'

'Travelling.'

'Who with?'

A cinematic smile lit up Bella's face.

'Dominic.'

The world took on a queasy tilt. Peach's mouth filled with saliva as she realised there was no spare self: the person who had sex with Dominic was in her skin. Mistakes were not imprisoned in a back-up life where being sorry set you free from them.

'But you broke up with Dominic, you said he was a dick.'

Peach felt sick, she felt faint – finally she felt responsible and it was every bit as excoriating as she deserved.

'It turns out I was wrong. We've been talking a lot on the phone and . . . Peach? Are you okay? You've gone all white.'

It was like looking into icy water from a high ledge.

Making a pact with her body.

In a moment I will jump. The waves are waiting.

Peach leapt into the cold unknown. 'I slept with Dominic.'

She couldn't confidently say she was still breathing. Time stalled, the impossibly long moment between injury and pain. A noisy silence vibrated between them as Peach waited for Bella's wrath.

But Bella didn't move. Bella didn't speak. She stood completely still, growing paler and paler as if she was turning to ash, as if she might blow away. Translucent white sadness made her look delicate and dead as she stared catatonically at the carpet.

'Did he . . . force you?'

'No.'

Bella's eyes focused emptily on the floor as if blind. It seemed as though something very important had broken inside her head.

'Bella, please.' Peach did not know what she was asking Bella for.

'Bella, I'm sorry. I love you.'

Bella spread her hands and shook her head. She gathered up big fistfuls of nothing and rubbed them on her face. Then in a voice small and distant as the sound of sea in shell, she said, 'Don't you *ever* say *that* to me again.'

Downstairs, the front door opened. Mum called out, 'Hello!'

'Are you going to tell Mum and Dad?'

They heard Mum climbing the stairs. She appeared in the doorway. 'Why aren't you at work, Peach? Ian needs help in the studio today.'

'I'm leaving, Mum,' said Bella.

'Why? What's going on? Have you two had a row?'

Peach said yes, Bella said no.

'You have,' said Mum. 'Come on, make up, there's no need to go, Bella.'

'I was leaving anyway,' Bella said as she left the room.

The morning after the opening, Ben had swaggered into the gallery, grey, hungover and vengeful. The first thing he'd said was, 'Can I trust you, Peach? Think carefully.'

Not asking Peach if she trusted him. Or wondering why she'd acted in a way she never had before. Not in ten long years of unquestioning subservience.

'I *cannot* employ people I don't trust.'

The night before the numbers had been different. The economy included bigger things than numbers. That morning pounds and pence were back at the centre of the universe.

Peach realised Ben was going to fire her. That financially she was as unable to afford to lose her job as, the night before, she'd been emotionally unable to afford to do nothing.

Cry then, she'd told herself. You need this job so cry.

'I'm sorry, Ben,' she blurted, crying easily because she was miserable.

'Oh right, right then, well,' Ben had been unprepared for tears, 'well ... that was unacceptable, Peach, last night, *totally unacceptable*, pissing off Ivan Rook of all people. I had to knock a thousand pounds off a painting for him and what were you even ... I mean, what were you thinking? You're normally so ... reliable, not ... I don't expect *that*, and I don't expect ... *this*.'

He gestured to Peach's tear-stained face as if pointing to a heap of dung.

'No ... I gave myself a scare really ... I'm just ... ' Do it, Peach, perjure your principles, sell yourself out for the cheapest possible price, do your most vulgar trick, he doesn't deserve you to spend a cent more of yourself. 'I'm very hormonal and I'm lonely and ... '

Ben looked delighted. Textbook female behaviour which could be condoned because it was pitiful. Tolerated because it was perfectly unchallenging. 'Do I have your assurance that *nothing* like that will *ever* happen again?'

'Of course, Ben, I'm so sorry.' The words cold vomit. Peach choked them out.

He perched on the edge of the front desk like a groovy teacher and a look came over his face that Peach hadn't seen in years. One she used to see when Ben was younger; still as motivated by art as money.

'Look, Peach, why don't you take a day off, sort out your *illness*.' His tone genuine concern, like he was peeling back his monster mask to reveal the human underneath.

'I need ... you know, not *need* but it's important, see ... you understand how it is, how things really are, all this *stuff* lately, people being ... *sensitive*, *over*-sensitive, I've always really valued the fact that you're not like that. That you *get it*.'

'Get it?'

'Yeah, I've got to surround myself with people I can trust because they, *you*, realise how life really works. People like you get things done without complaining. People like you understand life's not fair and do what I pay them to without banging on about *feelings* and all that.' He waved his hand dismissively. 'Can I trust you to go back to normal?'

'Yes.'

'Great. Prove it then. Fire the intern.'

'Her name is Grace.'

'Okay. Well, fire Grace then. And get me a coffee.'

Chapter 32

Once Bella was gone, Mum came up to Peach's room.

'I don't know what to say to you.' Mum sat down and balled her fists in her lap. 'Bella wouldn't tell me what happened between you, but something obviously did.'

'She was leaving anyway.'

Mum's mouth moved like she was chewing something foul. 'How can you be so uncaring, Peach? We won't see your sister until Christmas now. You haven't been yourself at all these last few weeks. You're usually such a nice child.'

'I'm seventeen.'

'Peach, when I had children, I promised myself I wouldn't be like *my* mother. She never got to know me. She was far too busy knowing what was best for me – enrolling me in secretarial school when I had a place to study art, trying to set me up with her friend's boring son when I was already seeing your father. I have tried *so hard* not to be like that with you but—'

'Why wouldn't you let me go to art school then?'

'Photography's a nice hobby. There's no need to spoil your enjoyment of it by putting it under all that pressure.'

'What if I think it's more than a hobby?'

'You have to be so talented, Peach. You have to be *so* talented to succeed.'

A throb of rage surged through Peach's brain. 'And I'm not?'

'Oh Peach, I don't know. Even *if* you *were* really good, it's so competitive. You'd have to work so hard. Be so resilient. And so, so responsible.'

'I can work. I can be responsible. You don't know how just how responsible I can be, *Mother*.'

Mum suddenly snapped, 'You weren't very responsible with my . . . the camera I lent . . . gave you.'

'God's sake, it was a fucking accident.'

'Don't you swear at me, Peach, after everything I've tried to—'

'Oh. *Fuck. You.*'

Peach's mother clasped her own hands and flexed her arms as though preparing to perform a contortion.

'What did I do to deserve this nastiness?' asked Mum.

'What *did* you do, Mother?'

'I ask myself that all the time lately, Peach Lewis.'

Mum stood stone still letting her breath maul raggedly through her nose.

'Ooh. The full name manoeuvre. What's next? A bit of I'm not angry I'm disappointed? You're playing the hits.'

Mum's right hand shot up as she was preparing to testify; she looked at her hand. She looked at Peach. She made a fist round the things her hand itched to do and let it drop. 'I am sick of you.' Her voice was poisonous with curdled love.

'Good,' said Peach. 'The feeling's mutual.'

After Grant Biddle humiliated her, Peach walked into the swimming pool café where Mum was waiting. She'd asked what time she called this and tapped her watch. Peach turned her eyes to the floor and shrugged, so embarrassed it felt as if even her hair would have liked to disown her.

She asked what Peach had been doing. Peach twisted the straps of her backpack round her knuckles, shrugged, said, 'Swimming.'

Mum had said, 'You'll catch a chill and it will all be your own fault.'

It put a stopper to the words Peach would use to tell Mum what had happened. They jugged up in her. Clotted and sore.

Later in her bedroom, she incarcerated all her stuffed animals in the wardrobe. Afterwards she asked Mum if she could have her hair cut short. Not quite understanding what compelled her, wanting Mum to ask her what was wrong. But she didn't. Not that time.

When Peach left the birthday party where Barry Jones assaulted her, Mum did ask what was wrong.

Peach took the seatbelt between her lips like a horse with a bit because she was afraid she'd tell Mum before she'd decided to.

Mum had said she could tell something was up, stop doing that with the seatbelt please. Take it out your mouth, you're not teething.

Peach cried, 'A boy touched me. I didn't like it.'

Mum's knuckles went white on the steering wheel.

'Men, boys have *needs*,' she'd said, 'They behave like dogs sometimes. Better not to start things.'

And she didn't say *you* started something. Didn't say Peach had made Barry feel like he could do what he did. But it felt like what Mum meant was: *you* should not have provoked. Or if not provoked, allowed. Or if not allowed, then found yourself in a *situation* where your mutually exclusive *needs* collided.

But what Mum had said was, 'It was not very nice. Let that be a lesson.' Then she'd put the radio on. And it felt to Peach like Mum told her: you are a toilet, a place for others to put things in, should their physical needs require alleviation.

Mum had always talked about girls who got a degree and girls who got a reputation as if that amounted to the same thing, or implied one cancelled the other out. And Peach realised that all her life she'd been receiving poison pen letters and valentines that arrived in identical envelopes written by the same correspondent: Mum.

Now Peach was going to show Mum just how much havoc her correspondence could cause.

Peach put *The Holy Bible* on the stereo and let 'Faster' rampage through her blood. She was ready for a life after this one.

Chapter 33

All night, Peach barely slept, watching the digits creep and gallop on her alarm clock until morning lit a frame of fire to the curtain edges.

She picked up her lipstick and put it down, yanked fishnet tights out of a drawer and stuffed them back. She torpedoed the urge to look attractive for Nick by reminding herself of the way he'd driven off. She was too enervated and fatigued to care about her appearance anyway. She chucked on ripped jeans and a Manics shirt.

As she walked, she had no idea what she was about to do. Or not. The streets appeared dimensionless, imbued with the malevolent peace of an empty swimming pool.

At Ian's, Nick was already back. He and Ian were in the living room surrounded by breakfast dishes and newspapers. Jazz whooped from the speakers. It sounded like the musical equivalent of scribbling, compounding Peach's jittery, over-caffeinated feelings.

Nick disappeared behind a broadsheet when Peach walked in.

'Where the hell were you yesterday?' demanded Ian.

'Didn't feel well.'

He rolled his eyes. 'I *do* hope you're better. Come with me, there's a lot to do.'

He marched out of the room. Peach hung on a moment.
'Hi Nick.'

'All right, mate,' he said, face still obscured by *The Times*.

Peach felt as dog-chewed and slobbered on as the toy monkey Solomon used to hump in the kitchen.

On the way through the hall, she encountered Mum arriving. 'Is there anything you want to say to me?' Mum asked.

'Is there anything *you* want to say to *me*?'

Mum snorted as if Peach was ridiculous and turned her back.

Peach stormed into Ian's studio.

'Feeling all right?' he asked disinterestedly.

The hidden papers infested the grate in Mum's office.

Peach smiled at Ian, the innocent beam of a diligent angel.

Ian lifted smashed parts of failed sculptures from a hopper. Almost indiscernible from completed ones. He showed Peach how to shove and punch clay to make it useable again. An unwelcome image of his meaty hands insinuating themselves under her mother's clothes: fabric falling, zips being pulled.

Ian left Peach to squash and knead clay while he pushed wood through a noisy saw. With her fingers bogged in terracotta, Peach thought: how dare they?

She didn't really experience it as interrogation but as outrage; the defiantly utter being of a creature under threat, the powerful rigidity of something about to be crushed.

Then she washed her hands, watched bloody-looking water disappear down the sink and walked out while Ian obliviously fed planks to the blade.

Nick was half asleep on the couch.

'Can I have a word, Nick?' she asked.

'Not a great time, mate.' He turned onto his side.

'Oh, okay then, I found some interesting stuff about Patty yesterday but never mind.'

'Mate,' he sat up and smiled, 'you're such a cool little unit.'

Quick, pathetic pleasure came over Peach in such a druggy rush she knew it must be poison. But Nick was looking at her again, *really looking*, and the desire for him to continue eclipsed her reticence.

She unlocked the door of Mum's office. She steered Nick inside.

'So, Nick—'

He was looking at a photo of Patty on the desk, not at Peach.

'Isn't she beautiful; I can't believe I'll never meet her – I feel like I know her.'

'She *was* beautiful.' Peach had never hated another woman as much as she hated long-dead, two-dimensional Patty right then. 'But there's a lot you don't know about Patty.'

Peach let the implications inflate.

'Like what, what've you found out?'

The grate and its concealed contents scintillated in the corner of her vision.

'I don't know for certain. I found some papers and they seem important but I'm not sure what they mean.'

He drew close. 'You look worried. Sad. Whatever it is has freaked you out.'

'I don't know what to do.'

Nick cupped Peach's jaw. 'We're friends, right?'

She pushed her face against his hand. 'We *are* friends. But this involves my family.'

'Mate, how? In what way?' He ran his thumb across her lips. Thrill became fear. Some things only shine because they're sharp.

'I can't say. I want to, but I can't.'

'You could tell me as a friend. Maybe it's not as big a deal as you think. Maybe I can help you.'

Peach could taste his skin.

288

'But if I tell you as a friend you might still use it as a journalist.'

He retracted his thumb, looking stung. 'You think I'd do that?'

'I don't know. How can I understand anything about this? A few weeks ago, I was still at school.'

'Let me help you figure it out.'

'It's not as easy as that.'

'Mate. I want to understand. You seem so worried – I hate that. But I can't help if I don't understand. It might not even be relevant. You're probably stressing over nothing.'

He shrugged and gave Peach a barbed look which suggested she was a silly little child.

'It's not nothing,' she snapped petulantly. 'What if I told you ...'

'You can tell me anything.'

'No.'

He shook his head. 'Just tell me what you're on about or forget it, mate. I don't really get what you're playing at. I reckon you're making a big deal out of nothing.' He yawned the way Peach did when she wanted someone to know they were worthless.

Peach squirmed on the taut line of it.

'What if Patty's death wasn't an accident?'

He snapped to, eyes popped wide. 'What makes you think that?'

'I think Patty found out Ian was having an affair. She crashed her car on purpose. It says suicide on her death certificate. And she was pregnant when she died.'

Nick dry washed his face with his hands, wiping them up and down his cheeks. 'So many questions, uh, I, where, what, how to start? Mate. *Mate*.'

'How though? Or like, no, how? People would know. Surely.'

'Who cared? Do you know what a big deal her death was at the time? None, no big deal, not at all. The "Right Way Home" singer dies in tragic accident. That was the headline. Two paragraphs on page five. No one cared much, remember?'

'Right. Yeah. I mean, of course. It'll be in the public records, just no one bothered to look before.'

It felt like hours since last she breathed. Public records: this wasn't as dangerous as she'd thought.

'It's all out there if you want to have a look.'

'Of course, I want to look. I'll *need* to. Christ ...' he mused, more to the room than to Peach. 'I'm meant to fly to Germany tomorrow but maybe I can get someone else to go, this is massive but ...'

'What?'

'Aw man, Ian, just, mate, I felt connected to him, like we'd had these amazing conversations about him and Patty and their life and her death. We were even talking about me doing a book someday. In light of this, it was all complete bullshit.'

'I guess if someone tells the same lie for long enough it probably starts to feel like the truth. Like once you don't have to consciously think how does this lie go? Then you completely forget that it's a lie at all.'

Nick was bunched up over his own body like the whole thing was causing him physical agony. 'You're right. I always said you were a cool little unit. What a huge heavy load for you. I'm glad you told me. My poor little mate. No wonder you were freaking out.'

He gave Peach a look which was so much *at* her it was *in* her; it filled and lit and lifted her like a hot air balloon.

'That's not even ... Nick, it isn't everything.'

She approached the grate.

'What are you doing?' Nick asked.

Peach's fingers felt gigantic as she fumbled with the screws holding it in place. 'I hid the stuff here while I was deciding what to do.'

'Clever,' he said admiringly. 'What's in there?'

The grate fell free with the clink of stolen coins. She pulled out the papers, heavy and lethal as a weapon.

'The affair, Nick. It's all in here. Letters. A notebook of Patty's full of stuff she was writing about it when she died. It seems like . . .'

He put his arm round Peach, the kindest most solid thing in the world. 'I'm here. I've got you.'

The perfection of the tragedy brought tears to Peach's eyes as she handed him the papers. 'It was with my mum. It *is* with my mum.'

Nick released Peach from his clasp and it was a sudden blast of ice, winter rushing in. 'Are you completely mental?'

Her body turned to bitter liquid; she felt like she would shit and puke and faint. 'What? Why are you saying that? Why are you being horrible?'

This was like her first fuck: realising a fraction too late that she had impulsively careered into a profoundly important experience.

Staring at the documents in Nick's hands, Peach wondered if it was sanity or madness to make a wild grab for them. Words she could disown; but the papers were a cold hard fact in the world and they weighed more now she wasn't holding them.

'I'm still a journalist! Why would you drop your own mum in the absolute shit like that?'

'But you're my friend!' Peach's words were the astonished cry of a creature receiving the wound it will die of.

'Yeah, sort of, I mean, of course, but it's not that simple now, is it? Now you've told me it's pretty complicated. You must realise that.'

Peach saw Nick's eyes turn flinty, his journalistic instinct set hard.

'What's complicated about this if we're friends? You said you'd help me,' Peach wheedled, her voice the frightened noise of someone jolted from a nightmare of falling to discover they are falling in the real.

'Give that back,' she said and made a demand with her palm, 'you can't have it.'

'Mate, I've got it.'

Peach flew outside herself with a nauseating bird's-eye view of what she had done.

'I'm obviously not your mate. No one is. You're just a horrible journalist pig.'

'I'm trying not to be a prick here, mate, but you're making it tough.' Nick was hard as the surface of the earth and more dangerous than its molten core.

Peach started to cry. 'Nick, please. *Please*. I'm begging you. Give it back.'

He was beautiful and frightening. He shook his head slowly like he was sorry she existed.

'Haven't you still got your story without this? Enough of Patty's story to bring her the recognition you think she deserves.'

'But there's another story underneath – better, more dramatic, more likely to draw people in. That's how it works. And also, it's the truth. I care about the truth.'

He spoke like he was swilling the words round his mouth to see if they tasted right while they were kicking holes through her.

'But Ian, but my mum, but me. What about me?' Peach grizzled and knew she was despicable: broken, unable to walk upright on the surface of this.

'I'm sorry for you.' Nick came close, showing Peach his face was really his face and not a mask. The worst, most painful thing was that compassion and chagrin were real on him. 'I'm sorry you've made such a crazy mistake.'

Every time Peach thought she could cry no harder she found a higher gear and greater acceleration.

She wished she could hate Nick but she was busy hating herself.

'Look at the state of you, kid,' he said, making a mitten of his sleeve and rubbing at Peach's cheeks as if she was a mucky toddler.

'What are you going to do?'

'*Mate*. I don't know. I never wanted to be a bad guy. I loved it here. I liked you a lot. You were my cool little unit.'

That's already a ghost, Peach noticed. How quickly things shift tenses. The meaning of who you are can change in the space of a day and not even be the worst thing to have happened. It takes a single second to knock the whole world out of shape.

She remembered the photo of her parents with Patty and Ian, thought there would be no picture to remember this summer by. Just the endless blurring and sharpening of images which would come and go in her mind as long as she lived.

'What's going to happen now?'

'You're going to have to tell your mum. I won't do anything. I'll say I'm going for a nap. Make myself scarce. You talk to your mum then we'll take it from there.'

'You'll take the stuff and leave.'

He threw her an honest what-the-hell face. 'Even if you think I'm a bastard, just take a moment – what would a pig journalist like me do? What do I want?'

'I don't know.' Peach was a withered balloon.

'I want the story. I want people to talk. I've got leverage here to make that happen.' He tapped the documents like a dodgy dealer closing a shady transaction. 'I'm not going to leave before I get Ian to talk about this, am I?'

Within the repulsive logic Nick described, his offer seemed almost generous. 'Why are you doing this?'

'Because I'm a journalist, mate, but I'm not a total cunt.'

Chapter 34

Mum was a blurred shape moving under the plastic skin of the greenhouse like a fish in a tank.

The weather was blistering, sky nakedly blue. Peach crossed the lawn with her insides made of rain. She wished her body would crumple onto the grass, green blades whispering against her sightless eye as day carried the hours away without her in them, like a missed bus heading to a destination she'd never wanted to arrive at anyway.

The greenhouse was hot as a furnace. The herby bitterness of geraniums permeated the atmosphere. Peach stepped inside. Mum stood far at the opposite end with her thumbs in the soil.

'Mum.' Peach's voice was a squeak in a jar.

Mum turned. She stood with her hand in a plant pot like a strange glove.

'Peach, I'm sorry. I got cross last night, and I'm sorry I was grumpy earlier, I think I'm just—'

'I've done something really bad, Mum.'

Peach's mother cocked her head, a curious birdie twitch. 'To Bella?'

'No, with Nick.'

'That sleazy little—'

'Not like that, Mum.'

'What are you talking about then?'

'Oh Mum, I told Nick about you and Ian and now I know that was the wrong thing to do but I didn't know that when I told him and I'm sorry please forgive me.' Words spewed out of Peach. She lunged towards her mother and stopped.

Mum tensed. The pot became a boxing glove.

'Ian? Me?' Mum recoiled, hand still stuffed in the pot.

The greenhouse was like an oven, the chemical smell of baking plastic mixed with earth, the optimistic tang of living plants.

'Your affair.'

'What?' Her bird head stayed on the side, twitching like a frail scared thing which was going to flutter away.

'I know you've been having an affair with Ian. I found the letter you wrote him. And I saw the pictures, and I read Patty's notebook. And I showed them to Nick.'

'Peach!' The pot left Mum's hand. It whistled through the air towards Peach and landed just shy of her toes.

Her mother's anger was more blistering than the scorched air. A worm made slow progress across the soil at Peach's feet as if nothing in the world was urgent.

'Do you have any idea what you've done?'

Mum launched another plant and it struck the plastic pot at Peach's side with a timpani flourish. She was a terrible shot.

'I'm sorry,' Peach wailed, 'I thought I was doing the right thing. Getting it out in the open. But poor Dad, Mum, I shouldn't have told Nick, but poor Dad, how could you?'

Another pot missed Peach by a mile. Shifting from foot to foot, Mum tested the rhythms of her fury. 'It was him. Them. My husband and my best friend.'

Peach crouched down. Made herself small so there would be less of her for the shock to scald.

'They were screwing each other the whole time. At our wedding reception, every time I was in hospital giving birth, he even slept with her after I found out what had been going on and gave him a week to choose, gave *myself* a week to choose.'

Such deceit. Looking and seeing merged. Like an optical illusion – two faces resolved themselves into a vase, a duck became a rabbit. The contents of the note, the strange caginess about who was there the day Dad got them Solomon, Mum and Ian's intimacy: it rearranged itself into a new and awful understanding of how things had really been. How they really were. Peach's scalp crawled with electric ants. Pins and needles scintillated in her fingers and toes and her face went numb. 'I thought—'

'*Clearly.*' A pot landed on the ground a couple of feet away.

The air was suffocating plastic, a bag on the face, in the mouth up the nose and Peach couldn't breathe. She kept heaving and crying. If she cried hard enough maybe she could cry all her mistakes out. Or die. Just die from crying.

'Mum, Mum, I'm so sorry, I'm so sorry, I'm so, so, so sorry.'

Teardrops landed on the earth at her feet where the worm was still slowly making its way across the ground like there wasn't any dying here.

'All these years spinning plates and calling it a vocation. I am *not* going to clear up the mess. Ian can do it. Your father can do it, the feckless bastards. It's their turn. I quit.'

'When I saw you and Ian were so close I—'

'Young girls. That's what Ian likes. Undergraduates, interns: girls like Bella – she's just Ian's type. And Magda. She had the measure of him. She couldn't get out of here fast enough. Didn't you notice? God he's embarrassing; the oldest swinger in town. I've been propping him up since—'

'Patty killed herself.'

'Ah, you really had a good look through everything then.'

'So she did kill herself?'

'Oh Peach. I don't know if she meant to. Patty was like a spoilt child. I think it was a gesture that went too far, a cry for help.'

For a moment the atmosphere softened and cooled. It was easier to breathe. Then a stoniness coarsened Mum's tone. 'She was throwing a tantrum because your father chose *me*. Chose *us*. I think she was trying to get him back, or to get back at him.'

'But what about the baby? Was it ... who was?'

'I don't know.'

'But Mum—'

'You'll never know, and I'll never know and nor will your dad or Ian.'

'But how can you stand not knowing?'

'Because sometimes you have to choose things you know over things you never will.'

'You're such an amazing person, Mum.'

Mum started growing redder and redder, Peach felt her own face grow sweaty and hectic in sympathy. 'I *used* to be a person, Peach. I used to be a human in my own right. A human and an artist and fuck. Fuck!' Mum screamed fuck at the top of her lungs. The heat of it felt like the pressure wave from everything Peach ever loved blowing up.

I have no one, Peach thought. Bella hates me, Mum hates me, and Greg will too when he finds out what I've done. And Dad, she realised, he wasn't really Dad. His niceness? Gutlessness. His good nature? Indolence. Riding around on Mum's back like a parasite, the spineless disgusting creep. Peach never wanted to see him again. She burned with how she had bereaved herself. She was the most alone it was possible to be – alone with the worst person in the world for company: herself.

'Let this be a lesson, Peach – don't exist for men,' Mum said. Peach looked up at her mother.

Dominic and Nick and Dad and Ian: their faces ghosted in front of her mother's and Peach knew she could never let herself be an empty vessel for men to tip their needs and wants into. Vengeful feelings against her mother transplanted themselves into Peach's certainty that she wouldn't sleepwalk into needing men, letting men need her. Would never become some stolid, practical nag with housework under her fingernails. She could see how close she had come to founding her self-esteem on their attention. Understood how easily she could have wrecked herself in that life until the day she woke up with her dreams floating dead in the water of what men needed her to be.

Soil congregated on her mother's hands. She looked like she had aged at least a decade. 'I feel like I killed our family,' Peach cried.

Mum looked at the earth collected on her fingers and blew. 'Stand up.'

Peach stood up on legs which held no promise of continuing to perform any such feat.

'It broke down a fault line. I think Bella's always suspected. It was probably always going to come to the surface someday.'

'I wish it hadn't been my fault.' Peach had never wished anything more. She wished she could vomit herself out.

'I brought you here and made you do my "job", I should have known you'd be bored. Watching you do it has made me realise how dull it is, it's not even really a job. It's an obligation I should have left behind years ago.

No wonder you went snooping. I'm surprised I haven't lost my mind.'

Mum seemed like she was looking through Peach, like they were both staring down the barrel of what life could be if you weren't careful. Suddenly Peach understood life could consist of blindly promising to live better; live the way you'd meant to while tedious necessities grew large enough to displace your dreams and cram you into a corner of yourself. Duty could consume your existence before you even realised; life could be filled with nothing you intended and everything you tried to avoid.

'I'm sorry for everything.' Peach really did mean *everything*.

'You were still at school a few weeks ago. I know you feel so grown up but you're only a child. I never should have interfered. I'm sorry.'

'How can you apologise after what I've done? How can you be kind to me when I've ruined everything?'

'Because I am your mother, because I love you even though you've been awful lately, because you and Bella and Greg have made all the bad things worthwhile.'

'But you can't mean that, that's like something from a book or a film, real life doesn't have happy endings.'

'This isn't a happy ending, Peach. Everything is a bloody mess and I could gladly strangle you right now. But you are seventeen and I am your mother, and in many ways, I got you into this. Besides, nothing will ever make me stop loving you.'

'What about Dad? Do you still love Dad?'

Mum looked at Peach. She bunched her mouth into the shape of that smile which isn't a smile; the one that means a person is overwhelmingly sad but courageously trying not to be. Peach thought that expression should have its own special name.

'Of course. I've loved him since the first time we met,' Mum said and tried to rub earth from her fingers where there wasn't any.

At that moment Peach realised love is not a word – it's an entire dictionary. That sometimes love means all the beautiful, noble, unconditional things you hope it means. But that it's also possible to give the name love to being used to someone. That it's possible to give the name love to not knowing what else to do with yourself. That sometimes people say love when they mean dependency, and that sometimes you have to call things love because sad situations need happy names to make them endurable. At that moment Peach learnt love is the same as dark matter: a substance that holds the universe together which we do not understand.

As if Mum could hear her thoughts, she said, 'Peach. You know, there's something I wish someone had said to me when I was your age. I wish someone had told me I was enough. Be enough for yourself, Peach. That's a parachute which will always open, it will always save your life.'

Peach sobbed.

'Do you hear me?'

She nodded. There was a sound like footsteps in snow. Mum crossing the gravel towards her.

Peach's chest filled with a big miserable joy it could barely contain.

Mum put her arms around Peach. Peach wanted to ask her so many questions, tell her so many things. She wanted to be sure of herself, but in the absence of such certainty she was simply grateful to be sure of her mother, who was made from a stronger material than the ground on which she stood, capable of greater sums of love than could ever be counted or repaid.

As Peach's mother held her in the afterwards of what she'd done, the day heaved hot hours by. Shadows moved across the lawn, pointing towards the house. Towards the house and everything that had happened there, everything that had not happened yet. But in that moment, nothing else existed but the uncomplicated act of a mother forgiving her child: a child who had made a mistake and was profoundly sorry.

Chapter 35

Peach has always thought that if her life had been a film, it would have ended there. A close-up of Mum and Peach embracing. A camera on a crane would have lifted away from the greenhouse. An aerial view of the house, the garden, speeding up into space, leaving behind the straightforward redemption of unconditional love.

But it was not a story. It was life. So, instead, it carried on: recriminations and reverberations resounded through the years, diverted the course of Peach's life, and carried her along like a river, depositing her in this moment, in the place where it all began.

'Why now, Nick?' Peach asks him.

'Mate.' Nick sits down heavily.

Weeks after Peach entered the greenhouse as one person and left it as another, Nick's article on Ian and Patty appeared in the *Observer*. Every Sunday the paper was delivered and every following Friday parts of it were still scattered through the house. Until a Sunday in September when it slipped through the letterbox and disappeared. Peach rifled through the outside bin. It had been treated like a murder weapon – wrapped in plastic, stuffed right down to the bottom.

With the paper juddering in her hands Peach discovered

that Nick had exposed Patty's death as suicide, revealed she had been heartbroken at the break-up of a long affair. But he didn't reveal with whom.

'You know,' Peach says, 'I never did understand why you didn't put all the gory details in your article. What stopped you then that isn't stopping you now?'

'Me,' says Bella, her face a strange admixture of guilt and shame.

'You?'

'We had ... Nick and I ... I was so angry with you and you were so crazy about Nick and he came into the Marquee one night and I wanted to punish you so I ... we had a ... *thing*. For a while that autumn, when the articles were coming out.'

Realising how long she has held Nick in her heart, Peach receives Bella's revelation in the knees. They bulge under her weight like they have liquefied. She can see from the way Bella and Nick avoid one another's eyes it ended bitterly.

'Are you okay, Peach?' asks Bella.

Before she can answer, Nick says, 'Something about you stayed under my skin.'

Bella doesn't quite look pleased exactly, but there is a just perceptible brightening around her eyes and mouth.

'You were *so young*. But there was something about you though, like, something just, fiery and sweet and *raw*, and I couldn't, you know? The look on your face when you realised what you'd done. You were only seventeen.'

'I was twenty-one!' says Bella. She looks at Nick who is looking at Peach.

Then Bella calls someone a cunt and it doesn't seem to matter who.

And Ian says, 'That's not how it happened! I begged him not to for Eleanor's sake.'

'Yeah, well, that too, obviously, but still,' Nick says, looking less disgraced than Peach thinks he should, 'and because you said you'd give me access to all the photos and documents, so I could write a proper book.'

'We're doing that now,' says Ian.

'Yeah but,' Nick's voice is spoilt-boy whiny, 'it's because of this Magda film, and with their dad sick, I'm not sure if it doesn't seem a bit—'

'You didn't seem to have a problem before they arrived, and it's all been very convenient hasn't it, me inviting you here when you'd been thrown out by your—'

'Yeah, no sure, Ian.' Now Nick looks shamefaced. 'No, it's cool.'

Peach reaches out a hand. 'Do you really want to be his, I don't know, Nick, his—'

'Amanuensis,' says Ian.

'Ventriloquist's dummy,' says Peach, 'his mouthpiece. Really?'

A vast disgust swells and ebbs in Peach, leaving behind lenient damnation for Nick's self-interested subservience to Ian. She's in no position to judge: Peach didn't fire Grace, but she *was* going to. By text message.

She was composing some weasel mea culpa when Grace sent a message of her own thanking Peach very much for looking after her and asking her to tell Ben Gardener exactly where he could shove his internship. Then Peach went back to work on Monday and let Ben think she had fired her.

It left Peach feeling as if there were greasy thumbprints on her soul. Ben made it clear she was on probation and indebted, demanding more from her in exchange for less respect from him. Like a dog that had killed, there was a blood hunger in him, a gluttonous cruelty to his conduct.

'It's all for Patty,' says Nick, 'I'm doing it for her, you know? Her story's never been told properly. She deserves it.'

Peach makes a sceptical face. 'But Patty's been famous for years now, Nick,' she says, 'she doesn't need you to rescue her from oblivion. Everyone knows who she is, and what are the things on the tapes Magda has, the things Ian is so worried about? Are they things you want to defend? And who are these other women he mentioned; what do they want to say? Why don't you just take part in Magda's documentary?'

Nick looks like a sulky toddler and says, '*I* wanted to do it.'

'What about Mum, after everything she did for you, Ian, what about her?' asks Bella.

Mum meant it when she said that for once she would not mop up after everyone else. After Ian's big retrospective that autumn, poorly reviewed and attended, Mum left her job with him. Then eventually she left Dad. She waited for Greg to finish school. She helped him pack his bags for university. Then she packed her own.

'Your mother made it very clear to me by her behaviour that she felt no loyalty to me, so why should I extend any to her?'

'Weird, Ian.' Bella is like white cloud, darkening and thickening, filling with storm. 'Weird, because I seem to remember you saying when we got here that you were trying to do Mum and Dad a favour and that doesn't quite chime with—'

'Enough,' says Peach, 'enough.'

This demeans them all. No one is a victim here. No one involved in the events of 1994 has clean hands.

The only person who bears no responsibility is Greg.

When Peach went away, she stranded Greg in a siege atmosphere. She experienced it herself when she came home to visit. An atmosphere fetid with unspoken animosity, silence interleaved with whispers – thin smiles, brittle cheer.

Peach had allowed herself to believe that because Greg didn't know the cause of the sudden iciness that descended on their parents, he was fine. Took his lack of histrionics to mean he was unperturbed. Now she can see they all told Greg who to be: demanded passivity and stability – all other roles had been cast.

They had forced him to be a supporting character. Though life was not a film, people did write scripts for one another.

Throughout the decades, Dad has carried on playing himself with no regard for anything that happened. Immovably useless and relentlessly affable. He maintained a flimsiness that made him impossible to catch, a defencelessness that made him impossible to admonish. And because of that, Peach's idea of him has always refused to accommodate the true enormity of what he had done. In her mind he remained less responsible for what happened than Mum or Ian or Patty or herself.

In some way, Peach realises, Dad has never been less remote than he is now. Now that he's a shell of himself, it seems to Peach he has always been that; a hiding place for the man she didn't really know and never really will. And in some way, he was always behind glass, silent, inert, impossible to reach.

'Let's go, Bella,' says Peach, 'there's nothing for us here. Let's leave this pair of pricks to enjoy their haunted house.'

'And what about me?' thunders Ian, and he appears to Peach as the Wizard of Oz: a scared old man trying to exert a power he is afraid he does not possess. 'I *am* writing my life story, whether you like it or not.'

'Well, exactly, Ian, aren't we all?' laughs Bella.

Peach and Bella begin to walk, and Nick says, 'Wait a second, maybe we should stay in touch, mate, like in case you change your minds about getting involved.'

'We won't,' says Bella.

'But *you* will if you've got any sense, *mate*,' says Peach.

She and Bella walk out of the house and step into the morning. Now that it is fully light, Peach can see what a wilderness the garden has become. Sugared with first frost of autumn, cobwebs gleam with dewdrops. Tumorous fruits decay on jagged bramble bushes. Wasp-bitten apples turn hag-faced on a lawn strewn with yellow leaves.

The day before Peach left home, she moved restively through the house, trying to convince herself that home still meant the things it always had.

Peach stood by the willow where the family had buried Solomon's ashes, back when things she had taken for granted were only starting to disappear. She offered a passionate prayer to a god she didn't believe in. The purest communication with numinous forces a faithless person can achieve: she prayed for everyone she loved to somehow, one day, *please*, be okay.

Afterwards, she stumbled upon her parents. Framed by the living-room doorway, clothed in heavy light, her mother and father embraced. Peach saw how life looked without her in it and was glad without understanding why.

This morning, Peach understands that all her most agonising experiences – unrequited love, hatred, guilt, blame – are all a loss of perspective, detail lost in darkness like a photograph taken with the camera set to the wrong f-stop. A narrowness of aperture which created the gloom in which Peach has grown and tended disappointments like a mushroom farmer.

She knows that true sight occurs when looking and seeing converge. And what she sees is her sister who, walking ahead of her to the car, appears almost unchanged since the summer of 1994.

What she sees is herself. She and Gwen went to see the Manic Street Preachers not long ago. Richey, like Patty, absent: a void into which other people project their dreams. Sean and Nicky and James looking like cool dads, playing music that raced through Peach's blood like medicine and fire the same as it did when she was seventeen. The crowd surged as a single entity, and Peach felt unearthly kinship with the teenage girls there, who were only just embarking on their lives, and from behind with their leopard-print coats and bleached hair, looked almost the same as her.

Peach feels like a camera with the aperture opening, all the things she can never change and all the things that maybe she can rush into her like bright white light.

She wants to say something as they climb into the car, she wants to say so much as they drive away, but Bella speaks first.

'He was a fucking disaster in the sack,' she says, 'Nick.'

'Well. You did say he would be.'

They laugh. They laugh and laugh while Bella drives Peach away from the town where they grew up.

As they reach the motorway, merging with the traffic of strangers leaving and arriving, Bella keeps almost falling asleep at the wheel. And more than anything, Peach wishes the one act of care she could offer her sister is to drive her back to the hospital, to let her rest as they travel together towards whatever is waiting for them there.

'Bella,' says Peach, 'can we try?'

'Try what?'

'To start afresh? After all this. Get to know one another?'

'I know you,' says Bella sadly.

This is it, thinks Peach, there will be no second act. Just a Mike Leigh version of the Mahabharata. Until Dad dies, then Mum dies and there's nothing left to force us together.

Then Bella takes her hand off the steering wheel and squeezes Peach's knee. She holds on for a long time.

And Peach rubs her wrists as though she has been released from handcuffs.

Acknowledgements

There are so many people to whom I owe thanks for helping me bring this book into being.

For every part of this book which I created alone, there are a thousand other, equally important parts of it that only exist because of the skill, care, intelligence, effort, generosity and kindness of other people. This list will be long because it deserves to be.

I would like to thank my agent Jo Unwin who is endlessly wise, unstintingly honest, deeply kind and also very funny. She saw the potential in me and this book before me or it were quite good enough, and her precious time and brilliant advice, so generously given were instrumental in allowing me to write the book I always wanted and to become a much better writer.

And to everyone at JULA; Milly and Donna who are always smart and friendly and brilliant and make every phone call and email to the office a pleasure. And I extend special thanks to Isabel Adomakoh Young whose acute and thoughtful feedback on an early draft was invaluable.

Sarah Castleton, my amazing editor, a pole star of a person who makes me and my writing feel valued, cared for and understood. Her skills and sensitivities as an editor and human being are life-enhancing and I am extremely fortunate that she is my ideal reader as well as my editor and friend.

To everyone at Corsair and Little, Brown who have worked hard and treated me wonderfully.

Thanks to Tamsin Shelton for incisive, insightful copy-editing.

To Elizabeth Reeder, Zoe Strachan and Kei Miller at the University of Glasgow whose sage teaching of craft and critique I have appreciated and employed every day since I graduated.

And to my fellow students of the MLitt who gave feedback on the earliest roots of this book.

To Cove Park for a residency which breathed new life into my work.

To Cheryl Field; always the perfect combination of dearest friend, wise owl and indefatigable cheerleader, who lavishes me with support of every kind and makes me welcome in her spare room.

To Stef Smith, fantastic artist and co-conspirator who treated me as a fellow writer even before I'd proved myself to me, let alone anyone else, and whose advice is always good.

To my parents Sheila and Bob who brought me up in a house full of books and reading that instilled a lifelong love of language and imagination which has never let me down.

And to every one of my friends, the people who gave encouragement and commiseration, shared every joy and worry and never once expressed doubt that I could do this, for pints and coffees, conversation and so, so importantly laughter: Andrew, Alec, Gail, BM, Fergus, Suzi, Chris, Lyndsey, Neil, Marie, Ralph, Dana and Heather.

To my cats for the significant balm of knowing nothing about human things so that the world falls away when I walk in the door. I know they can't read so this seems faintly ridiculous, but cats are genuinely important.

To my therapist for helping me to achieve and maintain sufficient sanity and self-belief to keep writing.

To the Manic Street Preachers who I have never met but who whose music and words saved my life when I was a teenager and were my first evidence that being oneself was a good thing and a powerful one.

But most of all profound thanks to Jack, without whom none of this would have been possible: generous to the marrow, supportive in every possible way, whose love is priceless. The one person who makes words feel inadequate to me because he has simply given so much of all the important things.

BETTWS